THE
ASTROLOGY
HOUSE

THE ASTROLOGY HOUSE

A NOVEL

CARINN JADE

ATRIA BOOKS

NEW YORK LONDON TORONTO SYDNEY NEW DELHI

ATRIA
BOOKS

An Imprint of Simon & Schuster, LLC
1230 Avenue of the Americas
New York, NY 10020

First Atria Books hardcover edition July 2024

ATRIA BOOKS and colophon are trademarks of Simon & Schuster, LLC

Simon & Schuster: Celebrating 100 Years of Publishing in 2024

For information about special discounts for bulk purchases, please contact Simon & Schuster Special Sales at 1-866-506-1949 or business@simonandschuster.com.

The Simon & Schuster Speakers Bureau can bring authors to your live event. For more information or to book an event, contact the Simon & Schuster Speakers Bureau at 1-866-248-3049 or visit our website at www.simonspeakers.com.

Interior design by Kyoko Watanabe

Manufactured in the United States of America

1   3   5   7   9   10   8   6   4   2

Library of Congress Cataloging-in-Publication Data
Names: Jade, Carinn, author.
Title: The astrology house : a novel / Jade.
Description: New York : Atria Books, 2024.
Identifiers: LCCN 2023044320 (print) | LCCN 2023044321 | ISBN 9781668045961 (hardcover) | ISBN 9781668045978 (paperback) | ISBN 9781668045985
Subjects: LCGFT: Thrillers (Fiction) | Domestic fiction. | Novels. Classification: LCC PS3610.A35689 A94 2024 (print) | LCC PS3610.A35689 | DDC 813/.6--dc23/mg/20231124

ISBN 978-1-6680-4596-1
ISBN 978-1-6680-4598-5 (ebook)

To Ian, Luke and Chyler:
no house, not even The Astrology House, is a home without you.
Thank you for every day and every adventure.

When an inner situation is not made conscious,
it happens outside, as fate.

—C. G. JUNG

SUNDAY

THE FINAL DAY

The house is a wreck.

In the kitchen, a fly buzzes around a bowl of rotting fruit on the counter. Coffee grounds dust the espresso bar. The abandoned fridge beeps, its door ajar.

In the foyer, a size-seven Golden Goose sneaker rests on its side, laces outstretched and tangled in knots. It stands out from the orderly line of yesterday's driving loafers and platform wedges near the door.

A thick chunk of books is missing from the meticulously kept library, yanked from the shelves. A trail of novels drips like tears from the library to the living room. On the couch, pages have been ripped from their spine and strewn about like confetti. Wind rattles the windows.

Beyond the walls of the Victorian house, the storm accelerates. Lightning slices through the sky to the ground, quick and sharp as an epiphany. The roar of thunder arrives, angry as the fight that churns outside.

Six remain. They move around the backyard as if in a poorly choreographed ballet, tiptoeing through their confused desires, shifting loyalties, and volatile emotions. The chaos of the storm cannot outpace the fury convening at this spot. Here, the people will do more damage than the weather.

All signs indicate that life will change in the next instant, but the astrologer would counter that viewpoint.

She would say everything that happened at 4:44 p.m. on Sunday, August 25, had been building, gathering momentum, and taking shape over time. Two days since they arrived. Six months since that fateful call. Ten years of pain.

Life did not change in that instant. The moment had simply arrived. The moment that drove one of them to murder.

TWO DAYS EARLIER

FRIDAY

ARRIVAL DAY

WELCOME TO THE STARS HARBOR ASTROLOGICAL RETREAT

Your custom weekend itinerary is as follows:

DAY 1—FRIDAY
+ **2–4 p.m.**—Tour and suite assignments
+ **4 p.m.**—Welcome Circle: Fate Has Brought You Here
+ **6 p.m.**—Couple Compatibility: Aimee and Adam (Cancer & Scorpio: Charm and Mystery)
+ **7 p.m.**—Stars and Charts Astrology Dinner
+ **8 p.m.**—Individual readings: Adam, Eden, Ted

DAY 2—SATURDAY
+ **9 a.m.**—Astro-smoothies
+ **10 a.m.**—Individual reading: Farah
+ **11 a.m.**—Sun Worship: Bringing Out Your Buried Masculine Rage (women only)
+ **12 p.m.**—Couple Compatibility: Farah and Joe (Virgo & Taurus: American Royalty)
+ **1 p.m.**—Couple Compatibility: Margot and Ted (Pisces & Aquarius: Passionate Planners)
+ **3–5 p.m.**—Individual readings: Aimee, Margot
+ **7 p.m.**—Dinner under the Stars
+ **9 p.m.**—Moon Men: Bringing Out Your Feminine Receptive Nature (men only)

DAY 3—SUNDAY
+ **12 p.m.**—Winery tours
+ **2 p.m.**—Individual readings: Rick, Joe
+ **3 p.m.**—Couple Compatibility: Eden and Rick (Aries & Leo: Setting the World on Fire)
+ **4 p.m.**—Farewell meal

RINI

When I was in kindergarten—before I knew about birth charts and death dates, when I still had a mom, a dad, and a big sister—I learned a vital life lesson: *you get what you get and you don't get upset.*

Anyone willing to pay my rates for a night at the Stars Harbor Astrological Retreat has probably never heard that pithy rhyme. This weekend's group, in particular, were likely taught the opposite lesson.

In the study of the main house, I spread out manila legal folders for each of the guests across the desk and light my vanilla-ginger candle for integration, inviting my studies about these eight men and women to become part of my recall knowledge for the weekend.

Adam and his sister, Margot, attended Horace Mann, then Yale, then Columbia grad school—law for her, journalism for him. I imagine their teachers jauntily lecturing that *you do not have to accept what the world gives you.* That they can—nay, they must—keep strategizing and negotiating until they receive exactly what they want. *Carpe diem.*

They have no idea what a privilege it is to live like that.

Adam's wife, Aimee, and Margot's husband, Ted, have similar pedigrees. Aimee is Manhattan born and bred, while Ted abandoned his working-class roots twenty-one years ago when he enrolled at Yale and never looked back, marrying higher than he could climb alone.

Ted works at Goldman Sachs with another guest, Rick. Rick's wife, Eden, is a wellness influencer to the rich and famous, blue-check verified and followed by every actress who has ever won an Oscar, as if green juice leads to gold statues.

The next guest is a woman named Farah, an obstetrician of some fame, which I had no idea was a thing. She has a lower profile than Eden, but research has revealed she's delivered babies born with more net worth than 99 percent of the country's working adults. The next generation of privilege starts inside the womb, and Farah is the first to get her hands on them. Her husband, Joe, is a local politician with his sights set on the White House. As charismatic as he is ruthless, according to the news.

This might be the single most influential group I've ever hosted, and yet none of that alters my plans for this weekend.

My phone pings with a message and I reach for it too quickly, knocking my pen to the floor. It rolls six inches to the east. If my older sister, Andi, were here, she would ask me why I still haven't called Eric to take a look at the floor. A slope could indicate a rotted joist, I know that. Andi would point out that knowing the issue isn't the same as fixing it. Eric's status as my ex-boyfriend makes it complicated to call in favors from my contractor.

Flustered, I grab the pen and look at the preview of a text from Margot, the designated organizer for this weekend.

Confirming foam (or preferably latex) pillows, my brother is allergic to feathers.

If Margot and her crew had learned the correct lessons at those fancy schools, they'd have thought about their obligation to leave the world a better place than they'd found it. Instead they learned they sleep better with hypoallergenic pillows. I leave her text unread. We'll deal with it when she arrives.

No matter who my guests are, I always maintain a pleasant smile and an even tone. That's the unspoken code between guest and host. They demand things, I nod, and we call it "vacation," not "entitlement." Most guests are content to figure out their minor inconveniences themselves, but I can tell I'm going to have to enforce the rule with Margot: the limit is three requests a day.

I don't think I've made three requests of anyone else in my entire life, never mind three in a single day. I started working odd jobs at the age of sixteen, using Andi's ID, and it wasn't long before I dropped out of school to help pay the bills. Two years later, on the morning of my eighteenth birthday, my mother handed me a deed for three acres of waterfront property on the North Fork of Long Island. The property had been placed in trust for Andi and me from our absentee father, set up in his grandest gesture of guilt.

That day, I called in sick at the diner, and Andi and I drove out to survey the property. It didn't take a building inspector to see that the 7,500-square-foot house was uninhabitable. The windows were broken, the roof sloped, and most of the shingles and siding were missing.

You get what you get and you don't get upset.

I never heard from my father again. His youngest daughter was legally an adult. His support obligations, as tenuous as they'd ever been, were over. Happy birthday to me.

I didn't sell the house as land per the suggestion of my father's hack lawyer who handled the transfer. I didn't even consider it, because in the ruins I saw a ticket to a better life for Andi and me. I withdrew all the money I'd earned and hadn't given to my mother, and spent it on moving to Greenport and the renovations needed to turn the crumbling beauty into a rental vacation home.

Quickly, I learned that my savings weren't enough, so I relied on an old personality trait in a new town—I hustled. I got a job waitressing at Claudio's Seafood Restaurant while Andi consumed YouTube tutorials on plumbing and drywall. We survived on twenty different shapes of pasta, and in our spare time, scrolled through Pinterest for painting and decorating ideas.

With grit and favors, many mistakes, and one contractor-turned-boyfriend, we restored the home to its original Victorian design. Over three years we added modern, practical touches, like central air and floor-to-ceiling windows to show off the water view. Once again, it wasn't enough.

I put so much planning, hard work, and heart into the renovation that I was deflated when my bucolic pictures resulted in nothing more than weekend bookings. We never made it out of the red during that first summer we were operational, and by the Fourth of July I had to beg for my shifts back at Claudio's. And it got worse.

That winter, a pipe burst in the house, gushing and threatening to flood the basement. It was a bigger job than we could handle, and money was tight. I called the kindest plumber and proposed an astrological reading—a discipline I'd been studying since I was fourteen—in exchange for the work. He scoffed and hung up, but called back an hour later. He said that if I could scrape up the money for parts, he'd kick in the labor if I impressed his wife. After a ninety-minute session, she declared me a witch (apparently a good one) and promptly sent all her friends to me.

For the rest of the winter, I was a part-time waitress, an astrologer to the locals, and a room renter to tourists. On a lark, I combined my roles into one. I included an astrological dinner party for any stay of three nights or longer, with an option to purchase chart readings for shorter stays at $250 a head. The house was booked every single day that summer. With one celebrity sighting a few years later, the Stars Harbor Astrological Retreat was an official success.

I have built a prosperous career using this once run-down house, along with my study of astrology and experience in the service industry. I have learned to persevere in a way none of my guests would when faced with my challenges. I've ignored messages from the Universe that I should curl up in a ball and surrender my dreams. But even with that fortitude, this weekend will test the limits of my belief in the cosmic interplay of fate and free will. What will happen, and what can I do about it?

The front gate chimes, alerting me that the first guests have arrived.

I cannot afford to be a coward.

STARS HARBOR
ASTROLOGICAL RETREAT

ASTRO CHEAT SHEET

GUEST NAME: Margot

SUN SIGN: Pisces

MOON SIGN: Capricorn

RISING SIGN: Aquarius

AGE: 37

OCCUPATION: lawyer

RELATIONSHIP TO OTHER GUESTS: married to Ted, sister to Adam

SPECIAL NOTES: with her Pisces stellium, boundaries are not strong. What will push her to take a stand?

MARGOT

This is my picture of heaven: a cushioned Adirondack chair outside a gigantic Victorian home on the North Fork of Long Island where every room has sweeping ocean views by day and a wood-burning fireplace, expertly lit by the owner of the home without us having to risk a splinter, to keep us warm after we watch the sun set. Guaranteed cozy nights, as promised by the haven host, Rini.

"Doesn't it look amazing?" I turn the phone to my husband.

"Margot, we're going to be there in five minutes," Ted says.

"I hate waiting," I huff. I close Instagram and toss my phone in my purse, but not before the date flashes on my locked screen. "I can't believe this weekend is twenty-seven years since my parents died."

Ted glances away from the road to check on me. "It's a long time, but also not?"

I nod. Twenty-seven years and I can still see my father laugh at my precocious monologues about life. Twenty-seven years and I still wonder if I'm making my mom proud.

"It's weird that this year feels like a hard one. Twenty-seven is so unremarkable."

"Grief doesn't follow a timeline."

My long-suffering husband smiles without taking his eyes off the road ahead of us. His tall, stocky frame and stable demeanor are the anchors in our rough seas, and we've had our share of those lately. This weekend, the tides will turn.

Stars Harbor Astrological Retreat popped up on my radar thanks to a fortuitous social media ad. After another month of failed pregnancy tests, I impulsively booked the last weekend of the summer at Stars Harbor, which was available due to an unexpected cancellation. Somehow, all of our schedules were open. It felt like fate.

Fate. In my twenties I would have said fate was for lazy people, people who don't put in the work to get what they want. But as I get older, and coincidences no longer seem random, I've started to wonder if I'm missing an intangible ingredient required to make things happen. Maybe the answers are in the stars, as Rini promises.

I'm not sure I believe in astrology yet, but I am nearing desperation. I have questions I need answered. The Stars Harbor testimonials raving about Rini's astrological accuracy were as important to me as sunset snaps over the water. Guests boasted that they'd come back year after year for equal parts relaxation and life insight. Ted thought the included astrological reading was nothing more than a parlor trick, but I took it seriously.

This weekend I will secure my future: to have a baby, and to get my brother back.

The car's navigation alerts us that our destination is one thousand feet ahead. Ted makes a left into the driveway marked STARS HARBOR ASTRO- LOGICAL RETREAT. He squeezes my hand as we wait for the beechwood gate to open slowly.

"It's to keep the deer out," I say, repeating the owner's words.

"Well, good, because it doesn't look like much of a match for anything else," he says, kissing the back of my hand. The gate is tall but flimsy, the mechanics no more sophisticated than a lever and a crank. It looks like it would splinter if Ted pressed the gas and barreled right through it. And we drive a very tame Audi.

The gate exposes a long and decadent gravel driveway, a river of small brown-speckled white pebbles, like my favorite Toasted Marshmallow jelly beans. The edges are lined with bricks of light gray stone.

Ted barely lifts his foot from the brake as the gate recedes and we take in the lush flora. Soon, the white clapboard Victorian home appears as if it's rising out of the sparkling ocean in the distance. The structure is accented with black shutters, a black roof, and a circular turret. On the ride out east, I felt slightly disappointed that Stars Harbor was not painted Easter egg colors of turquoise and purple with sunshine yellow, like some of the other versions we'd passed. But the truth is, I prefer things in black and white.

My legs stick to the leather seats after three and a half hours of traffic, but I swing my door open and peel myself out of the car. I raise my arms overhead and stretch my spine tall. Behind us sits a tiny cottage where the owner must live.

"Turn around and look at that view," Ted says.

The manicured lawn sprawls out hundreds of yards to the sparking blue water. Evergreen trees in the distance to the east and west obscure the neighbors. The distant shoreline of Connecticut is twenty-three nautical miles away. Ted wraps his arms around my waist and I lean into him. It's like we're the only people in the world.

"Hello," a young woman calls. She waits for us at the grand front entrance of the house. The double doors are made of dark wood with raised glass panels etched in a vine motif. There's a projecting pavilion above the entry door laced with greenery. It's even more stunning than the photos.

"Rini?"

"It's Ree-knee, short for Serena," she says.

On the phone I imagined an uptight, snobbish woman who fancied herself "refined." If I'd had to guess, I would have said she was older than my thirty-seven years. Much older. An empty nester. But in person, Rini barely looks like she could legally buy alcohol.

"Welcome to Stars Harbor, Mr. and Mrs. Flynn," she says.

I was the one who made the reservations, so she thinks my last name is Ted's last name too.

"Please, call us Ted and Margot," I say, electing to keep it casual. Rini opens the front door and waits for us to step inside. My gaze lifts to the candelabra-style chandelier hanging from the twenty-foot ceiling. Below it is a spiral staircase like a strand of DNA. The flooring is a wide blond-wood herringbone. Very elegant.

"This is lovely," I say.

"I'll give you a little tour, and then you can get settled," Rini says.

We pass the sweeping staircase on the left, and on the right, a unique round library I saw posted on BookTok. Outfitted with books in every color from floor to ceiling, it looks like a candy store.

"This will be Adam's favorite," I say to Ted, nodding at my brother's titles on her shelf.

Rini shows us the classic white kitchen with its stocked fridge, and then the stately study that smells of leather and old textbooks.

"This is where you'll have the private astrological readings," Rini says.

Ted claims the game parlor as his spot because it has billiards and shuffleboard in addition to full-size *Ms. Pac-Man* and *Frogger* machines. I can't choose a favorite. Each room on the first floor is swathed in jewel tones, emerald green, ruby red, sapphire blue, and citrine yellow, like a real life Clue house.

I notice that some of the windows are small and thick with imposing panes while others are expansive and frameless. I ask Rini about the stark difference.

"These rooms were part of the original house, built in 1894," Rini says. "This area of Long Island gets summer storms and violent winds during hurricane season. Now, we have better methods of protection, but then, they had little choice but to limit the windows."

Rini leads us past the formal dining room to another living room.

"Wow," Ted and I say in unison.

The Stars Harbor showstopper is the floor-to-ceiling windows. It's as if the high tide could bring the ocean inside.

"Ironic, isn't it? That modern touches allow for the centuries' old natural beauty to shine," Rini says.

"That's the Atlantic?" Ted asks.

"The Long Island Sound, an estuary of the Atlantic," Rini says. "Shall we get upstairs to the suites?"

The back of the house also boasts twenty-foot ceilings, with a second staircase, this one built into the wall like a colonial, camouflaged.

"Was that a servant staircase?" I ask.

"You know your old houses," Rini says. "We kept it for subtlety. Is there anything more unsightly than a housekeeping cart blocking your room? You won't see that here."

We follow Rini to the grand staircase in the front of the house. I run my hand along the smooth stained wood. At the top we land on plush cream carpet.

"I've got you set up in the Gemini Suite," Rini says. "I assure you it's the best room in the house."

Ted and I both nod. He'll take her word for it and collapse on our bed. I will satisfy my curiosity by looking in every room before the others arrive.

"In case you are inclined to explore, a reminder that the suites in the second wing on the east side of the staircase are not open to your group," Rini adds.

"Why not?" I ask.

"Because you have all you need in this wing," she says with a smile.

Rini opens the door marked GEMINI with a symbol beneath it. The walls are painted seafoam and the curtains are a bold yellow-and-green pattern. The bed is framed by a gold slat headboard and has an ivory duvet. It's tasteful, an understated Versailles, but the kind of piece you'd be sick of after a few months at home.

"I'll leave you here, Mr. and Mrs. Flynn."

I clear my throat, preparing to speak up.

"It's actually Margot Flynn and Ted Williams," I say.

I notice Rini glance at my ring finger.

"You'll change it when you have children," she states.

"I don't think so," Ted says kindly but firmly.

"It's fine," I interject.

Normally I would have engaged in a prolonged debate, dismantling her antiquated ideas around surnames that treat women like property. Or I would have probed into how hurtful her comment could be to someone facing infertility. But neither lawyer Margot nor trying-to-conceive Margot has been invited on this trip.

Rini isn't a stranger on the street offering unsolicited advice. Her comment might have been a hint. After all, she's an astrologer who has read my future chart and was so bold as to reference my future children. That has to be a good sign.

After Rini leaves the room, I open the door to the Juliet balcony overlooking the Long Island Sound. A flock of honking geese takes flight into the cloudless blue sky.

"I'll grab the luggage," Ted says. "You should go down there and relax. I see an Adirondack chair with your name on it."

I place my purse on the desk in our room and grab my library book. I turn left in the hallway past the other suites: Aries, Capricorn, and Cancer. The doors are all closed, but I peek inside. The Aries Suite intrigues with its pops of red for fire, while the earth-toned Capricorn Suite is dark and brooding. The Cancer Suite is painted a calming blue but has a tacky plastic shellfish mounted on the far wall. Rini was right, we got the best room.

I skip down the back staircase and am greeted by the view out the immaculate floor-to-ceiling windows. I step through the sliding glass door and position my Adirondack chair to face the still-as-glass water. I'm about to crack open my book when I spot Ted opening the back door with two fingers. He carries a beer for himself in one hand and a glass of iced tea for me in the other. I meet him halfway across the lawn.

"Thanks, honey."

I lean in for a hug and press my head to Ted's chest. He wraps me in his arms, the can of beer cool against my back. He touches my chin so I look up at him. He kisses me and I shiver, despite the warm sun beating down on us. I gesture for him to sit in the chair next to me.

Vacation is the perfect time to raise a certain difficult topic of conversation, and our host has served me the perfect opportunity. Ted reaches over and kisses the top of my head. I rest my ear on his shoulder.

"I think I'd like our kids to have my last name," I say into his shirt without looking up.

"Really? Over a decade together and you've never mentioned that. I love that you still surprise me."

Rini might dismiss me as a progressive Manhattan-raised brat, but she doesn't understand. My brother and I are the last living Flynns in our lineage. Adam's got three girls, and I'll plant the seed of responsibility in them to keep their name, the way I have, but I'd like to help carry on our surname too.

Family is everything to me. Adam and I lost our parents tragically when we were in elementary school. Nana raised us and was lucky enough to see us graduate from high school, but she passed away when I was twenty. For so long, my brother was my whole world. Then Ted came to save me from myself. Now I have three wonderful nieces. The last, most perfect piece, will be children of my own.

"Do we have to decide right now?" he asks.

"Yes, right this instant. Yes or no."

I break my serious glare to show him I'm kidding. We laugh together. It's a moment I want to hold on to. I've been so focused on my clients, and getting pregnant, and my brother's erratic behavior, that I've lost the best parts of myself. I want them back.

I rest my head on the Adirondack chair I've been dreaming of and show my face to the sun. Ted and I sit in comfortable silence for a few minutes, but my brain can't help itself. When I'm feeling good, it flies to the future. It's been two weeks since my last ovulation cycle, tracked on both my Ava bracelet and the Ovia app. Could I be pregnant at this very moment? I promised Ted I wouldn't bring any tests—it's one weekend—but I'm rethinking that now. When Adam gets here, we'll sneak off to one of the 7-Elevens on the main road. Adam will come with me for a pack of cigarettes, his own contraband.

My phone vibrates in my pocket. When I dig it out, Adam's number blinks on my screen. I swipe right.

"You off the expressway yet?" I ask. "That's when the real traffic starts."

"Uh," Adam says.

My heart races without a conscious thought. Swatting away his excuses has become an automatic response.

"Adam, do not tell me that you're stuck at work, or you have to clean the gutters or wait for a furniture delivery. I will not hear your lousy reasons. Not this weekend."

Adam's down cycles usually pass in a month or two, but he's been blatantly ignoring me for six months. I have no idea what's gotten into my brother, but it stops on this trip. I need to get him alone and have a real conversation with him. I can't do that if he's not here.

"Chill, I'm coming," Adam says. Despite my harsh words, he sounds like he's in a good mood, teasing me for fun. He continues speaking, but I catch only every fifth word. Something about a train. Or did he say *rain*? Neither of them makes sense. The sun is shining and he should be in his car.

Rini had warned us that the house would assist us in unplugging from our busy everyday lives, but I thought she meant with beautiful vistas, drinking excursions, and friendly competitive games by the fire, not zero cell towers. I step through the sliding door, hoping there's better reception inside. Through the windows across the house, I spot my brother's Acura SUV already parked in the lot in front of the house.

I end the call and throw open the front door as the trunk slowly rises.

To my dismay, I hear Aimee's and Farah's voices.

"Why are you driving my brother's car?" I ask.

"It's Aimee's car too, isn't it?" Farah says.

"No, traffic wasn't bad. How about you?" Aimee asks, pretending we're having a different conversation.

Farah and Aimee grab their bags in tandem. Aimee wears a bold cobalt-blue jumpsuit that screams *I'm here to have fun*. In opposition, Farah wears a tailored white shirt and linen pants with a statement necklace that exudes refined elegance—the outfit of someone who would look down her nose at Aimee's child-free weekend antics. And yet, the two women are inseparable. I invite Farah to our family getaway every year because her boys are best friends with my nieces, but her company provides distraction for Aimee. With her around, Aimee doesn't get pissy at my sibling inside jokes and shenanigans with Adam. But really, it weirds me out, the two of them. Who becomes best friends with their OB?

"Adam called, but we got cut off before he could tell me when he's getting here. I thought you were him," I say.

"Obviously," Farah says. She can't watch Aimee struggle with her roller bag on the gravel and takes it from her.

"He had to be in the city today. Some big meeting with his agent," Aimee says.

At last count, Adam was at least thirty thousand words behind schedule on his new book, and a lashing from his agent wouldn't be a great start to our bonding weekend.

"So he's on his way?" I ask, wishing I could have heard him better when he called rather than relying on Aimee.

Farah scoots past me while Aimee stays behind.

"He said he's taking the train," she says.

"He's taking the train in the future or he's on it now? Our readings start in a couple of hours."

Aimee puts her hand on my shoulder and leans her weight on me.

"You'd know better than I would," she says.

I thumb my cuticle in worry. I grab my phone out of my pocket.

Are you on the train? I text Adam.

There's only one train east a day. Are you kidding me?

I press the call button, but it goes straight to voice mail.

It's not my fault, Margot. I'll come tomorrow.

Tomorrow morning? I type the question mark, my heart breaking through the phone.

A minute passes. Two. No response comes. The screen blurs with my tears. The rage slips through me, quick and silver like mercury. I don't process the surge until I lift my arm and whip my phone down at my feet. I glance through the window to check whether Aimee or Farah saw, but instead I catch my reflection. The wild eyes and deep frown are startling on my face, but they are familiar. I look like my mother.

I swoop down to pick up my phone. The device stands lodged at an angle in the perfect lawn like an axe stuck in the wall at one of those bad-idea concept bars. While I brush off the dirt and grass, I spot Rini watching me in the distance. I wave as if to communicate all is fine. Rini doesn't wave back.

STARS HARBOR
ASTROLOGICAL RETREAT

ASTRO CHEAT SHEET

GUEST NAME: Aimee

SUN SIGN: Cancer

MOON SIGN: Libra

RISING SIGN: Virgo

AGE: 37

OCCUPATION: social media influencer

RELATIONSHIP TO OTHER GUESTS: married to Adam, best friends with Farah

SPECIAL NOTES: unexpected Sun, Moon, and Node synastry with Farah. What's the connection?

AIMEE

Farah and I set our bags down near the steps and I kick off my shoes to drag my feet through the thick green lawn. Together we walk around the astrology house to the ocean view.

"I wish I could bottle that fresh-air-and-saltwater scent," I say to Farah.

"Already planning your next caption?" Farah grins ruefully.

The three-hour drive to Stars Harbor Astrological Retreat took nearly four, due to the number of times I forced Farah to pull over to the side of the road to capture Instagrammable moments.

At an idyllic little farm stand, I hopped out of the car, the dust from the unpaved road coating my slides, and craned my neck, looking for a toddler I might be able to pass off as one of my own three girls.

"Is she too tall to be Dylan?"

"No, but too blond," Farah said. "But that could be Clara in the blue stripes over there."

I spotted the little girl near the sign for the pick-your-own strawberry patch. "You are a genius," I told Farah.

I angled my phone for several perfectly framed shots of me smiling over the little girl's back as she crouched with a basket of berries in the distance.

"Aren't you billing this weekend as a romantic getaway, not our usual group family vacation?" Farah asked. I was surprised at the bitterness in her voice, but then again, I don't normally rope her into my photo shoots; she doesn't have the patience for the banality.

"I'm not posting these now. They're for next week. It's called scheduling content," I said.

"I wish I could pre-deliver a baby so I could build in a little breathing room for next week."

"Last one, I promise."

The rest of the drive to Stars Harbor, I felt a bit nettled. My posts may appear frivolous to Farah, but a lot of hard work goes on behind the scenes to create lucrative content.

Since leaving the women's magazine where I started my career, I've made a living posting to social media about the superficial parts of motherhood—how to remove ketchup stains, how to sleep train, how to make the perfect cake pops for classroom birthday celebrations. But there is nothing shallow about being a mother. Not for me. It's the most rewarding, soul-searching journey I've ever taken.

Farah does not share my views about motherhood as a vocation, or social media as a job. Farah is a doctor, the most traditional of professions. She doesn't have a clue about an influencer's challenges in the parenting space. I have to keep tabs on the newest trends in clothing and gear, amass thousands of adorable shots per week when my subjects are cranky for the majority of the day, and manage a regular posting schedule for my sponsors down to the ideal hour of day to maximize the algorithm.

But Farah and I are drawn together by our differences, not repelled by them. We share a mutual respect for our individual choices. So I know it wasn't my extended Instagram photo shoot that was bothering Farah on the drive. She sounded stressed, frazzled even, as she navigated traffic. Rather than peppering her with the questions on my mind, I gave her the space to work it out.

Now, seeing her open expression as we look out at the ocean, I ask, "Hey, is everything all right?"

Farah glances at me and then back at the horizon. "Beckett darted out in front of a car yesterday," she says after a pause. "I was putting Cole in his car seat and Beckett took off across the street. A Mercedes was barreling past, but their emergency system kicked in. Stopped on a dime."

"Was he okay?" I ask, horrified.

"Yeah, but he cried because he saw the ice cream truck and then it was gone. Not because he almost, you know, died."

I can't help but laugh at Farah's dry delivery. She seems pleased by the break in the tension.

"He's fine, I'm fine, everyone's fine," she says. "Joe asked me if I was on the phone. He thinks it's my fault."

"Joe is a politician; his default is blaming other people."

Farah doesn't say anything. She clearly feels responsible. Her read on Joe might even be a projection of her own guilt.

"It must have been so scary," I say.

Farah nods. "I still hear the tires squealing in my head."

I let the moment stretch out between us. Farah's eyes are trained on the ocean ahead. I know there's more to the story, but I trust that she'll tell me when she's ready.

"So should we go meet this astrologer? You googled her?" Farah asks, changing the subject.

"I would say I can't believe you didn't, but of course you wouldn't."

"I don't have time for that nonsense," Farah says.

"Okay, so what are you picturing?" I ask.

"A wrinkly old woman in a muumuu?"

"Exactly. But she's young and she's wearing cute pants."

I flash the photo of Rini on her website. Her shiny brown hair is swept over one shoulder. Wrapped in a red peacoat, she sits on the front steps of the black-and-white Victorian home, staring straight into the camera with a closed-lip, mysterious smile.

"She looks so normal. How'd she become an astrologer?" Farah asks.

"That's every twentysomething's dream job," I say. In the days leading up to this trip, I had googled the astrologer obsessively, and now I pull up some of the best headlines to read aloud. "'Young entrepreneur revives hospitality on the North Fork and zoning law changes thwart her competition.' 'What can't she do? Success in the stars for this whiz kid.' She sounds like an ingenue, while I wasted my youth partying and churning out articles with clickbait headlines for thirty bucks a pop."

Farah brushes my arm with her fingertips. "Oh, Aimee, you're still young," she says. As always, Farah sees through to the core of me.

"Forty is on the horizon," I admit.

"In three years."

Ignoring Farah's insistence, I fixate on Rini. Her youth isn't the only thing nagging at me. I zoom in on the picture with my thumb and pointer finger, but I can't place her, or the feeling.

"Well, I'm glad we're doing this. The house is certainly pretty," Farah says. "Shall we check in?"

It's not our usual modern luxury resort, but it is charming. The Victorian house on the bluff. Green manicured lawns. The ocean in the background. The graveled road leading to the house is framed with tall knotty trees, their limbs gnarled in disjointed directions. The character of this home is so real that it greets us at the door, along with the astrologer, who introduces herself.

"This place is beautiful," I say. As for meeting Rini, she doesn't look as vaguely familiar in person.

Rini leads us around the first floor, pointing out the amenities and specialty rooms with practiced perfection. I notice the library is stocked with every Audra Rose novel in print and smile to myself. Rini couldn't possibly know it's my Adam who writes as Audra Rose, but he will be thrilled to see his thirteen published books displayed like treasure.

We ascend the grand staircase to the second level, where Rini explains that we are forbidden from using any of the rooms in the second wing unless we want to incur "exorbitant" housekeeping charges. Farah laps it up; she loves rules.

"What about the turrets?" Farah asks.

"There's no access to them," Rini answers tersely, as if she's been asked that a million times before.

"Too bad, I bet the view is amazing from there."

Rini leans in conspiratorially. "Can you keep a secret?"

Farah and I nod at the same time. Farah might be discreet, but I'm the one who's as impenetrable as a vault.

"They're purely decorative," Rini states.

"Why? That's such a waste," I say.

"The zoning code would have recategorized me as a three-story B and B rather than a two-story vacation rental and that would have subjected me to more regulation without adding any bedrooms for increased capacity."

"Ah, well, from the press it sounds like you've done right to stay in the good graces of the zoning authorities," Farah says.

Rini clasps her hands behind her back, and I wonder if they teach that in Hospitality 101.

"Well, that's it for now. Any questions?"

"None, thank you," Farah says.

"Actually, yes," I say at the same time. "She's an obstetrician. We were at a farm stand earlier, and she said something that stuck with me."

"What did I say?" Farah asks.

"You said you wished you could pre-deliver a baby."

"That was a joke."

"I know you were teasing me, but I thought, 'Isn't that what a scheduled C-section is?'"

"No, that's not the same as banking content for TikTok."

"I didn't want to argue about my 'work,'" I say, putting air quotes around the word like she does.

"Ladies?" Rini interjects.

I shoot Farah a look that asks her to be patient with me, the way I am with her. I turn to Rini to explain.

"When we filled out the forms for our readings, you asked for our date and time of birth. If a birth is planned ahead of time, do you think that messes up the baby's destiny? Or what about the mother's destiny?"

A previous Aimee would have ridiculed the idea that our fate was fixed by some unseen force. Old Aimee knew what she wanted out of life and did everything in her power to achieve it, from submitting extra credit for higher grades in school to breaking up with Adam when he didn't propose on the right timeline. My specific actions led to my Columbia acceptance letter, and to Adam showing up the next week with a diamond ring. Nothing could have carried me somewhere I didn't want to go. And nothing could have stood in my way of where I wanted to be.

Yet in the last few years, I've found myself believing more in woo-woo ideas like fate and karma. Even this very conversation feels like evidence of their existence. How many times has Farah seen a post of me and the girls go up on social media during the exact minute we're outside her office having lunch? Enough to know I schedule content ahead of time, and she's never once said she wishes she could pre-deliver a baby. Not until the moment I have an opportunity to ask an expert. An unseen force has to be at play.

"Aimee, you didn't have C-sections," Farah says, confused.

She's right, obviously, but the question is a metaphor. Could I have made a choice a long time ago that altered this very moment, and I'm the idiot who thinks she's still driving the bus? Are our futures determined by our pasts? I can't bear to hear the answer to that direct question, so I ask about C-sections.

"What an interesting inquiry," Rini says. I smile.

All I've ever wanted is a picture-perfect life. The recipe for which is a lot of hard work in the setup, dozens of tries to get it right, and a sprinkle of good lighting.

Place the devoted romance-writer husband by my side. *Snap.* One magazine-worthy duplex on the Upper East Side of Manhattan. *Snap.* One yummy baby. *Snap.* Another angelic girl. *Snap.* A third perfect daughter. *Snap.*

Me, front and center. The best light, the best angle. *Snap.*

Lately I'm scared that the next time I capture a shot, the camera shutter will close and—poof—it's all gone. Collapsed under the weight of a mistake so old that it predates Instagram Stories. A choice that won't disappear after twenty-four hours no matter how I try to archive it.

STARS HARBOR
ASTROLOGICAL RETREAT

ASTRO CHEAT SHEET

GUEST NAME: Farah

SUN SIGN: Virgo

MOON SIGN: Libra

RISING SIGN: Leo

AGE: 38

OCCUPATION: doctor, ob-gyn

RELATIONSHIP TO OTHER GUESTS: married to Joe, best friends with Aimee

SPECIAL NOTES: dominated by Fixed and Earth signs. Is she incapable of change?

FARAH

Holding back from Aimee is as unnatural to me as posting on social media. I become awkward and two-dimensional. My tone never lands. The ride to Greenport alone with Aimee should have been the highlight of my weekend, and yet I feel a knot in my stomach that is both caused by Aimee and one I cannot untangle without her.

A mother's intuition is different from other gut reactions. It's something that cannot be tested until you have children of your own. I didn't expect mine to be strong, because I'm too logical to listen to some vague "feeling." But I also didn't expect that intuition would never find me. Over eight years into motherhood and I don't "know" things the way Aimee does. I've seen her look at Clara across a table and dash away for a bowl to place under the girl's chin the very moment she throws up. Meanwhile, I had witnessed nothing more than Clara eating, playing, and laughing. What did Aimee know that I didn't? What gene does she have that I'm missing?

Aimee knew I wasn't telling her the whole story about Beckett, but she has no idea how much more I'm not saying. That's why I welcome the existential argument she and I are having in the hallway of this astrologer's house. When we're talking about C-sections and fate, I don't have to hold back for fear of what I'm missing that should be obvious.

"Are you suggesting we're all here acting out some predetermined script, like dinner theater?" I scoff.

I don't believe in destiny, and even if I did, scheduling C-sections for my work is not toying with the universe. The mother has as much free will in the date and time as I do. Life is made up by a series of concrete choices.

"I'm asking if the past determines our futures. And I'm asking Rini," Aimee says.

We both look to Rini, who has a playful smirk pulling at her lips.

"Why don't we move this conversation to my study?" she says. I wonder if we're embarrassing her with our petty bickering and she's trying to hide us.

Rini's study looks remarkably like my office at work. Two green leather chairs positioned in front of a massive walnut desk. A tufted couch against the side wall. Hundreds of textbooks line the space behind Rini sitting at her desk. It smells like knowledge: woodsy with a hint of vanilla, the scent of decaying paper. Aimee and I sit in the chairs across from Rini.

"I want to try to answer your question. I do think the rise in C-sections will have a lasting impact on society," Rini says.

"How?" I challenge.

"The Sun is the primary source of consciousness for people born during the daylight hours, while those born after sunset are led by the Moon. Very simply, the Sun represents father; the Moon, mother."

"And she schedules C-sections between the hours of ten and four," Aimee says.

"I'm a senior doctor. I can make my own hours."

"I'm just saying, those are clearly daylight hours, even in the winter," Aimee says.

This conversation is starting to feel wrong, not like a distraction, but a lure into a trap.

"The result will be a generation for whom fathers will play an increased role—for good or bad. Their absence will be more heavily felt by their children, or on the positive side, their contribution will have a more beneficial impact," Rini argues.

"Don't you think that's because of science? Birth control allows mothers to do more than produce children. And in turn, societal progress allows companies to do more to retain mothers. That doesn't have anything to do with elective C-sections."

"So no matter what, in the future, mothers will be less important in their children's lives? That's devastating," Aimee says.

Rini has been carefully watching Aimee and me volley our words, and now her aloof demeanor gives way to a hearty laugh. She's looking at us in a way that makes me uncomfortable. She wasn't judging us earlier; she really sees us. That scares me.

"As you know, the first astrological highlight of this weekend is the compatibility reading," Rini says.

"Adam and I volunteered to go first," Aimee says.

"I never do this, but what if we compared your charts right now?" Rini asks. She folds her hands over her papers in anticipation. I get the sense she's as giddy about breaking her own rules as anything else.

"You mean a reading of us?" Aimee says. "That would be so fun."

"Fun? I'd say inappropriate. We aren't a couple," I say.

My face burns with embarrassment.

"Compatibility is not limited to romantic relationships. In fact, I do Zoom consultations with Fortune 500 C-suites," Rini says.

"So, what, you get people fired for being the wrong astrological sign?" I ask.

"There are no bad astrological signs. I guide them to better empathy and communication."

"Farah, loosen up," Aimee says. "You aren't going to charge the group for this, though, right? Margot would have a fit."

"No, and it won't even be a full experience. But watching you two, I am utterly fascinated by your dynamic. Do I have your permission to merge your charts?"

Aimee nods her head with furious excitement. What am I going to do, say no? I mutter my consent.

"I always say our friendship was fated," Aimee adds.

Aimee and I clicked at her first OB appointment almost ten years ago. I was four months pregnant, six weeks ahead of her. We bonded over our very different experiences of early gestation. She was tired; I was energized. She craved sweet; my mouth watered at sour. That first appointment lasted over an hour and neither of us wanted it to end.

I regretfully informed her I would be on maternity leave when she went into labor, but in the end it didn't work out that way. I was going stir-crazy during the day with the baby and returned to the office on a limited schedule after six weeks at home, and chance would have it that Aimee's was the pained face I saw the first time I returned to a birthing suite postpartum. Everything in my life felt upside down—my body, my daily routines, my marriage, even the whole experience of delivering a child felt different. Standing at the bottom of Aimee's bed, I roared with her during every tension-filled push as the baby's heart rate dropped. I was deeply invested, as if my own birth plan was unmedicated labor and delivery with no medical intervention, which, incidentally, it had not been.

When I shouted at Aimee that she could do this, I was talking as much to her as I was to myself. I actually welled up with emotion as the baby crowned. By the time she released in a warm whoosh, a single tear streamed down my face. Thankfully no one was looking at me in that moment, but it was a first I haven't repeated since. It's not simply at work that I contain my emotions; it's who I am. I didn't shed a single tear when my own sons were removed from the womb. That day brought something out in me that hadn't existed before, though time has proved it was more Aimee's influence than happenstance. She has an effect on me, more than I care to admit, as evidenced by the fact that we are now randomly getting an astrological compatibility reading.

"Aimee, you're a Cancer Sun, and Farah is Virgo—that's a sextile and an obvious match. In addition, both of your Moons are in Libra. But the real magic between your charts is in your North Node–South Node placements."

"What does any of that mean?" Aimee asks.

"For one thing, Farah, you might feel slightly hurt that Aimee raised such a big, introspective question to me when the two of you had clearly never explored it."

"Absolutely not. I was surprised, that's all. She knows I had two scheduled C-sections myself and she never asked me about destiny."

"Don't take it personally; she was caught up in the moment. Given more time, she would have come to you with a conversation like that." Rini directs her attention to Aimee. "Unless you feel she's too closed off?"

"She is closed off, but I like prying her open," Aimee says with a smile in her voice. I feel myself flush and scratch my neck to hide the red splotches exploding on my skin.

"You talk about anything and everything, and no matter how different you are, you never feel like you're talking past each other. You're always seeking the connection," Rini adds.

"So that's not the margaritas?" Aimee laughs.

"Aimee, as you mentioned, Cancers can encourage Virgos to let loose and tune into the flow of their intuition, while Virgos offer Cancers grounding without feeling bound or stuck."

"That's so us," Aimee says.

Rini shuts her laptop and checks her watch.

"I need to get a sound bowl and prepare for my welcome."

"Aww, that's it?" Aimee says. "What a tease."

"She already said it wouldn't be the whole experience," I say in Rini's defense.

Rini closes her folder and pushes her chair away from the desk. Before she stands, she stops herself.

"I know I said that was it, but I can't leave without explaining your North Node and South Node synastry. It's remarkable for two best friends."

I wait for her to elaborate, because the only nodes I know are bean-shaped bits of your immune system.

"Your North Node symbolizes the forward trajectory of this lifetime. It marks the character traits or energy you need to embody to fulfill your soul's mission. Your South Node symbolizes what some people refer to as past-life karma. The experience, knowledge, and baggage you are born with."

"And ours are the same?"

"No, they are opposite. That's what makes it incredible that you've found each other."

"Why?" Aimee asks. I have the same question lodged in my throat.

"Farah's North Node is your South Node, and your North Node is Farah's South Node. Said another way: you carry into this lifetime what she needs to learn in this lifetime, and she carries into this lifetime what you need to learn in this lifetime. Not all of us get a guide like that."

"Friendship soulmates," Aimee says. She reaches for my hand and I attempt a smile.

"Thank you, ladies," Rini says as she stands.

"For what?" Aimee asks.

"Letting me break my own rules. That was fun," Rini says.

Rini opens the door, and outside we hear Eden and Rick. Aimee's expression sours. She hates both of them, Rick the finance bro and Eden the wellness influencer. They look the part to me, but Aimee is turned off by their new-money choices. Wearing Alexander McQueen on their backs and Stella McCartney on their feet, while carrying Chloé bags, is one of their most disgraceful violations according to Aimee. Rini whisks the fashion victims off for a tour, leaving Aimee and me alone.

As of this moment, the only two people not present for this weekend getaway are our husbands.

"Let's see what trouble we can get into," Aimee whispers.

She scurries out of the study and I follow her, forcing myself to say something that sounds like me. The old me. The normal me. The me who had never heard any of what Rini shared.

"Should we go upstairs and claim the best suites?" I ask.

"They're already assigned," she says.

Side by side we stand, taking in the view outside the magnificent floor-to-ceiling windows. In the backyard, Margot rests her head on Ted's shoulder in adjoining Adirondack chairs. They have their eyes closed as they soak in the warm late-day sun. It's rare for me to see Margot with her husband. It's sweet. Whenever I'm around, it's brother and sister, Margot and Adam, who pair off. I was a psychology major in undergrad, and they haven't invented a label for the dysfunction between those two, even for siblings.

But the Margot distraction doesn't last long, and the astrologer's words repeat in my mind. *You talk about anything and everything, and no matter how different you are, you never feel like you're talking past each other. You're always seeking the connection.*

That has been true for the better part of our long friendship. But lately, despite what Rini said, I've been silent. Holding back. Like earlier—that's an easy example. Aimee said the incident with Beckett was scary, and I agreed, but I wasn't honest about why.

I can no longer ignore Beckett's impulsivity, especially in light of other behaviors Joe and I have both brushed off: he's highly distractible, he loses things constantly, he's prone to epic meltdowns, he has a short attention span. These traits aren't uncommon in any young child. *Especially a boy*, Joe says. Then why do I feel like I'm missing something that's right in front of my face?

That's the shameful secret I could never share with Aimee—that I don't know. I don't know if this is all in the range of "normal"; I don't know if Beckett needs behavioral support or medicinal intervention, or how to get either without scarring everyone involved because I say the wrong thing in the wrong way. I don't want to treat him like a patient; I want to care for him like my child. I'm just not sure I know how to do that. My analytical doctor brain overrides any nurturing thoughts I might have.

I'm aware I could lose Aimee if I continue to hold back from her. And I'm withholding much more than my inner monologue around motherhood. The space between us grows with every opportunity to share that I ignore. It could quickly become an uncrossable gulf. But there's a chance—maybe even a greater one—that if I reveal my secrets, I could lose Aimee anyway. Forever.

STARS HARBOR
ASTROLOGICAL RETREAT

ASTRO CHEAT SHEET

GUEST NAME: Ted

SUN SIGN: Aquarius

MOON SIGN: Capricorn

RISING SIGN: Gemini

AGE: 39

OCCUPATION: investment banker

RELATIONSHIP TO OTHER GUESTS: married to Margot, best friends with Rick

SPECIAL NOTES: key air placements mean he could be overly intellectual. What motivates him to take action?

RINI

Standing in front of the stone fireplace of the front parlor, I hold the wooden dowel in my left hand, cradling the small bronze singing bowl in my right. Firmly, I press the dowel against the outside rim and move my wrist in a circle, generating a quiet hum. Some of the guests stop and look around to identify the source of the sound. I roll the dowel up and down the circumference of the bowl, changing the tone from high to low. The sound builds the faster I move the wood around the edge. Finally, when everyone has abandoned their side conversations, I hit the side of the bowl bluntly. A single sharp noise echoes through the room.

"Welcome to the Stars Harbor Astrological Retreat. Please take a seat on the couch; there's room for all of you."

I wait until everyone takes their places. Margot sits alone in the center of the semicircle. She's wearing a cotton sundress with a full skirt. Her hands are casually tucked in the pockets, but I know Margot is feeling anything but laid-back. Her anxious expression begs me to begin.

Khaki-clad Ted sits next to his flashier coworker Rick. Ted wears a staid black Bonobos-type shirt, while Rick has donned a textured camel-colored button-down better suited for an electronica DJ. Rick has his arm proprietarily wrapped around his wife, Eden, who is relaxing in head-to-toe Lululemon. Aimee and Farah sit together on the next cushion to the right, leaning back and slumping into the soft cream cushions with their wine dangling precariously in their hands.

"I see we're missing two. Shall I come back?" I ask. "I prefer to wait until the full party is here."

"I'm eager to get started. We can fill Adam and Joe in when they arrive," Margot says.

"*We* prefer to stay on schedule," Ted adds. Margot's eyes shine with what seems to me like gratitude for her husband's support. Her chart already showed me that even though she's bossy, she has trouble speaking up for herself.

"Of course." Ignoring a prickle of irritation, I take a deep breath to steady my racing heart. "You get what you get and you don't get upset. In other words, there's no point in pretending away or contorting around your core identity."

"But how do we know which parts of ourselves are our core identities and which parts are choices?" Eden asks.

"Eden, let me give you an example of the interplay between your fate and your free will. Your second house is in Cancer, which means you are destined to work with unconventional streams of income."

Rick shakes his head. "You could say that because you know she's the founder of the Eden Mitchell Method. A badass fitness instructor who's also a deep-thinking life coach," he says.

"A wellness influencer," Eden corrects.

"Rick, your second house includes Leo," I say. "Ever since you were a little boy, you dreamed about having a lot of money and success. It is directly related to your sense of security and self-esteem."

He scoffs. "I'm an investment banker. That's not exactly going out on a limb."

Margot clears her throat and raises her voice. "Rick, we're not here to have Rini prove herself to you. Can you let her continue without interruption?"

I nod. Margot thinks she's interjected and saved the day, but she doesn't realize this moment has its own rhythm in every group. The naysayer challenges me; the type-A sets things back on track. I return to Eden and my original point.

"Eden, when you were born, as I mentioned already, it was decided that you would work through unconventional streams of income. At the time of your birth, the job of 'wellness influencer' didn't exist. There was no working from home. There was no online community through social media. And even if there was, you could have been a bartender who chose to sell craft cocktail boxes online, and that would have satisfied your destiny. It didn't have to be about exercise and nutrition."

"We have choices," Margot says.

"But we also have destinies," Aimee says.

"I'm here to reveal your core identity and to highlight the areas you have the most to work out during this lifetime. *How* you do that is up to you."

"What if we're experiencing issues that couldn't have been obvious when we were born?" Margot asks.

"Very little is obvious when we're babies, but as adults we have the capacity to dig deep inside rather than looking for external blame or fixes. Can I impose some of *who I am* on my current situation? If not, how can I bridge the gap between where I am and where I need to go? This inquiry will stop you from moving from one situation to another and repeating the same mistakes."

Eden excitedly chimes in. "It's not just jobs and partners. People jump from Peloton to CrossFit, from gluten-free to Paleo, and they're making the same mistakes. Different diet or exercise fad, same person unwilling to look deeper than the number on the scale."

I see Farah roll her eyes, but I don't miss a beat.

"People are always searching out there for answers." I frantically look around, eyes wide. "But when you gather insights," I close my eyes, take a deep breath and press my hands together moving up and down in front of my torso, "then the path forward becomes clear," I say.

"And how do those questions reconcile with 'You get what you get, but you don't get upset'? I take that to mean we can't challenge it," Farah says.

I couldn't have planted a better student.

"Some things are set in stone. Farah, with all those Fixed and Earth signs in your chart, you are never going to be impulsive and radical. For you, change will always be organic and practical. But metaphorical mountains can be moved. Slowly, deliberately, but still drastically."

Margot soundlessly sits up straighter, giving off intense *pick me* vibes.

"Margot, with your Pisces stellium, you're never going to take off and live the nomad life. Not unless you can convince your whole family to go with you. Because you need them like you need air in your lungs."

"What about me?" Aimee asks.

"With your Libra Moon and Leo Mercury, appearances are important to you. Not just because they're pretty and nice, but because you believe they influence what's underneath the surface. A tidy desk leads to a tidy mind."

"I don't use a desk, but for sure I get this."

"Thank you for saying that. That's exactly what I mean. This weekend, in my study and at dinners, what I tell you will be true. It is, I promise. But only you can decide what it means. In your situation, in your life."

For a moment, I let them ruminate on what I've said. The responses from this group are similar to every other one. There are some, like Rick, rolling their eyes harder than ever. Others, like Margot, stare at me, desperate to hear more. Aimee tries to catch Farah's gaze but Farah sees nothing; she's turning inward.

"This weekend there will be surprises, even for those who don't believe. You can't control the people around you. These readings will conjure unexpected emotions, unforeseen actions, and even more shocking reactions. This is a normal result of that which is buried rising to the surface. Some of you will feel blindsided, while others will feel vindicated. This is your fate."

The din of side conversation rises. The guests' curiosity has been stirred, and they're swirling in the mix of expectation and reality.

I reach for my sound bowl and dowel before continuing. "You get what you get and you don't get upset. But you *can* get even," I say.

The front door slams shut and seconds later Adam walks into the room with his weekend bag slung over his shoulder. Margot's face breaks into a smile, which she then rearranges into a scolding grimace. Adam dutifully notices the gathering and plants himself in a wingback chair near the bar cart.

"Better late than never," he says.

Aimee jumps up and falls into her husband's lap. "Rini, you mean getting even like revenge?" she asks.

"More like Newton. Every action has an equal and opposite reaction. Karma is waiting to see how you'll correct any lingering or past imbalances."

I whack the bowl again, louder this time, signaling the end of my welcome initiation.

"Compatibility readings will take place in the living room that flows to the dining area. Cocktails and appetizers will be available, and these readings are open to the group. You're all friends, right?"

This time I catch Farah and Aimee's eye contact. They know they got away with a lot earlier: an extra reading, private for them.

"I'll see you in two hours," I say to the group.

I exit the house through the front entrance, knowing I left an impression. I doubt they've noticed the seeds I've planted, but I look forward to watching them spread over the next two days.

STARS HARBOR
ASTROLOGICAL RETREAT

ASTRO CHEAT SHEET

GUEST NAME: Joe

SUN SIGN: Taurus

MOON SIGN: Virgo

RISING SIGN: Sagittarius

AGE: 42

OCCUPATION: politician, state senator

RELATIONSHIP TO OTHER GUESTS: married to Farah

SPECIAL NOTES: weak first house. Does he have real potential as a leader?

FARAH

Rini dismisses us and everyone scatters. Margot follows Rini to the front door, asking about the tropical storm gathering force in the Caribbean, which Rini assures her she's tracking. Adam grabs his bag and heads up the stairs to his suite, while Rick and Ted head to the game parlor. Aimee, Eden and I remain.

"Did you see your welcome-day horoscopes?" Eden asks. "They were on our pillows."

"We haven't been up to our rooms yet," I say.

"Was it good?" Aimee asks.

"Mine was, but it was so generic it could apply to anyone." Eden pulls the card out of her pocket and reads, "Welcome, Aries. The first sign of the zodiac, you're both the rebel and the leader, which means you don't have to explain yourself to anyone, but you do have to set a good example for others to follow. It takes a special kind of power to make your own rules, so don't forget to play by them."

"That doesn't sound generic," I say, knowing I would never make my own rules for anything.

"I also found a tarot card, " Eden adds.

"You found a tarot card? Is this place full of woo-woo clichés?"

"What was the card?" Aimee asks.

"The Lovers, but it was facedown on the floor, not displayed or explained. I thought it was weird, like it had been randomly dropped there," she says.

That doesn't make any sense. Everything in this house has been meticulously arranged.

"We're going swimming. Wanna come?" Aimee asks Eden to my surprise and disappointment.

"I think I'm gonna read a little before I shower," Eden says, and heads upstairs.

"It's just us, then," Aimee says, rubbing her hands together.

She's clearly excited, so I don't bother to point out the obvious: that neither of us is wearing a bathing suit; that while the sun is warm, the air has an ocean chill in it; that we don't have towels; that we haven't properly settled in.

Without a care in the world, Aimee has already flung open the French doors leading to the water. Besides, Aimee never misses the obvious—she just doesn't care about it. She'd say, *Farah, nothing good has ever been obvious.*

I watch her run toward the beach grass at the edge of the water. She doesn't check to see if I'm coming. It would be my loss if I wasn't.

The Stars Harbor dock juts out from the sprawling green lawn like a T. Down the center, solid planks run fifty feet out over the water, held up by bulkheads painted white. A ramp is affixed to the right side holding a floating jetty intended to rise and fall with the tides, a launch for a smaller speedboat or fishing cruiser. The left side of the T is another solid dock and is meant to provide access to a sailboat or small yacht. There are no boats for us, but I wonder if other guests come with their own.

As she runs, Aimee hops from one foot to the other, kicking off her slides. She glances back at me, and though I can't hear her over the wind, I can tell she's giggling. She wiggles out of the pants of what I thought was a one-piece jumpsuit. The top piece transforms into the shortest dress ever.

I break into a jog to catch up with her.

Aimee leaps off the end of the high dock, her legs scissored wide, her arms loose above her head. There's a moment she's suspended in the air when she looks like she's flying, and there's an expression of joy on her face that defies adulthood. Gravity takes over then, and she's pulled under the water with a thwap.

"Come in," Aimee calls, her head poking through the water's surface. "It's so refreshing."

"That's fish pee," I tease.

"Okay, Moana," she says, calling out my movie reference.

We've set our kids down in front of Disney's *Moana* four dozen times over the years to have some time to talk.

"Are you worried about the kids?" I ask.

I leave my boys every day for work, including one weekend a month. I don't need a break from them the way she does, but Aimee's excitement was contagious when she convinced me to come without them. Now, looking at this water that the boys would love to be splashing in, I'm having doubts. I already spend too much time away from them.

Aimee flips from her breaststroke onto her back with her arms in an exaggerated windmill motion. "I'm literally floating. Do I look like I'm worried about the kids?"

I shake my head with a cackle. "You most certainly do not."

Aimee grins from the water, the golden-hour glow lighting her skin. She bobs up and down with the gentle waves. I glance back at the house and clear my throat.

The front and the back of the house are completely different styles, I notice. The front has textured white clapboard siding, with small, identical windows, whereas the back of the house is wood planks, painted blueish gray. The entire center section has glass windows. Two wings spread out from the center with Juliet balconies dotting each side, like a boutique hotel. It gives the house character I didn't expect. Original. Not cookie-cutter construction. I'm impressed with Margot's selection.

A scream shatters the quiet.

"Something is wrapped around my leg," Aimee shrieks, then screams again.

Heart hammering, I step off the grass onto the dock.

"Is it still there?" I ask.

Maybe it was seaweed. Aimee has the tendency to overreact.

"Yes, it's still there. I can feel it." Aimee swims over and grips the floating dock for balance. I can't see anything from this angle as she inspects her leg.

"Oh my God, it's an eel," she says.

Aimee scrambles to climb onto the floating dock, to no avail. She can't get a solid grip. She pushes up as hard as she can, but her palms slip and she plunges back into the water.

"You have to swim to the shore," I shout. I can no longer see the top of her head. She's disappeared under the water. I cup my hands around my mouth. "Aimee, can you hear me? There's no ladder; you can't get up here."

I wait but I see nothing. The water is too green and murky. Visibility can't be more than a few inches past the surface. As the seconds pass, the pressure mounts. It's vital to get someone drowning out of the water immediately. I kick off my shoes.

I'm about to dive in when Aimee breaks through the surface, gasping. "Help me!"

Aimee reaches out and I wrap both my hands around her thin wrist.

"Push your feet against the side of the dock," I say.

"Farah, hurry. There's more. They're all over me." Her voice is laced with panic. A calm washes over me, as it does every time I deliver a baby.

"Listen." My doctor voice echoes off the water. "Brace yourself and use your legs to help me pull you up."

Aimee leans back and wedges her toes in between the planks on the side of the floating dock. I crouch down and grab her second hand. Together we leverage our leg muscles to launch her up to safety.

She lays her cheek on the warm wood, her breath ragged. I drop down to sit in front of her.

"Are you okay?" I ask.

Aimee nods and stands, inspecting her thigh. Green slimy reeds cling to her shapely legs.

"Looks like you got caught in some vegetation," I say.

A splash ripples through the water next to the dock.

"Do you see that?" Aimee points.

Sure enough, a black eel serpentines away under the surface.

"Gross," I exclaim.

"That's not the type of snake in the pants I was hoping for on this trip, if you know what I mean." She laughs.

I shake my head. Aimee loves a crass joke.

After her first two girls, Aimee specifically, greedily, asked me to confirm that she had to wait the six weeks her doctor recommended to have sex again. But after the third, she didn't ask at all. All she talked about was how the baby was having a hard time latching and she'd never had any nursing issues with the other two.

Weeks later over a second bottle of wine while Aimee had her shirt open, a mechanical pump attached to both breasts so she could "pump and dump," I learned she and Adam hadn't had sex since the baby was born. But that was six or seven months ago, and the baby was no longer feeding at night so I'd assumed Aimee would've rectified that situation.

"Still?" I ask.

"Yup," she says.

Normally I'd ask questions. Doctor questions. *Do you have any pain? Are you struggling with desire?* Or friend questions, like *Is that his choice or yours?* But what comes to my mind are inappropriate questions. *What's changed, Aimee? Is it the same thing I feel?*

Aimee leans back to shake the water out of her hair and I lose the nerve to ask anything at all. I can't stop looking at her. Her flushed cheeks. Her long neck. Her shirt is wet and it sticks to her body. Her nipples stand erect, and instead of ignoring this normal female response to cold, I imagine leaning down and putting my mouth over one of them and closing it, tasting her in my mouth.

The vision comes in a flash that feels real but not at all, the way one pictures jumping off a balcony when looking down from a great height. This, I realize, is an apt visual metaphor for seducing my married best friend while being very married myself, to an elected official no less. I'd probably come out in better shape after launching myself from a balcony.

"Well, that ends on this trip," Aimee says. She picks up her pants and shakes them out in the wind.

"I'll alert the presses," I say.

"Oh, don't worry, I'll do that," she says with a smile.

I strain to match her grin and swallow the surge of jealousy that's jumped from my stomach to my throat. We make our way up the lawn back to the house.

The first time I had a thought like the one I had on the dock was three months ago. It was of me and Aimee touching. Not a friendly intimate gesture like an affirming pat on the leg or our shoulders brushing from standing too close. I pictured her sucking my fingers while we made margaritas. A flash that came and went while I squeezed lime into our salt-rimmed glasses. I was surprised, but pleasantly so. Who doesn't want to be touched? And the truth was Joe had been doing a lot less of that lately. A split-second thought was hardly cheating. Besides, I'd never had any conscious interest in women, nothing I'd ever felt compelled to act on, so I didn't view the thought as something that threatened to upend my whole life. But they haven't stopped coming.

If I had friends to confide in other than Aimee, they'd tell me this was an early midlife crisis. And this wasn't about my professional integrity, or my firm belief in monogamy. But I know it isn't about any of those things. This nascent obsession is about Aimee. The way she's wormed herself into my life, my heart, my fantasies until I start to believe I'd rather die than hold myself back from her for another day.

AIMEE

Impulsive people have no room in their minds for regret. Consequences are acknowledged and then set aside like the shirt I wore when jumping into that murky water.

Who cares that my hair stinks to high hell, like a mechanic's garage in a swamp? I've definitely got a mark from that repulsive eel, but Google tells me its bite is no more harmful than a jellyfish sting. I'll shower, put some ointment on my leg, and open a bottle of rosé. It will be like it never happened. Except that my body will thrum with the exhilaration of following my impulse. It feels amazing to give in to pure desire.

"I can't believe you did that," Farah says as we walk across the lawn to the back entrance. She opens the door and playfully shoves me inside the house. I stumble over the threshold and remember it's not either of ours. I freeze.

"What?" she asks.

"Do you hear that?" I whisper.

She shakes her head, listening obediently.

"That's right," I say. "It's quiet here. No crying, no whining, no petty fighting."

Farah huffs. "You scared me."

I throw my arms around her and squeeze until Farah chuckles. We hug with the joy of two mothers reconnecting with their old selves. Our child-free selves.

Like Margot, Eden is also child free, except her status is by choice, while Adam says Margot is struggling to accept that she might not be able to conceive. She's my age—not too old to get pregnant by a decade—but they've been trying for years. Farah says it's different when trying for the first time. In fact, she's warned me that my body is already too familiar with how to get pregnant, and since I haven't been on birth control in years, there could easily be a fourth if Adam and I are not careful. If we're not careful—and we resume having sex. That's an important requirement.

I do want to have a fourth child. A little boy would be good for sponsorship, but it's not even about that. Motherhood is a wealth of mystery. How is Clara Adam's physical doppelgänger, but acts exactly like me? How can she wear dresses and play in the mud, but our second daughter, Dylan, won't act fancy or be messy? And Baby Go is beginning to show herself as a whole other type, different from the first two. What would a fourth be like? But when I've brought up the idea to Adam, he's dismissed me, saying I have my hands full already. Each rejection is a small knife in my chest.

At the top of the stairs, Farah and I make a plan to coordinate outfits for dinner before retreating to our rooms. I find my bags have arrived in the Aries Suite, though I never saw a bellhop or house assistant bring them up. There's a thick white card tented on my nightstand next to a single white rose. I open it.

....

Welcome, Cancer! This astrological sign is rarely noted for its duality. We're familiar with the hard outer shell of the crab and the sweet tender meat inside, but they are rarely acknowledged together. Cancer is one of the most spiteful signs, while at the same time one of the most nurturing. You're not for everyone, but the people who get you are yours for life.

You're walking toward a major realization this weekend,
but it's your style to crab-walk sideways into change.
Don't worry—you'll end up exactly where you're supposed
to be, even if it takes a little longer to get there.

....

I turn the card over in my hand. The horoscope is just detailed enough to feel like it was written for me at this exact moment in time without sounding invasive. I slip the card into the novel on my nightstand and take a shower.

In the gorgeous white-tiled bathroom, I appreciate the craftsmanship of this house. One of my Insta friends is a home renovator with six adorable kids, and I watch enough of her reels to know that Stars Harbor hasn't been torn down and renovated, but impeccably restored. Small details, like the delicate baseboards and the gold-legged pedestal sink, indicate the original design. Very thoughtful. Very expensive for that labor and know-how.

In the shower, I slough off the residue from that impromptu jump in the water. Farah was right that it was a bad idea, but I can't let being wrong stop me from being happy. From being me.

The hot water scalds my skin the way I like it. I'm lathering the coconut-scented soap under my arms when I hear a faint cry. A baby's cry. I wipe the steam from the glass door.

It's the unmistakable sound of an infant who doesn't understand that their needs are moments away from being fulfilled. The infant who doesn't comprehend that Mommy needs a goddamn minute to wipe, or to put a modesty shield over her engorged breasts. I shut off the water. Silence. I stand there until I begin to shiver, but the crying doesn't resume. I turn the water on to rinse off the rest of the soap.

I don't bother trying to comfort myself by rationalizing that it was the squeal of the hot-water pipes, or that the sound carried from a neighbor. This isn't the first time I've heard phantom crying. Always in the shower.

It must have something to do with the fact that it's the one place where I get close to actually relaxing. My sleep barely qualifies; it creeps in lightly or else washes over me involuntarily. I can't remember a single dream I've had since Clara was born eight years ago.

I turn off the water for a second time and step onto the thick bath mat. The crying is gone, but I hear the scratch of a zipper in our room. I open the door and see that Adam is rifling through his suitcase.

"You scared the crap out of me," I say. "Weren't you writing?"

"I need a break, okay?" Adam sighs.

"Of course you deserve a break, honey."

Adam scoots back on the bed fully clothed and props a pillow behind his head. He thumbs in his passcode, and the doomscrolling begins.

"Hey," I say.

Adam doesn't look up. Not a glance. We haven't had sex since the baby was born. To say that's the longest we've ever gone without is an understatement. After the first two babies were born, we were intimate in a matter of weeks. Six after Clara. Four after Dylan. Once I know the rules, I like to break them.

A year without having sex with my husband. Sometimes it doesn't sound like my life. Hearing myself think it, I want to open my mouth in shock, as if a girlfriend has just revealed her darkest secret. "Pre-motherhood me" would slap "mom me" across the face and tell me to get my shit together.

This means I understand why he doesn't look up. He stopped searching for clues of seduction or opportunity long ago.

"Hey," I repeat. I tickle his leg that hangs crookedly off the side of the bed.

"Yeah," he says, his thumb moving slowly up the side of his phone. "What's up?"

I loosen the knot in my towel and let it drop to the floor. *The people who get you are yours for life.* I let the affirming horoscope lift my self-esteem.

"You wanna?" I leave the question there, but finish the thought by crawling on hands and knees toward him. Adam looks up from his phone and fixes his face to hide his shock. I can see a smile pulling at the edges of his mouth.

"Now?" he asks, looking down at himself. "I've been on that germ-infested bus. I know you hate that."

I've been trying to shed my mother's germ obsession for years. Is he trying to reject me and make it my fault?

"These aren't our sheets. I don't care. Let's do it now."

I pluck the phone from his hands and place it on the nightstand. I lean down to kiss him and throw my leg over to straddle his lap.

"Really?" he says, unsure of where to put his hands.

It's a slow and awkward start, but I conjure up the memory of our first weekend away together. He covered the bed with rose petals. We took a long bubble bath, drank champagne, and talked about our dreams. It was the performance of romance, but it worked like a charm. And it grew into something more real and somehow more wonderful.

Our bodies move in a familiar rhythm. Even after a year, it's like riding a bike. I notice a distant look in Adam's eyes, almost like he isn't really there. Does he think of the same memory I do? Or something else? Or some*one* else?

Desperation wells inside me and I moan loudly, put on a show worthy of an Emmy. Some people frown upon the performance of sex, but the underlying feelings are real. The freedom of being away from the girls, the release of stress, the promise of connecting with Adam again. Does it matter if it's slightly exaggerated? Heightened for effect? Good for me, I say.

Adam buries his face in my neck, and triumph courses through me.

Panting, I roll off Adam and pull the sheet up to my chin. I nuzzle into his shoulder.

"I'm gonna shower," he says, nudging me away from him.

"Already?"

I'm overcome with emotion that I let out only when I hear the thick glass shower door open and close. Adam turns on the water and the phantom cries begin again, fainter this time, but they're still there. My picture-perfect life doesn't feel so perfect right now. Where did it go wrong? Could I lose my husband? Could the girls lose their father?

Before I had kids, I was the impulsive person who left no room in her mind for regret, but I've since learned that a mother can drown under the weight of one bad decision.

STARS HARBOR
ASTROLOGICAL RETREAT

ASTRO CHEAT SHEET

GUEST NAME: Adam

SUN SIGN: Scorpio

MOON SIGN: Scorpio

RISING SIGN: Aries

AGE: 38

OCCUPATION: writer

RELATIONSHIP TO OTHER GUESTS: married to Aimee, brother to Margot

SPECIAL NOTES: influential water and fire in this chart. Too much fire and the water boils over; too much water extinguishes fire. Which is the threat?

ADAM

need to live the love I write. It's what has made my romance writing career so successful, and something I have found impossible since Aimee got pregnant with our third. Aimee's life, her whole world, has become the girls. Even her career. She went from a women's rag writer ("How to Blow a Guy in Ten Ways!") to a momfluencer ("Check Out These No-Fail Sleep Training Tricks!"). For the past year, there have been no late-night plot brainstorming sessions for my novels. No date nights for romance. No connection.

The Aimee and Adam of our first meeting would be so disappointed.

Thirteen years ago, fresh off my MFA, I was writing obtuse literary fiction about a dark, damaged man alone in the world. I drank in dirty corner bars during daylight hours, rejections from agents ringing in my ears. I was at such a bar on the Upper East Side of Manhattan when she walked in with a friend.

Music played loudly from an ancient jukebox that hadn't been updated since the early 2000s. The bar was not a nightclub by any stretch of the imagination—or it wasn't until Aimee and her friend squealed at the crooning of Dave Matthews Band. Before that, no one had moved a shoulder or bopped a head, let alone stood up and danced like the two of them. To say they looked out of place was an understatement.

Especially Aimee. She was beautiful and she knew it. Half the guys in the room swarmed to her like flies to a rotting banana, but I stayed put, playing it cool.

I chatted up the bartender about the NBA finals, ignoring her. She sidled up close enough to sip my beer.

"I played basketball," she said.

"Oh really?" I said. She was the same height as my six-foot frame sitting on my bar stool. Five four, tops. "Was that in college?"

"In elementary school," she said in total seriousness. "I was a point guard."

I suppressed a laugh, and she bounced her hand up and down, dribbling an imaginary basketball. I watched her with a mix of confusion and awe. She must have enjoyed the look on my face, as she proceeded to crouch low, still bouncing her imaginary basketball, and weave in and out of the crowd as if they were defenders on the court. She was so low that I lost sight of her head, but I could track her path by the stream of people being jolted in the backside by this whirligig of a woman.

She returned to the spot at the bar next to me, her face flush with excitement. I was stunned, wondering who this woman thought she was.

"I know that feeling you have right now," she said.

"You have no idea what I'm feeling right now," I said. "Because I don't understand it myself."

She took my beer right out of my hand and shook her head, telling me I was wrong about my own thoughts and feelings.

"I can help you name it," she said.

"Okay," I said, waving down the bartender. "Let's get you one of your own."

Aimee returned my beer, now half-empty.

"So you're feeling deep intrigue," she said.

"Let's google that one, just to be sure it's the exact right word," I said.

"Oh, it's the exact right word. I know it."

"Intrigue," I read from my phone. "One: 'arouse the curiosity or interest of; fascinate.' Similar to *tantalize, engross, charm, captivate.* Opposite to *bore.*"

"Spot on," she said.

"But wait, there's a second definition," I said.

"Go on, let's hear it," she said. The bartender delivered her beer, which she sipped with confidence.

"Okay, 'intrigue,' two: 'make secret plans to do something illicit to someone.'"

Aimee smiled up at me.

"Don't lie—you felt that too," she said.

I tilted my head back and let out the laughter that had been building since she said she played basketball in elementary school. She smiled wider.

"And that." Her eyes sparkled in the dim bar lighting. "That laugh right there?"

"Yeah?" I asked.

"That's love," she said.

I didn't believe her that night, but I had been charmed by the outlandish comment. In the end, she'd been 100 percent right. I fell in love with her during that very first exchange. It wasn't until years later that I understood why. Aimee is more powerful than I am. The world does not bend to her; rather, she forces the world where and how she wants. No one that powerful had ever chosen me.

But her power over me is weakening.

When I get out of the shower, Aimee is waiting on the bed. I quickly dress, avoiding her face pleading for a cuddle.

"I'm gonna get back to writing." I gather my laptop and drafting notebook.

"Oh, okay, good luck," she says, twirling her hair on the pillowcase.

Aimee thinks she made me the success I am today. It was her idea for me to start writing romance. *Why don't you base a character off me?* she had joked after a particularly brutal rejection from an agent. *You're a hopeless romantic.*

Yes, it was her suggestion that got me devouring everything from modern-day bodice rippers to happily-ever-afters for unlikable women, but I started reading because I was between projects. Once I began, I was enchanted of my own accord. Impressed too. I wasn't aware of how much craft went into those meet-cute beats, how many subgenres had exploded onto the scene, and how much nuance existed within the basic tropes. We didn't exactly study romance in my MFA program, but there was so much to sink my teeth into.

When I began writing in the genre, every bit of my past clicked into place. I'd been rewriting the tragedies in my own life since I was a kid. A therapist told Nana it was an excellent coping method to make sense of my parents' deaths. To slay my father like the dragon I saw in him. To rescue my mother who died and my sister who would never be the same. I wrote to let them live the lives we deserved. This was the career for me.

Aimee was my muse, but those days are over. She hasn't read my latest published book, and she hasn't asked about this current draft. Aimee had once been my first reader and she gave great notes. She'd help me fix plot holes; she'd make sex scenes not just titillate, but advance the plot. Aimee made it part of her work to create content in our real lives that was fertile ground for my novels.

Until that creative well dried up. No, that's not the right metaphor. Aimee built a dam. She diverted all the water to our girls, leaving me parched at the bottom of a depleted riverbed. She gave the bare minimum so I didn't die of dehydration. Which was exactly what that scene was about in our suite. The first time we've had sex in nearly a year.

She thinks having sex one time fixes everything? Where's the intimacy? Where's the investment? If she wants to be forgiven for the blinders she put on after the baby, it's going to take more than this. More than sex on her terms because the girls aren't here. That's not real life. And it's not real love.

I grab a beer from the stocked fridge and poke around the house, looking for the library Margot mentioned, but I never get past the view. The sun is huge and round, buoyed above the water. The sky is blazing orange and pink. I leave my laptop and notebook on the dining room table and open the French doors. Outside the air smells salty and fresh. A few early crickets sing as I walk to the dock. I pick up a discarded clamshell dropped by a seagull and skip it across the dark water.

Out of the corner of my eye, I see a woman exit the small cottage south of the main house. Assuming it's the host, I wave. The woman registers me but does not acknowledge my friendly gesture. I lower my hand and rub my head to cover the rejection. That kind of bad attitude might earn her a gruesome death in my next book, perhaps as an innocent bystander taken out as my lead rescues his love interest from danger.

On the dock, I attempt to soak in the beautiful sunset that pulled me outside, but I'm agitated by mosquitoes.

"Hey, bud."

I hear my brother-in-law's voice behind me and realize I'm not alone. I kick another broken shell into the water. It lands with a plop.

"Hey, Ted," I say.

Ted trails his best friend, Rick. They carry triangular pieces of wood with a small round hole in the top. The sight shifts my mood.

"You guys playing cornhole?" I ask.

"Not really," Ted says.

"Sure looks like it."

"What Ted means is we're throwing around some beanbags while we put back some beers. Not keeping score. Nothing competitive," Rick says.

"Where's the fun in that?" I laugh.

I should be in the library writing the book that's due in a matter of weeks, but this opportunity strikes me as more important. A not-so-friendly game against one of the most fake macho guys I know. Rick, with his show muscles, trying to overcompensate for his five-foot-seven stubby frame. This is a perfect outlet for my pent-up frustrations.

"What about a speed round, first to five wins?" I offer.

Rick looks at Ted, who shrugs.

"You two go for it. I'll grab more beers," Ted says.

It feels good to chuck these beanbags across the lawn and feel the countdown to five bearing down on me. It helps to direct and focus my anger, rather than letting it spill all over. I nail two throws in succession. Rick's toss is short and slow, exactly like him.

I'm laughing at my own joke when I toss my third bag. It misses the platform completely. The next one lands on the box but stops before falling in the hole. I channel my energy into my last shot. This beanbag hits the one lying flat on the platform, and both slide in.

"Yes," I say with a fist pump. Ted cracks open a can and hands me the beer.

"Thanks, man," I say.

I take a sip and place the can at my feet. I'm up two and refuse to get anxious. I stay steady and calm. Until Rick lands another.

Since all my beanbags are in the hole, I have to walk across the lawn to retrieve them. As I hustle back to my tossing spot, Rick's wife, Eden, steps out through the French doors at the back of the house.

"Babe, do you know where my green dress is? I can't find it," Eden asks.

"It's hanging in the closet, zipped in my garment bag." Rick tosses a beanbag that plops through the hole.

"Okay, thanks," Eden says.

"No, baby, stay," Rick calls out. "You're my good-luck charm. I only need one more."

"Me too," I say. "I only need one more too."

Eden doesn't glance my way.

"Tiebreaker determines the winner here," Ted says.

Rick takes his shot, but he rushes it and misses. Now he's got to collect his bags and I have some breathing room. I manipulate one of the bags in my hand, massaging it before patting it into a nice flat flying unit.

"As riveting as this game is, I don't have time to watch. I've gotta go shower," Eden says.

"Love you, babe," Rick responds.

I toss the beanbag, and from the moment I release, I sense it's a winner. I trace its perfect arc as it comes down exactly in line with its target. Rick stops halfway to watch, his hands full of retrieved beanbags. My shot was perfectly aligned for the distance, but it falls slightly to the left of the hole.

"Don't blame the wind," Ted teases.

"You saw that, though, right? That gust came out of nowhere."

"What are you manly men doing?" Aimee shouts from the balcony. She's wrapped in a robe, drinking a glass of wine. Farah appears by her side.

"We're mowing the lawn," I say.

Aimee laughs too loudly at my joke. Her exuberance was something I once adored, and now it fills me with ugly irritation.

I ignore Aimee and let another beanbag fly, but I miss the mark by two feet. Finally, she showers me with the over-the-top affection I once craved and all it's done is make me frustrated. I'm the only guy who gets laid and then afterward needs to take the edge off.

I squeeze the life out of my last two beanbags and watch Rick eyeing his target. He takes a practice underhanded swing, warming up his arm. We both release at the same time. Rick's beanbag sails through the hole with an imaginary swish, while mine lands soundlessly in the grass.

"That's the game," Rick says, finishing his beer.

"It was a good one," Ted says.

"Rematch," Aimee says. "You'll get him this time, hon. Best two out of three."

"Nah, we're good," Rick says.

"What's the matter? You scared, Rick?" Aimee taunts.

"Stop it, Aimee," I say.

My tone was harsher than I'd anticipated, but I don't apologize. Aimee disappears from the balcony, and I glance down at the crumpled up beanbag in my hand. Although the game is over, I swing my arm forward and release. I watch the beanbag fly through the air, and for a split second, I imagine tossing Aimee away too.

MARGOT

No, I was not happy that Adam "surprised" me with his arrival. But am I mad at him for saying he missed his train when he was on the bus? Of course not. I'm thrilled my brother's here, and I've all but forgotten that I lodged my phone in the grass after our texts.

I think it's sweet that Adam cared enough to want to surprise me. He gets how important this weekend is for us to connect. He made the effort to get here even though it meant figuring out plan B. The love between me and my big brother is deep.

Adam had always been the prince of the family, and my father the king. My mother and I suffered quite a bit of tension, vying for the attention of the same men in some weird familial way, but I've rarely dwelled on that since they've been gone.

I was born fifteen months after Adam, and the story goes we were inseparable from day one. Best friends and confidants. Not all siblings are this way. Some are jealous of the new person in the family. Not Adam. Some younger siblings feel overshadowed by the older one. Not me.

That's not to say Adam doesn't drive me crazy on a regular basis, and he never hesitates to tell me when I've aggravated him, which is quite often, since he finds help and guidance "annoying" when it comes from his little sister.

We aren't immune to the rifts that siblings experience, but our parents died when Adam was nine and I was eight, and after that we fused together like two halves. It wasn't a choice; it was survival. It's been that way since the day we moved from our Westchester County home to our Nana's townhouse in Manhattan.

Prior to that tragic day, Adam and I had been shipped off to Nana's dozens of times—for our parents' date nights, or, according to Adam, for them to fight without scarring us. Probably both on the same occasion. But when we arrived the first time after Nana had been granted sole legal custody, Adam insisted we do things differently. Just me and him.

We snuck out the open front door, hidden between movers carrying out King Louis chairs to make space for our stuffed animals and twin-size beds. He held my hand as we tapped down the limestone steps, his chin glued to his chest, my tongue held firmly between my teeth.

A few minutes later we rang the bell like we were strangers. Nana opened the door, annoyed already. She'd been looking for us inside.

"Please, kind ma'am, we are little orphans with no place to go. Could you find it in your heart to take us in?" Adam said. I bowed my head to hide my laughter. Adam punched me in the leg.

"We could help you with the dishes and dusting," I said to Nana, ad-libbing. "And we have so much love to give."

Nana stood silent, unmoved by our performance. We expected some laughs, or scolding for tracking dirt into her house. Instead, Nana touched our heads and shook hers. Her eyes glistened. I heard her voice catch in her throat when she told us to get inside and wash our hands, that dinner would be ready soon.

She tried to act normal, but I knew we'd done something wrong. I wrapped my arms around her belly and hugged her hard before running past. Later I could point to that moment as when I first understood that despite my unbearable loss, I would have to spend a lifetime absorbing other people's discomfort when I told them I was orphaned in the second grade. Adam found new life in dramatizing our stories; I kept it all inside like a good girl.

"I'm so glad Adam made it in time for dinner," I tell Ted as he emerges from the bathroom, towel wrapped around his waist. I lean my head to the side to loop my earring through the hole.

"Yeah, we got in a quick game of cornhole while you were in the shower," Ted says, unpacking his suitcase while looking for boxers.

"I can't wait to hang out with him," I say, flattening my hair in the back.

"This shirt for dinner?" Ted holds a blue button-down. I nod. "What is an astrology dinner anyway? Are we going to eat things from the zodiac?" he asks.

"Crab for Cancer," I say.

"Isn't Pisces fish?"

"That's me, cold fish."

"No way," Ted says, wrapping his arms around me. He hates my negative self-talk. I kiss him on the lips to lighten the mood. I'm not going there. Vacation Margot is fighting her way to the surface.

"Some meat for Taurus?" I joke. "Oh, a gorgeous crystal water pitcher for Aquarius."

"Are we allowed to have non-ovulating sex?" Ted nuzzles my neck.

"Later tonight, but it's already after six and I don't want to miss Adam and Aimee's compatibility reading."

"That will be some sort of magic trick," Ted says.

I lace my hands through Ted's and we walk downstairs together. I like to arrive fashionably late to social functions. Let guests have a glass of wine and mingle. Everyone's a little more relaxed; they're looking for someone new to chat with. It's all joy, nothing forced or strained.

When we descend the spiral staircase and enter the grand living room, that's exactly the scene in Stars Harbor. My brother's leaning on the bar, swirling his red wine. Aimee and Farah are perched on the love seat, a bottle of rosé on a small table in front of them. Eden sits on a swivel chair, sipping a pink drink while rocking left to right with the heel of her boot. Rick stands behind her.

Rini sits in the center of the cream-colored circular couch, her back straight, her two feet planted firmly on the plush rug.

"There they are. Our first couple in the compatibility spotlight," Rini says.

"I thought my brother was first."

"I volunteered, but Adam's in a mood," Aimee says, glancing back at Adam. "We'll go tomorrow. Besides, Rini gave me a preview earlier and she is *good*."

Ted steps down to the sunken wooden floor and extends a hand so that I can land safely in my heels.

"A preview?" I ask.

"Rini was giving us the house tour and mentioned a few things. It wasn't a big deal," Farah says.

"It was so. She said we're friendship soulmates and our bond will last a lifetime. How can you say that's not a big deal?"

Rini pats the sofa next to her. Ted and I share an oversize cushion on the left side of the circular couch. A cocktail waiter appears and asks what we'd like to drink.

"Since you're soulmates, maybe now you'll stop using her as your lady doctor," I say. I'm relieved the line lands with some humor, because I feel all sorts of judgy about their relationship and it's hard to hide.

"Aimee's not my patient," Farah says, matter-of-factly. She sounded more defensive about the extra reading.

"I was in the hospital when you delivered Clara," I say, confused.

"Yes, but once we became best friends postpartum, I suggested she move to another doctor in my practice. I haven't seen Aimee professionally in over eight years."

I study Aimee, who refuses to meet my eye. She sips her wine slowly, with great care. I know I'm not crazy.

"But you've said things to make me believe that she was still your doctor. You knew I thought it was . . . strange."

Farah pulls Aimee's wineglass away from her mouth to reveal a devious grin.

"You're so naive sometimes, Margot," Aimee laughs.

"From her chart, I'd say Margot is earnest," Rini says. Her simple kindness shifts the energy in the room.

"And Aimee does enjoy making herself out to seem worse than she is. Her bark is louder than her bite," Farah adds.

Adam places his wineglass on the bar with an ear-piercing clink. "Ha. Now who's the naive one?" he says. Adam lets his barb land without acknowledging Farah and Aimee. Instead, he stares directly at me. His attention is comforting.

The server arrives with a tequila soda for me and an IPA for Ted.

"I'd say it's time to get started," Rini says. "Margot and Ted. Pisces and Aquarius. At first glance this might look like opposites attract, Aquarius being known as independent and ambitious, while Pisces are emotional and dreamy, but you are united by your hardworking, never-surrender Capricorn moons. It's the exact right combination of qualities."

"It's worked for over a decade," Ted says, rubbing my knee.

Ted and I met while I was a first-year associate at Gannett, Horvath, Swine & Moore. I'd crashed Adam's annual Yale-alumni Manhattan bar crawl at Dorian's after we'd wrapped a law firm event at Quality Meats. I was complaining to Adam that my graduating class didn't do impromptu reunions when Ted interjected.

"If you want one, you should organize it yourself," he said plainly.

"Margot, this is Ted," Adam said.

I nodded at Ted and sipped my gin and tonic through a tiny black straw. I could see his impulse to shake my hand, perhaps the way his corn-fed father had taught him to do, or his favorite professor in school, but he wisely resisted. He had good awareness of social cues.

Adam was pulled away to the bar while Ted and I stood around the small high-top table. The music was loud, the crowd even more so.

"You look like the kind of woman who could make that happen if she wanted to," Ted shouted.

"Well, I'm busy making many things happen, Ted, things bigger than a bar crawl."

"Like?"

I leaned in close to him. I could smell his cologne over the mixed stench of bleach and alcohol in the bar. I inhaled so deeply it made me dizzy, but I never lost my train of thought. I exhaled out my answer.

"Being the youngest partner at my firm, and then a top rainmaker by fifty, *after* I settle in as a hot young wife and mother to four without slowing down one bit."

"Ambitious and family focused, a rare combo," Ted remarked.

"Is it?"

"Unless the kids are just a vanity play and you have no intention of spending time with them."

"Four of them?"

"Good point. But maybe you're excessive."

From another man that might have been code for "too much," but the twinkle in Ted's eye told me it was a challenge. He dared me to be too much for him. He wasn't going to scare easily.

"Family is everything to me," I said.

"Well then, you pass all my criteria. I have met my match."

"The question is, Have I?" I said, flirting. "Are you a lawyer too?"

"Investment banker. Morgan Stanley."

"And you want four kids?"

"I'm an only child; it's part of my God-shaped hole."

"Your what?"

He tapped his suit pocket and gestured with his head. I followed him under the flat-screen TV hanging from the ceiling to the red EXIT sign at the side door. It was a gorgeous summer night, the kind where you could feel that people had been stuck inside all day, bathing in the air-conditioning of their office buildings, waiting for the moment to feel the warm, thick breeze and remember again they were primal and human. It was almost as loud outside as inside, without the relentless bass of the music.

"I hope you didn't bring me out here to show me any hole on your body."

Ted smiled and slipped a vape pen out of his breast pocket. He offered it to me first.

"What is it?" I asked, knowing I wouldn't accept it no matter the answer.

"Little bit of weed."

"Weed is for lazy people," I said.

"Coke is for the gunners?"

Touché. A cliché for a cliché. In reality, I wasn't into any substances that made me feel out of control.

"I thought you were going to arrest me," Ted said.

"Is that what you think lawyers do?"

"I'm not an idiot, I was trying to flirt."

Ted took a pull off his vape and stared at the people in the pizza place across the street. I touched his arm and waited for him to look at me.

"So was I. We've gotten off track. Are you into God, is that what you're trying to say?" I asked.

Ted shrugged. "I wasn't speaking literally. It's a metaphor."

"For what?"

Ted exhaled a plume of smoke, directing it up toward the sky. It floated like a thought bubble over his head. I could tell he was intrigued by my persistence, my willingness to go there with him, but he had to calculate how much he wanted to reveal and how soon.

"I come from a simple, secure blue-collar family in Michigan. Parents are still together. No chaos. No poverty. No abuse. And yet still I'm driven to extremes."

"Extremes?"

Ted laughed. He had a nice laugh.

"I wouldn't be extreme to you, but according to my parents and everyone I grew up with in my town, I am. They want a nice solid life. I want it all. Success, money, family, love. A big, huge life. Not the illusion of it, but the real thing. Even if it takes time to build."

We fell hard and fast after that night. From then on, every weekend would begin with a date night on Thursday, and we wouldn't leave each other's side until Monday morning, even if we spent it with rotating groups of friends. This weekend away to Stars Harbor is a natural extension of those early years.

"I knew she was smart and fiercely loyal to her family, but when I learned she was funny, I was done," Ted explains to Rini.

"And same for you?" Rini asks me.

I blush. "It wasn't quite that."

"Ah, it was your sexual compatibility. Your Venus signs are well aligned."

"Didn't know you had it in you, buddy," Rick says, slapping Ted on the back.

"I'll say this," I say. "The thing that I loved was that this was a man I could count on to be a rock in tumultuous times, but who also had emotions and heady stuff he grappled with."

"In bed," Rick says.

"That's his Scorpio Mercury," Rini says. "He works things out in intimacy. Sex communicates his wants, his fears, his plans for the future, everything he's going through. But you struggle with communication, Margot. Not only are you a Pisces Sun, but your Jupiter, Mercury, and Venus are all in Pisces. That's a stellium."

"What does that mean?" I ask.

"It means a lot of things. That you live in a fantasy world and reality rarely lives up to your expectations."

"True, but I pivot quickly. What else?"

"That means other people's pain is your pain and other people's joy is your joy."

"Isn't that called love? You share in the good times and the bad times."

"For you, it's not only love. You feel this way with strangers. This level of empathy is karmic. In reality, I'd go so far as to say that you feel things ten times deeper and stronger than the person experiencing it firsthand."

Tears sting my nose when Rini shares this hard truth.

"The problem is you keep it all inside. You're an emotional vault. Other people love that about you—you share nothing of what they tell you. But *you* need to share more."

"*Need* is a strong word," I say. My attempt at a joke doesn't land.

"It's the right word," Rini says.

I smile and try to act casual, but she's right. There's no limit to the pain I can take on. It distracts me from my own.

ADAM

Rini sits behind a desk in her big bohemian dress, her hands folded over a stack of papers, and I wonder what she's hiding under there. She appears aloof and disinterested, perhaps in an attempt to get me to spill my guts. I walk around the study, surveying the hundreds of books that stretch out behind her.

"Well, well, well, you seem to love changing up my itinerary," Rini says.

My reading wasn't supposed to be for another hour, but I wasn't hungry as they set down the food for dinner so I asked if we could get this over. It was the only moment I saw Rini look flustered, but she agreed without hesitation.

"Thanks for being so flexible," I say with a wink.

"I'm actually surprised you didn't opt out of this reading," she says, ignoring my charm.

"Really? Why?"

"You're a double Scorpio, Sun and Moon. Very secretive. I wouldn't expect you to open up in a thirty-minute session."

"Is that so? Says who?"

"Ancient wisdom."

She's not wrong, but I'm not going to roll over and show my belly in the first five minutes. I pull out the chair across from her at the desk.

"Secrets are the driving engine of a good story," I say. "We need to know our hero has a secret, and we turn the pages to find out what it is, and how he will overcome his reasons for hiding it."

"In my work, I find that secrets thwart or change your fate," Rini says.

Fate. That was a word I hadn't thought much about until *her*. With the girl in the scarlet-red dress, how could I not believe in fate?

"What if I don't want secrets anymore?" I ask Rini. "Are you saying I'm always going to have something to hide because I was born in November?"

"I said you were secretive, which is a personality trait. That could mean shy, introverted, or private. You're the one that brought up secrets."

She's right and I don't like it. I've already given her too much. I pull up my ankle to rest on the opposite knee. I let my foot jiggle, my loafer quietly tapping the edge of her desk.

"The path of your future is informed by your past acts. You are limited in how far you can go if you carry the weight of previous wrong-doing," Rini says, her head hanging low as if reciting a script.

"What is this past thing I'm carrying? Can you see it there in those dots?"

"The conjunction of Mars and Pluto that we're experiencing this week hasn't happened in ten years. The wounds you inflicted then—that's the past you need to pay for."

"Ten years?" I ask.

No way. That's ancient history between me and Aimee. I don't think about it, and she doesn't either. No Pluto or Donald Duck in retrograde is going to change that.

"Well, you've got that very wrong. I've paid more than my share. My debts are settled."

"Maybe you've been paying the wrong person. Because I see it clear as day. You have unfinished business to take care of before it blindsides you."

Rini makes a petulant face and a flash of déjà vu disturbs me.

"Ten years," I repeat. That was when I published my first novel.

This conversation is yet another reminder that the best parts of my life are hidden, including my life's work. But that's not the way I want it. Those were old choices, made by an old Adam.

"Let's say I'm done with secrets, but there are other people involved. And they expect a say in which facts remain secret."

"That presents a challenge, I see," Rini says.

"So what am I supposed to do?"

"You can only control yourself. And if you want to be released from your secrets, you need to pay for the wounds you've inflicted. Your future will not be free until you right the past."

I skulk out of the astrologer's room. *Your future will not be free until you right the past.* She's talking about letting go of Aimee before I can be out in the open with Scarlett, my girl in the red dress.

A few months ago, Ted and I were grabbing a happy hour special. Ted bailed after one drink like he always did, but I needed more time before going home to my home-turned-den-of-chaos. I had no problem drinking alone. Of all the bars in Manhattan, she walked into mine. She was wearing a sultry red dress among a sea of spring florals. I'd known her casually for years, but I don't think we'd ever had a real one-on-one conversation until that night. The connection between us was electric. Neither of us wanted the night to end, but we knew we couldn't stay at Lillian's Bar & Tavern, where I was a regular.

"You ready?" she asked as the Uber slowed in front of her West Village bar of choice.

I nodded, fully aware that I wasn't ready for anything this girl was going to do. She took my hand as we got out and led me to a dark, sexy speakeasy. It was crowded, but it looked like every person in there had only one thing on their mind.

We sat on a velvet love seat and ordered drinks. She smiled, but instead of it setting me at ease, the tension mounted. I had consented to resting the sanctity of my marriage in her soft hands. What was going to happen? It didn't matter. There was no choice but to let our desire lead.

"I've always thought this song is hella romantic," she said. I tuned my ear to hear Radiohead pleading to notice when I'm not around.

"Since I was a little boy, I've wished I was special," I said.

With unflinching eye contact, she put her drink down between us and pulled my face to hers. She landed the kiss of all kisses. Her lips were plumper than Aimee's, her tongue quicker. My heart raced with the excitement of beautiful novelty.

We shared one long passionate make-out session that night—forgivable by most standards of infidelity—but I knew we had crossed a line we could never take back. I wouldn't even if I could. Especially not because of what some astro-witch said.

Outside Rini's study, the rest of the house is as inhospitable as that disappointing reading. The seafood appetizers have congealed and give off a briny stink. But worse than the smell is the sound. Margot is going batshit lawyer on Eden about something. I don't know what they're arguing about and I don't care. All I want is a drink from the bar, but the bartender isn't there. I step behind the counter and pour myself an extra-large Jack Daniel's.

The bickering continues. I sip my drink, but it's not enough to match the escalation of Margot and Eden, who look just about ready to kill each other.

"Hey!"

The room quiets immediately. Relief.

"Settle down, Margot," I say.

Margot leaves the room. Eden slips into the astrologer's study. I drain my whiskey in peace and try to figure out how to unwind this mess I'm in.

STARS HARBOR
ASTROLOGICAL RETREAT

ASTRO CHEAT SHEET

GUEST NAME: Rick

SUN SIGN: Leo

MOON SIGN: Aries

RISING SIGN: Cancer

AGE: 42

OCCUPATION: investment banker

RELATIONSHIP TO OTHER GUESTS: married to Eden, best friends with Ted

SPECIAL NOTES: heavy masculine energy with all that air and fire. Watch him closely during the Moon Men exercise. Expect a breakthrough.

MARGOT

In the powder room I stare at my face in the mirror. I am holding it inside, aren't I?

Adam has never failed to back me up like that. He missed my argument with Eden while he was in his reading, but telling me to settle down was uncalled for anyhow.

Eden and I aren't close. We tolerate each other for the sake of our husbands, and when the four of us go to dinner, we always have a nice time. But tonight, in the presence of the group, she seemed to have something to prove.

I watch my expressions as I try to re-create how the conversation had gone so wrong.

It should have been a lovely dinner. As the group organizer, I'd lingered around the rustic wood dining table, waiting for everyone to take a seat and begin eating. The sizzle of fish skin wafted from an otherwise quiet kitchen. The smell of garlic in the air enhanced the depth of the merlot decanting on the table. A gloved server arranged a platter of vibrant salmon, yellow and green squash, and caramelized brown baked clams. The chandelier overhead was dimmed.

"Everyone looks fantastic tonight," I said. Despite this retreat being more casual than last year's weekend in Playa del Carmen, no one had dressed down. Farah's fitted dress had a plunging V to reveal heavy cleavage, while Eden's layered delicate charm necklaces accentuated her bandeau top. Aimee's backless pantsuit made me feel like a nun in my elegant emerald wrap dress. This group loved to pull out the stops on the first night of dinner.

With a scene as perfect as that, it was easy enough to forget about the ovulation tracking apps, the sadness at the anniversary of my parents' deaths, the distance from my brother. I kept it all inside. It fit there nicely.

And yet there were tiny sharp pieces that kept poking out. The confusion as to why my brother had lied to me that he wasn't coming tonight and then showed up in time for welcome remarks. Had he done it for the grand gesture? And the humiliation of being called naive when Farah told me she's not Aimee's doctor. Had Aimee said it for Farah's amusement? And the embarrassment from Rini's piercing insight that I felt things more than the people experiencing them. Was that code for *overdramatic*?

"The food is amazing and I'm so impressed with the service," Farah said.

"I hope no one is eating this," Eden said, scooping the salad. She pointed with her fork. "Do you see the glisten? That's an alarming level of oil, even if it was one enriched with omega-6 fatty acids. And blue cheese, the most toxic of cheeses."

"Eden, you're off duty this weekend," Farah said. "No need to police our food."

I could sense Farah biting her tongue out of respect for Aimee the momfluencer, but I'd bet Farah had the same questions about Eden as I did. She had posted a new "certification" this morning on her social media, and I'd wondered aloud to Ted, "Do people think Eden is qualified to provide health advice?" It wouldn't surprise me if she rubbed Farah the wrong way.

"So what's everyone hoping to get out of their sessions with Rini?" I asked, attempting to act the part of the conscientious organizer. No one answered at first.

"Well, for sure you're going to talk about having a baby," Aimee said.

"Why would you announce that?" I said. I'm sure that my tight voice was the only crack in my cool demeanor.

"Oh, come on, everyone here is aware you're trying to have a baby," Aimee said, unapologetic.

Even though it wasn't true, it felt like everyone knew we'd been trying to conceive for almost five years. Five long, painful years.

"I wasn't aware," Eden said.

I looked around for Ted at the other end of the table to rescue me, only to see he must have stepped out with Rick.

"The doctors"—Aimee made a face at Farah—"haven't given them any answers. I'm sure she's hoping this astrologer will."

"Who knew I'd be seeing a mind reader too?" I said to Aimee, with no sincerity.

"Astrologers aren't psychics," Eden chimed in.

"Astrologers can predict life events in the next year as they view the planetary alignments in certain houses of your chart," I said.

"And what if she tells you that you won't have a baby this year?" Eden asked.

"Then there's next year," I said, with forced nonchalance. I casually rubbed my thumb on the sweat of my wineglass and wished Eden would stop talking.

"The stigma around intervention is outdated, Margot," Farah said. "Even for someone as traditional as you."

Farah was right, of course, and even my own doctor doesn't understand why I haven't moved to IVF after five years. Only Rini could understand. Earlier she said I lived in a fantasy world, but I call it a utopia of my own making. And in my perfect world, conception is a miracle that doesn't require medical intervention. I want to live there a little while longer, even though I know at my age I can't afford to stay too long.

I smiled at Farah for her genuine input. She had surely faced patients with the same look of desperation I tried to hide.

"Thanks for saying that," I said.

"Well," Eden said. "Even with medical help, you aren't entitled to a child because you want one."

I picked up my fork and stabbed a cherry tomato drenched in balsamic vinegar. I felt the spew of seeds in my mouth before forcing it down.

"It sounds like you're mistaking my desire for something else," I said.

"That you seem to believe you deserve one," Eden said. "As if deservingness has anything to do with science."

"How about you, Aimee?" I asked, trying to bring the subject back to the readings.

"Me? I get pregnant every time Adam looks at me." She laughed, not picking up on my cue.

"You've always played by the rules to not get pregnant. Now you flip the switch and don't understand why it didn't happen on the first try," Eden said.

"I have a stable job, a great relationship, and a loving home—the right circumstances to bring a new life into."

"If you'd acknowledge your entitlement, it could free you. Maybe you'd actually get pregnant," Eden said.

Adam returned from his reading and walked over to the wet bar. His presence made me bolder. Whatever Eden was trying to do, she was not going to get me to snap. My composure is vital to my career as a lawyer.

"You know nothing about me, or my husband, or my family," I said.

"Hey," Adam interjected. I watched him expectantly, waiting for him to back me up. "Settle down, Margot," he said instead.

I stood and adjusted my dress. "Excuse me," I said plainly.

Now, I am hiding in the powder room, the bottled-up feelings hanging over me thick and heavy as a storm cloud. Eden should acknowledge her hypocrisy when her entire career plays on women's body-image issues by forcing pseudoscience wellness crap down their throats. What does she care if I'm desperate enough, after years of trying, to want an astrologer to tell me I'm going to have a baby?

"If you'd acknowledge your entitlement, it could free you," I say, mocking Eden.

You're mistaking my desire for something else.

Entitled.

You're mistaking my calm for something else.

Entitled.

I turn away from the mirror, unable to look at myself anymore. All that emotion is disgusting. I flush the toilet and run the water in case anyone is listening. My anger and hurt does not drain with it.

I want to go out there and tell Eden that entitled people don't work this hard. They just expect the result they want. They don't track every single day of their cycles. In the last five years, I've read more articles than I did in law school, educating myself on best practices. I want a baby so much, and I am willing to do anything to make it happen.

That is so far from entitled. She has no idea.

Next to the sink, I spot a hand towel dotted with fuchsia, ecru, and lavender impatiens. I hate it. I hate its pretty, happy flowers and its perfect folds.

I shove the dainty rectangle in my mouth, bite down as hard as I can, and scream.

STARS HARBOR
ASTROLOGICAL RETREAT

ASTRO CHEAT SHEET

GUEST NAME: Eden

SUN SIGN: Aries

MOON SIGN: Scorpio

RISING SIGN: Gemini

AGE: 30

OCCUPATION: wellness influencer

RELATIONSHIP TO OTHER GUESTS: married to Rick

SPECIAL NOTES: excess dualities—cardinal fire, fixed water, Gemini. Is she complex or is she split?

RINI

Eden steps into the study and I can feel the rage vibrating off her. I'm not scared, nor do I feel compelled to make small talk or calm her down. All I need to do is sit here with my regulated nervous system, and her senses will self-correct. Sitting in the chair across from me, her whole body leans toward the door. She stares over my shoulder into the rows of leather-bound books behind me, but I can tell she's listening rather than seeing.

"You won't catch any dinner party chatter from here," I say, knowing my study is the only room with no vent or dumbwaiter connection to any other part of the house. "And no one out there will hear what you say either."

Eden lets out a calming exhale and centers herself in the chair to face me.

"There's something about Margot's flavor of traditional that triggers me," Eden starts.

I nod, always happy to take conversational direction from a guest. "That's the transit of Mars through your first house of identity. You're playing with new ideas you were once afraid to look at. You're ready to take action on the things that set you off," I say.

Eden leans forward in her chair, her nodding fervent. "She's a wolf in sheep's clothing. She works like a feminist, talks like a feminist, but the more time I spend with her, I see the way her codependence with her brother has infected her entire worldview. She's so enmeshed with the patriarchy that she can't see herself apart from it."

"Like a fish who doesn't know what water is," I say.

"Meanwhile from what I can tell, Adam's trauma has made him dependent on his sister, such that he holds the matriarchy sacred. Margot is always talking about his over-the-top romantic gestures, from his first promposal to his engagement. He's the kind of traditional that the world needs more of, rather than Margot's poison. And the thought of her trying so hard to have children, to pass along her gross family values, it set me off."

"Any notion of traditional offends you," I say. "You've got *thought leader* and *rebel* all over your chart. On top of the Aries Sun, your chart is a classic splay formation."

"Really? I was born like that?"

"You can handle multiple lovers, and you prefer it this way." I say this with no judgment, and no voyeuristic curiosity either. A flat affect is gold for an astrologer.

"You can see that in my chart?"

"Your seventh house in Sagittarius demands freedom. You like to explore, and that's not simply about traveling the world or some such."

Eden shakes her head. "I promised I'd come into this reading with an open mind, but I didn't think you'd read my deepest thoughts. Rick and I have been polyamorous from the beginning."

Eden explains that they were both single when they met, but according to her, it was not by choice. It was because everyone they became involved with expected a monogamous relationship, and that led to the early expiration of good chemistry.

They were fed up with others wanting to tie them down, but also feeling the pressure to give in to monogamy—or at least the appearance of it—to have a shot at love. And then they found each other. Two people who wanted to be in a committed primary relationship, who were secure enough to let their partners, and themselves, remain open to other connections. It's the most compelling case for polyamory I've ever heard. And so refreshing, given the number of straight cheaters who ask me for guidance on whether they should choose their spouse or their lover.

"We got married six weeks after the day we met. What else did we need to know? It seemed beyond perfect," Eden concludes. I can see—on her chart and on her face—that there's more to the story.

"But right now there is opposition between Venus the planet of connection, and your Venus placement. Your expansive view of partnership is being challenged."

"Well, his name isn't Venus, but opposition, yes. We met at a wedding. He was wearing a tux, and for someone who hates tradition, you'd be surprised how riled up that gets me."

"You don't hate tradition; you want to make your own rules. And if tuxes get you going, then that's your thing."

"You could tell he knew it too. In his mind he was James Bond, both hot and cool. But after two minutes of conversation, it was plain to see that he could never stab a spy with a hotel pen. He wore his heart on his sleeve, at least with me. Don't get me wrong, he was hot enough to be James Bond, but there was a soft vulnerability. A boy in need of love."

"I don't see the issue, though. This seems ideal, or at least exactly what you signed up for with your husband."

"It could be. It should be. It would be, if it weren't for me."

"What do you mean?" I ask.

"Rick and I have rules. Rules as to who we get involved with, how we handle the new person, what we do for the primary partner. I've broken them all."

"Eden, why are you here? What can I help with?"

"I need a sign. Do I come clean to Rick?"

I'm not someone who believes in blindly telling the truth. Even when it sounds plain and clear, "the truth" is often murky and has unpredictable effects.

Come clean.

I have repeatedly held back important information from the people I love most. It can be safer to keep it inside. It can also be disastrous. I need to press Eden to think about which outcome is more likely for her.

"That's your free will. There's nothing in your chart that can answer that. So I'll ask the obvious question—why haven't you come clean already?"

"If I tell Rick, he'll put a stop to it immediately. When I imagine that conversation, I see Rick as one of the people I was trying to get away from when I married him. Someone who is going to impose his will over me, deny me what I want to do."

"But you both agreed to the rules."

"And we'd both broken rules before, but we keep each other honest. That's a vital part of polyamory, the openness of it. Now I'm just a plain old cheater."

"And yet the solution is simple. You can put an end to this deception in several ways," I say.

"There's something inside me that can't do it. I know I should, and yet . . ."

"And yet, what?" I repeat.

Eden and I have been so conversational and connected that I struggle to keep my frustration locked away. Eden gets to choose. She gets to make mistakes and try to correct them. I no longer have those luxuries.

"Unlike Rick, he's the first man who has ever felt like enough for me. He is so attentive, but also gives me my space. I think I understand monogamy now."

That was all I needed to spark more insight from her chart and drop my personal angst. I turn to her twelfth house, the unseen, the subconscious.

"Your rejection of monogamy might be a fear of rejection. Tell me about your parents," I say.

"I was an only child. A miracle baby. My parents smothered me with love. I've never met a man who could love me as much as they did, and in dating that felt like constant rejection. Even when we were in love, it wasn't enough."

"So multiple partners seemed necessary to replicate that intense love."

Eden nods solemnly. I let the impact of this series of revelations set in with silence. Which also gives me time to recover my own unwieldy emotions about love and rejection, honesty and protection. I shine on the optimism.

"Well, I have good news. You aren't choosing between two guys. You're choosing between two versions of yourself. You're caught between a loyalty to a past decision and exploring a future promise. Which Eden do you want to be?"

Eden's whole face lights up as soon as I finish the question.

"I guess you already know," I say.

After Eden leaves, I consider my own behavior. Which Rini do I want to be? *You get what you get and you don't get upset* doesn't mean you don't have choices. I never want to be someone who throws in the towel and gives up when they believe they know exactly what's going to happen. Where's the room for surprise? The room for growth? I haven't limited myself in building Stars Harbor, or planning this weekend's guests, so why have I done it with Eric, the love of my life? I've given up not only my free will, but his.

Before I summon Ted, I pull my phone from the drawer where I hide it during readings. I text Eric with the urgency I feel in my heart.

Hi, sorry to bother you. I might be having a joist issue with the floorboards in the study. Do you think you could drop by so I can show you? Schedule is the same as always.

I reread the text. It's got the urgency I feel in my heart, if not the words. *Gotta start somewhere.* I hit send and put the phone away before he can respond, but the joy I feel from taking action is undeniable.

When we are our highest, most practiced selves, that kind of lightning-bolt clarity comes from the wisest parts of the psyche. That's why I'm certain that text was the right thing to do, even though it will unwind the last six months of distance I've put between me and Eric.

I can only hope for Eden that she's not jumping out of one proverbial pot of boiling water directly into another, clinging to the belief that the pot will make all the difference.

AIMEE

'm trying really hard to focus on the positive: Adam is here on this trip, we broke our sex drought, and he got a bit of writing done before the first night's dinner kicked off. But Adam is quiet and refuses to engage after his reading. He responds in one- or two-word answers when I ask him a question, and draws away when I reach for his hand. I know in my gut that something is wrong.

Going into this weekend, I knew Adam and I weren't in our best phase, but I would have said we are rock-solid. That this is not a repeat of our first year of marriage. I had assumed whatever distance was between us now would be fixed with time away from the kids and some intimacy, but that hasn't been the magic bullet.

After dinner while everyone moves into the living room, refreshing their drinks and ambling around the first floor, I excuse myself to our room. I'm on a hunt for clues.

Maybe it's Adam's deadline that's got him on edge. I asked him if he'd figured out the ending yet and his stony gaze turned fiery. I wanted to offer to help brainstorm, but I didn't even read his last book.

The weight of this fact slams me. It's the first time I've ever skipped a book. Thirteen published novels plus three in a drawer that will never see the light of day—I've read every word. Yet I couldn't even tell you the names of the hero and his love interest in this last one. How has the past caught up with me like this all of a sudden?

At his last deadline I had a newborn, a preschooler, and a first grader. How much can he expect of me? The world. Of course I know he expects the world. It's what we promised each other.

"Hey," Farah says, opening the suite door a crack.

"I'm looking for Advil," I say, trying to hide the fact that she startled me.

Farah closes the door behind her, and the din of the party fades. "I have some. Do you want me to go get it?"

I shake my head but continue to root around Adam's things.

"Are you okay?" Farah asks.

I'm surprised that with those three words my anger and confusion turn into something else. Something ooey gooey. I consider telling Farah that I don't know what's going on between me and Adam. I can imagine saying I'm a little bit scared, and maybe increasingly desperate. That beneath those more obvious reactions might be deep sadness.

"It's my lashes. This one's irritating me," I respond while fixing my eye in the mirror.

Farah can tell I'm not fine, but she lets it go. That's when the emotion overwhelms me and I confess.

"I'm scared Adam's going to leave me and I'm trying not to lose it," I blurt.

"Oh, Aimee. What can I do?" Farah asks, the doctor always to my rescue.

I suspect she wants me to cry or bad-mouth Adam, but I've got something else in mind. "Help me go through his things. I need proof."

Farah is more game than I expected. She doesn't exactly love Adam, but I figured she'd object on the principle of invading his privacy. I was wrong about her.

"Did you try his laptop?" she asks. She sits at the small desk and opens his computer, staring at the keys.

"His last password was Clara321."

"Really?" she asks.

"Yeah, why?"

"His daughter's name is his password? I would have thought it was I'm-God's-gift-to-women321."

"Stop it. You know Adam is an amazing dad. He does everything I do. Just less of it."

Like you, I think unkindly. My stress is coming out sideways, but Farah doesn't notice. She types the password.

"Nope. Not it," she says.

For tallying points in the "everything is fine" and "everything is shit" columns of my marriage, the new password isn't helping even things out.

"Okay, we'll have to go analog. I'll grab his bag; you go through his briefcase."

"What are we looking for?"

"Receipts, statements, love notes."

"You think he could be having an affair?" Farah asks.

"No, not necessarily. But that's the only thing I care about. If this is just a mood, it will blow over."

"What do you think the astrologer would say about searching for proof of your husband's affair? Are you thwarting your destiny? What about his?"

My words from earlier, thrown back at me.

"Ha, ha. Listen, Little Miss Science. I'm not asking for the universe to step in. I'm seeking facts. Information. This has nothing to do with destiny."

I unzip the front compartment of his briefcase and pull out a stack of papers.

"Oh, this is good," I call out in relief.

"What is it?"

"It's an essay he's writing for *GQ* about a long, healthy marriage," I lie.

In reality, I've uncovered the first five pages of Adam's current work in progress. Although no one besides me, Adam, his editor, and his agent are supposed to know the true identity of Audra Rose, I would trust Farah with that secret. The only reason I don't tell her is because she would think even less of him than she already does, and I don't need that kind of headache. Farah's not the kind of woman who would have any respect for a male romance novelist. She's too old-fashioned for that.

I skim the first page and hug the stack of papers to my chest and close my eyes. Adam named his protagonist Scarlett. Like my scarlet fever.

Adam and I had been dating for a year when we went upstate to the Berkshires for some autumn hiking and cozy lovemaking. Instead, I got sick.

I worried that Adam might treat me the way my mother the nurse always had. She'd set me up in bed, with tissues, water, medication, and the remote control. She'd check on me every few hours with objective precision, like she had a chart at the end of my twin bed that she had to complete. It was confusing and lonely.

Or I was afraid Adam would react like my hypochondriac father, who wouldn't even look at me while I was sick but then would overwhelm me with hugs and kisses when my mother assured him I was no longer contagious. In different ways, I felt disgusting to both of them.

To avoid having Adam seeing me the way they did, I wanted him out of the hotel room. I told him to go to the museum without me. Go out to eat alone on the reservations he made. But Adam wouldn't hear about plans. He held my hand. He brought me a cold washcloth, and when my fever roasted it, he wrung it out and brought me another. Nothing he did was intended to make my sickness pass quicker. He did it for comfort. It was a love I'd never known.

People think you have to have horrendous things happen to you in your childhood to be messed up. I believe you can live in the same house your entire childhood, have an insurance broker for a father, a nurse for a mother, both gainfully employed but not overworked, neither of whom have any substance abuse issues, and you can still be royally screwed up too.

All you need is one part critical, cold, exacting mother (ironically all the qualities that made her a great health care provider), two parts dad with gushy need that is palpable but misdirected. I was smothered and ignored. Praised without reason, criticized without cause.

But Adam's love was measured. He comforted me when I was sick. He walked out of the room when I was lashing out for no reason. His love was within my control. Not him—I wasn't controlling him or his actions—but the dynamic between us had a logic I understood. And when I loved him the way he needed to be loved, we had a big, dynamic, intense connection. And when I didn't love him the way he needed, he abandoned me. I never want to feel his absence again. And now I'm sure I won't.

"It tells me Adam still loves me and wants our marriage to last as much as I do," I say to Farah.

He knows it wasn't only me who stopped giving that intense, dynamic love. Adam dropped out too. He became utilitarian, and there's nothing less romantic. To think, I used to be the one gloating to complaining moms at our wine nights that I held the secret to a strong marriage after kids.

Adam is a great father because he takes my instructions well. By previous generations' standards, he's a superstar. He drives the girls to ballet and soccer. But he doesn't exactly take the lead on anything. I don't sweat that stuff, because I want to be in charge at home. And when I'm done with the arduous work of the day, he greets me with the most important question: Red wine or chocolate ice cream? He brings my choice to me with a blanket and asks what I want to watch while I unwind. He takes care of me the best.

It hasn't been like that for a while. How long? Months? A year? Time with little children goes so fast and so slow all at once. No matter how long it's been, I'm not ready to lose Adam. Not to his career or whatever else might be creating distance between us. We are a happy family and we're going to stay that way. No matter what.

"So things are all good?" Farah asks.

"Not yet, but they can be still," I say.

Farah heads downstairs first while I shove Adam's papers back in his briefcase. I notice my pants and shirt strewn across the floor where I left them before my shower. It gives me an idea for a post. These aren't the right clothes for the job, but I have the perfect lacy black bra and panties. I rummage through my suitcase and place them on the plush cream carpet just so. I get the shot and type.

Being a mom is the greatest thing in the world, my purpose in life, but it's so important to reconnect with your partner. He's the reason this all exists. #ad #laperla #sexy #blacklace

RINI

I lied to Farah and Aimee when I said there was no access to the turrets. Well, I half lied. There's no access for the guests. But for me, there's a way. You must go down to go up.

Tonight, after the readings are done, after the staff from Claudio's has cleared away the food and drink, after every single light is switched off, it's my time.

I move through the shadows from my cottage to the main house. I quietly lift the well-oiled metal bulkhead doors to the utility basement. I pass the hot-water heater, the oil tank, and the panels of circuit breakers. In the back corner is a door. It's a simple hollow-core wooden door with no lock on it. If you wanted to kick it in, the fiberboard would easily give way, exposing the honeycombed plastic keeping it upright. That door opens to a narrow hallway. Three feet into this enclosed, damp, dark hallway is another door. This one is solid. You can feel its heft simply by touching it. You wonder if it's metal, and you're half-right. The door-frame is, and the solid-core wood is reinforced with metal bars inside. If you tried to kick it down, you'd break your leg.

I gather the chain from inside my shirt, where a key stays safe around my neck, next to the heart-shaped locket, and pull it over my head. I unlock the deadbolt and make my way up the winding staircase. Because the shaft is so small, like in a mine or a lighthouse, a spiral is the only type of rise that works in the space between an elevator (too loud) and a ladder (too tenuous). When I reach the top, I wait for my eyes to adjust in the new room. I tiptoe through the small bedroom and living area to the door between the kitchen and the bathroom.

After opening the unlocked door, I ascend the final staircase to the turret on the east side of the house. I close the door behind me and the metal frame squeals. Last time, I said I'd remember to bring the WD-40, but that didn't happen. I freeze and wait, hoping it's far enough away from the current guests' balconies to go unheard.

I take a moment to breathe in the salty air. I relish the hint of marshy sulfur scent that accompanies the extra-low tide of the moon. The back lawn and the dock are bathed in the moon's luminescence. I swing one leg over the thick wooden railing of the turret and then the other, careful not to snag any splinters. Atop the railing, I let my legs swing back and forth over the ledge below. Once I've been there long enough to know I haven't woken anyone with my skulking around, I hop over the railing and onto the ledge that circles the turret.

I'm untethered and high enough to feel slightly dizzy, but I hold on with my hands behind me. While my equilibrium steadies, I take a step onto the tiles of the steeply peaked roof. I walk with my arms extended for balance until I reach the middle. I slowly crouch to sit straddling the peak and slip my phone from my pocket. Still no response from Eric after three hours. He doesn't want to see me and I don't blame him.

I was born unlucky. Not "brick falls on my head as I stroll by my favorite coffee shop" unlucky. Not "struck by lightning" unlucky. Nothing that would go viral on social media. My life has mostly been "Alanis Morissette's 'Ironic'" unlucky. Black flies and myriad spoons. With the constant threat of death.

My father left our family when I was seven. A year later, my mother dragged me and Andi with her to Pittsburgh for a psychic reading. The psychic said my mother would meet and fall in love with a wealthy black-haired man who would rescue us and keep us safe in a tower in the city. My mother couldn't hide her joy. The psychic had promised three things she had always wanted but never had: true love, riches, and a lavish home. She was so happy, my mother tipped the psychic handsomely.

In a hushed tone at the end of the session, the psychic added that maybe my mother should consider spending more time with "the little one"—she nodded her head toward me next to my older sister—because I would die as a child. My mother's new smile crumbled for a split second, but she snatched back the cash gratuity and recovered her glow.

At the time, I must have thought the session was pretend storytelling until my mother met and married that black-haired rich man who swept us away to Manhattan. They divorced five years later, and my mom, my sister, and I ended up in a one-bedroom in Queens. The psychic hadn't said anything about it lasting forever.

An eight-year-old's brain can't truly process the idea of dying. It only knows that it is unsafe. As a result, I was on high alert at all times. Since I didn't know what danger I was looking for, I became scared of everything. It was simply how I moved through the world: afraid.

When my stepfather left us, my mother sought the counsel of an astrologer. Unlike the psychic who had rocked side to side with her eyes slightly closed, this astrologer was composed. She sat in front of stacks of books printed in languages I couldn't read. She studied a massive piece of paper, *a map of your mother*, she'd said. She drew lines with her finger and pointed to symbols of planets we'd learned in science class. She told my mother all sorts of truths, about her and her future, but something more amazing happened that day. My fear evaporated in that room.

Astrology was something I could study, unlike the psychic prediction pulled from thin air. Looking at the stars, my challenges could be found in the location of the planets in certain houses of my birth chart. Obstacles were explained by noting the angles these planets made to one another—the oppositions, trines, and squares. And yet, there is still one thing I can't find in my chart: my death date.

I pick up a stray acorn on the roof and toss it as far as I can. I don't hear it land. I shimmy over to the landing and pull myself up. But instead of climbing to safety, I stand on top of the railing so that my head pops above the turret's roof. With nothing above me I have to grip the edge of the roof from underneath. My fingers bend and burn, but I hold on tighter and spit into the wind. I let go of the underside of the tile with my right hand and shake it out. I switch hands, simultaneously grabbing the tiles with my right hand while I shake out my left. I lose my balance but stabilize by pulling myself closer to the turret roof.

I lean back farther this time and do the switch again. My left hand slips and I scramble to catch myself. My favorite purple pen falls out of my pocket and bounces off the lower roof with a click, click, click. I let myself hang there until sweat springs on my upper lip and my fingers cramp up.

I never mentioned the psychic's prediction to anyone. Not my astrology mentor, though I asked her for strategies in predicting death all the time, which she repeatedly dismissed. She thought there were some dark matters that should stay outside the purview of the practice. Namely, no forecasting elections and no death dates.

I never mentioned the prediction to my mother, and if she remembered what that psychic had said, she never let on. I certainly never considered mentioning it to my sister, who had enough trauma in her own life to easily forget mine. When I was sixteen and Andi in college, I witnessed my sister go through an incident so unbearable that she wished for death. It shocked me that she wanted the thing I was most afraid of. Andi shifted my perspective and I vowed to start living—really living, not just waiting to die.

I dove into work and figuring out my dreams, rather than waiting until I was a grown-up, since for me there was a good chance that was never going to happen. I earned my GED at my mother's insistence, but spent my time as a florist, a barista, a diner waitress, a house cleaner, and an astrologer's apprentice, all of which prepared me for my future success with Stars Harbor Astrological Retreat. I was exhausted but happy.

With each passing year, the idea of an early death transformed into nothing more than a tiny buzz in the background. I was able to ignore it—until I did a terrible thing. Something I couldn't take back.

I fell in love.

It was an accident. I knew to keep my distance, but that's impossible when you're essentially rebuilding a home from its studs and he's the best local contractor. Eric was so kind and generous. He loved this project before he loved me. We had that in common.

Every time Eric stayed the night or we texted throughout the day, there was a little voice in the back of my head telling me not to trust it. *You're going to die.* I couldn't relax into the safety he offered.

When Eric started talking about the future—moving in, getting married, having kids—I freaked out. I made it my mission to track down the Pittsburgh psychic my mother saw when I was eight years old. I had to know my fate, if not for me, for him. For us.

Six months ago, I found her online through Facebook. She'd closed down the storefront operation less than a year after my mother saw her. Yet during the financial crisis of 2008—when everyone had no money but desperately needed to hear about their future—her online presence flourished. I called her hotline and cut off her introductions to bluntly ask if she had gotten it wrong all those years ago, or if I had somehow.

"You told my mother I would die as a child," I said.

Metal clanked against the phone as she shook her head. A memory of her massive jeweled costume earrings flashed in my mind's eye.

"Pittsburgh, eighteen years ago, I've never forgotten you. I was a beginner then, and ashamed as soon as I said it. I wanted to help your mother, but now I would never reveal such information."

I was stunned. I expected to have to explain.

"But you were wrong," I said. "You said I would die as a child, but I'm twenty-six."

"I didn't say you would die as a child." Her words were drawn out and deliberate. "I said you would die too young."

Neither of us said anything for a long time. Time stretched out before us. How young was too young? In the state of New York, the age of consent is seventeen. At eighteen, you can vote. At twenty-one, you can drink. At twenty-five, you can rent a car. Hadn't I passed every adult threshold? Shouldn't I be safe?

Then again, in some sense I never was a child. From the moment I was born I could feel the invisible burden of being the baby expected to fix a broken family. My mother hadn't gone to college, and though she was proud of Andi for trying, she didn't blink an eye when I dropped out of high school to start helping to pay the bills. I grew up too fast.

Was the psychic's prediction wrong because I had never been a child? Or maybe karmically I was a child now, aging in reverse?

"I've been studying astrology," I said to the psychic. "I've seen a few things that can be interpreted as death. A cluster of planets moving into my eighth house. My Imum Coeli in Gemini, which is the sign of youth. Or is it something less obvious, like my Saturn's Return approaching?"

The psychic laughed. "I have no idea what any of that means, but I have been waiting for this call. I've debated what I'd do when it came."

She sighed and shifted herself. I heard her earrings jingle.

"How about it's not up to you anymore? You made that choice years ago," I said.

The faint scratch on the other end of the phone told me she nodded, but she didn't speak.

"I want a date," I added.

"My guides tell me you have done well with the information I gave you then. I've regretted it all these years, but they say you've done all the right things. They trust you."

"Tell me." My words were forceful and confident, more so than I felt. But I was afraid if I hesitated she would give me nothing.

"August twenty-fifth," she said.

Two days from now.

On the roof of Stars Harbor, I lose feeling in all my fingers. I point my toes until I find footing on the wooden rail beneath me. My arms burn and shake. I'm reckless and afraid. My fate says I will die the day after tomorrow, but I don't know when or how or why. My free will tells me that if I wanted to make the psychic wrong, I could. I have that power.

I could let go right now.

Instead, I use my remaining strength to haul myself back to safety. That's when I hear the rustling below, and low voices murmuring. I squint to see two bodies undressing in the silver moonlight. Their faint moans reach my ears even from here, and I recognize them both. I don't know why I find myself shaking my head. It shouldn't surprise me to see those two together.

SATURDAY

THE SECOND DAY

MARGOT

With wet hair, I descend the back stairwell of Stars Harbor. At the bottom, I run my hand along the painted wall, searching for the door to the storage space underneath. A nostalgic touchstone, it's the one closed-off area I don't mind invading in any new location. This morning, there's no one around to bother me.

The small square entryway isn't obvious. It's painted the same color as the wall and there's no frame. I press my palm flat and pop the door open. With a creak, I swing it open and look inside. There are books shoved in a corner, overflow from the library. There are also cleaning supplies and extra towels and linens. The space smells like my childhood.

I hear Farah and Aimee giggling down the front room staircase, so I quietly press the door shut. I sneak up the back stairs to avoid them. In my suite, Ted is out of the shower.

"I slept terribly. How about you?" I ask.

Ted shrugs. "I don't think I moved once. What was keeping you up?"

"I fell asleep quickly, but I woke up around midnight when I thought I heard voices outside, and then again at three a.m. I heard noises from above."

"Maybe raccoons in the attic. Remember when that mother took up shelter in our beach house to give birth? It sounded like they'd come through the walls."

Ted's not wrong, but he's focused on the wrong thing. "I probably couldn't sleep because I'm worried about Adam."

"He seemed fine to me yesterday, but he's bailing on golf this morning," Ted says.

When Adam started missing the occasional Wednesday night dinner, I'd been disappointed, but not worried. When he was a no-show at Clara's ballet recital last month, both Aimee and I covered for him, telling her that he was there but she couldn't see him in the dark. Not a high point, lying to my own defenseless niece, but when we got home it was worse. Adam was sitting on the couch, beer in one hand, the other down his pants.

Adam has always been prone to depression, and I think it's because he lives mostly in a fantasy world as a writer. Compounded by the fact that he writes under a pseudonym, which means no one knows who he is. It's like all his success exists only in his own head. At school functions and dinner parties, the question of his career ends with the lackluster grunt of "Writer." Meanwhile, in reality, his novels have sold millions of copies.

"It's this deadline. He doesn't know when to ask for help," I say.

Ted sighs and retreats to the bathroom while I cuddle up under the sheets again wishing I could start the day over. For the most part, Ted chooses to stay out of things with me and Adam, but occasionally he likes to offer a "gentle reminder" that maybe I get a little too wrapped up in my brother's life. When Ted emerges from the bathroom dressed in his golf shirt, he slides his wallet off the dresser and into the back pocket of his shorts.

"I think you might be projecting a bit?" he says.

"Fine, that's fair. But Adam doesn't always see the big picture clearly. He needs my perspective whether he wants it or not."

Ted sits down on the bed next to me. "I want you to take care of yourself before him for once. You are carrying a lot. Trying to create life."

He smooths the sheet over my stomach and kisses my belly button. I smile, but part of me wants to remind him that there's nothing I can "do" when "trying to create life." It's the worst feeling in the world. Helplessness. I consider reminding him that as of this morning I'm officially two days late, but I hold on to that to discuss with Rini, hoping she'll give me something more concrete to share.

I hear the back door open beneath our open balcony, and I check the time. Speak of the devil.

"That's probably Rini with our astro-smoothies, ready to kick off this morning's readings," I tell Ted. We walk down the stairs hand in hand. Ted peels off toward Rick, who is waiting for him with their clubs in the entryway.

"Still no Joe?" I mouth. Ted shakes his head.

I head toward the back of the house, but there's no sign of Rini in the kitchen. Aimee and Farah plan their day at the bistro table in the corner. I offer a polite "Good morning" before pouring myself a mug of coffee and getting ready to sprint out of the room.

"Anyone else awoken by strange noises in the night?" Farah asks.

"I was just saying this to Ted."

"I heard crying," Aimee says.

Rini enters through the French doors then, a silver tray of brightly colored smoothies in her hands.

"These are so pretty," Aimee exclaims.

Eden joins from outside.

"I saw you walk by with these and I was intrigued," Eden says.

"There's one for each of you, prepared to suit your astrological sun sign," Rini says, placing the descriptive cards in a line along the table next to the tray.

"Is this almond milk?" Eden brings the glass to her nose.

Rini passes a description card to each of us and tents the others in front of their smoothies for the guests not here. I scan the tropical ingredients in the Pisces smoothie.

"I can't have pineapple," I say.

"Oh? I noted there were no food allergies on your booking questionnaire," Rini says.

"I assumed that was for life-threatening allergies, like shellfish or tree nuts. I'm not going to die or anything."

"Does it give you a migraine?" Farah asks.

"Yes, how did you know?"

"The tyramine in pineapple can overpower the anti-inflammatory properties of the bromelain. Happens to about fifteen percent of my patients during pregnancy."

Pregnancy? That feels like a sign that this will be my month for the two glowing lines on my pregnancy test.

"You can have mine. I hate coconut," Farah says.

I accept the glass from Farah, but before I take a sip of the frothy white drink, I check with Rini.

"Does that affect my reading, drinking another sign's smoothie?"

Aimee laughs. "Wow, you are such a rule follower, Margot. Live a little and try some Virgo juice."

"Enjoy your welcome smoothies in any way you wish. The Sun Worship excursion is at eleven a.m.," Rini says. "Farah, your reading is next."

I carry my smoothie upstairs to my room and look for a place to set down my drink, but the glass is sweating and I don't want to ruin the furniture. I grab a couple of tissues from the nightstand and fold them into a makeshift coaster. I notice the fresh flowers on the desk and a note on my pillow.

....

Good morning, Pisces. When you leave here at the end of the weekend and everything is fine, it will be clear you spent all that time and energy worrying for nothing. Do you know you have the ability to change your outlook? Enjoy the next two days rather than working yourself up. Your problems will solve themselves.

....

Your problems will solve themselves? That's not a thing. Problems ignored become bigger problems. I toss the card back on the bed and hope Rini's readings are better than this laughable wisdom. At least I can hold on to the first sentence. By the time I leave, everything will be fine. I pray that's true.

On Ted's pillow, I see his horoscope card. He won't even read it. He wasn't impressed with Rini's reading last night, and now I don't know what to expect for mine. I collapse on the bed and stare into space, listening to the geese honking until my eyes focus on the flowers on the desk. How did they get up here if I saw Rini walk in with the tray of smoothies?

I think of the door I heard slam earlier. Rini must have taken a detour to our rooms using the back staircase before she got the smoothies. I scan the room for any other new touches, evidence of her presence. I spot a square on the wall in the space between the window and the bathroom. It looks like the laundry chutes Aimee and Adam have in their beach house, but bigger. There's no handle, no pull tab to slide, but I know how to open the tiny door.

As I did with the space beneath the stairs, I press my palm flat and pop the door open. There's a small white plate sitting on a gray box, and on the plate a single perfect raspberry. The scale of the plate makes the space inside the dumbwaiter look massive in comparison. I pick up the plate and inspect the perfect red berry with its tiny hairs and glistening skin.

Raspberry. At eight weeks, your baby is the size of a raspberry, the pregnancy sites proclaim. Next to the random plate is a brightly colored rectangle that reminds me of a mass card from church. I pick it up and turn it over. Upon closer inspection I recognize it as a tarot card, the word *EMPRESS* emblazoned on the bottom. I slide my phone out of my pocket and search for the meaning of the Empress. The Google sidebar makes me gasp.

Meaning: The Empress is traditionally associated with the divine feminine and maternal influences. If you are hoping to start a family, consider this your sign to buy some pregnancy tests. If not, The Empress can also represent the seed of new romance, art, or business.

I stick my head inside as if I could see the magical fairy who left me this perfect sign. Instead I see the pantry below through the cracks in the dumbwaiter shaft. My heart's aflutter reading those words. I want to run through the hallway waving the tarot card like Willy Wonka's golden ticket, but part of me also wants to hold it close to my vest. If this is a sign of what's to come, I have plenty of time to share. This moment is just mine. I put the card back in the dumbwaiter and wonder why it wasn't on the bed with the daily horoscope. I decide to investigate in my brother's room.

The first time I saw a dumbwaiter was when Nana brought us to the English countryside for spring break in high school. All the massive homes of the wealthy had these rope-and-pulley delivery systems so they could avoid exposing guests to the staff while they entertained.

I'll use this discovery as an excuse to reminisce with my brother. I knock on the door and push it open. I hear the shower running. I take a quick look around the room, but Adam has no flowers or horoscope cards. I search for the outline opening in his walls and spot it next to the closets. In his bathroom, the water splashes against the marble shower floor.

I sneak into the room and close the door behind me. I pop open the dumbwaiter and find a similar setup for Adam: a small glass vase of flowers and daily horoscope cards. No plate, no tarot. I'll have to ask Rini about that later, but for now my curiosity gets the best of me. With one more glimpse toward the closed bathroom door, I pick up Adam's card.

···

Good morning, Scorpio. More than most people, you know the power of connection—as well as the pain and shame of a disconnect. Repent (and don't deny it, as your ego wants) and deep healing shall occur. For both of you.

···

I hear the shower knob squeak and the water come to a halt. I rush out of my brother's room with glassy eyes. His horoscope confirms my greatest hope for this trip. That we will reconnect and it will heal us both. I don't even need repentance, I only want my brother back.

FARAH

Precisely at 10:00 a.m., I knock on Rini's study door. I announce myself the way I do in an exam room: a quick, sharp double rap. I crack the door and Rini waves me in.

The first time Aimee and I were in Rini's study I didn't notice the Tiffany lamp on each side of her desk. The shades are identical, multicolored at the top fading down into aqua blue. I'm reminded of the water Aimee plunged into yesterday. Lately, everything reminds me of Aimee.

"So, do you have any topics of intrigue this morning?" Rini asks.

"Actually, I do. Why is the back of the house different in style from the front of the house?"

Rini gives me a look of annoyance. "I meant about your life."

"It's a valid question."

"It's for privacy. It makes it harder to track down guests from the water because they're looking for the house they could see from the road."

"I thought it was poor planning," I say.

"Quite the opposite," Rini says with a slight smile.

"Very clever."

"Let's get into your chart. Your sun sign is Virgo. My teacher called them the healer of the zodiac. You're a doctor, is that right?"

"Exactly like I wrote on my forms for our stay, yes."

Rini doesn't look ruffled, but maybe she should be. Her reading better go deeper than the *Daily News* horoscopes, or this Virgo will have a field day on Yelp.

"You're a perfectionist grounded in reality," she continues.

"What does that mean?"

"You think perfection is attainable, not an out-of-reach ideal," she says.

"Oh, absolutely," I say. But she could have inferred that from my profession. There aren't a lot of sloppy half-assers who go to medical school.

"Capricorns are perfectionists who use it as a tool for self-flagellation. Pisces are more idealists than perfectionists. The differences are subtle, but important," Rini says, as if reading my mind. "You work a lot," she continues, "but not to stay busy like Leos or to outrun their pasts like Aries, but because you believe in what you're doing."

"What I believe in more than anything is science and the wonders it provides."

Rini nods. "That's your bigger reason. Your purpose."

I wait for her to go on.

"People can accuse you of being critical, harsh, arrogant," she says.

I raise my eyebrows at how blunt she is.

"But you never hear those words from people who are close to you," Rini continues. "It's an initial reaction to the fact that you're very practical. Cerebral."

I lean back in my chair and fold my hands at the back of my neck. I understand why she starts with personality traits. She's winning me over. If I were naive, I'd consider buying a bridge from her by the end of the weekend.

"Yes," I concede.

I might be impressed, but I'm not giving her anything. I've seen these things on TV, where the person says something vague like *I see a man*, and the other person gives it all away: *My father, he died when I was fourteen and we had a strained relationship.* Then the charlatan runs with those insights, and the duped thinks they're witnessing a miracle.

"What's the deal here?" I ask bluntly. If she wants my buy-in, she's going to have to give me a peek behind the curtain.

"I'm not sure I understand the question," she says.

"Do you just deep dive on our social media or do you hire a private investigator? That seems impractical for every guest."

"I don't know anything about my guests other than what you provide on your booking forms and what I see in your birth chart. And that's far more complicated than knowing which horoscope to read in a magazine."

"How?" I ask.

"Your Mercury sign is how you communicate, your Venus sign is how you connect, your Mars sign is how you take action. Together these give me a more nuanced picture of who you are as compared with every Virgo in the world."

"And what's a Mercury sign?"

"It's the zodiac sign and house where Mercury was situated when you were born."

"Mercury the planet? So there is some connection to astronomy?"

Rini explains the origins, limitations, and unique wisdom of astrology, and I realize the mistake I made when I came into my readings. I had the kind of attitude I hate in new patients. They treat me like I'm here to sell them something, as if I personally profit from epidurals or C-sections, when I'm a professional trying to give them the best prenatal care and birth experience.

At this point in my career, I have nothing to prove. However, first-time mothers, as they typically are, do—and by all means, I'm not going to get in their way. I give them the tools to know what's happening, and to trust me enough to take over if things go sideways. Rini might deal in magical thinking, while I operate in the realm of researched science, but she and I aren't as different as I'd imagined.

"Most people come in here with lots of secrets," Rini says. "Women who have a favorite child, crushes at work, desires for their spouses to lose weight. Little secrets. But you have a major secret that you're holding back."

I watch her, waiting for more. She looks up from her papers. I avoid her gaze.

"It's marked in your eighth house," she says. "That house governs household finances, sexuality, and death."

She puts emphasis on the last word like that's the bloody scalpel, but my heart skips at *sexuality*. I don't say anything. I can't. Honestly I'd rather she think I was a murderer than an almost-forty-year-old questioning her sexual orientation because she's in love with her best friend.

"The Venus transit through your eighth house is happening now," she says.

"And that means?"

"This secret connection is something you've recently realized. About three weeks ago."

"My dream," I blurt out without thinking. That dream.

"You had a vision?" Rini asks.

"Vision?" I shake my head. I don't have visions. I won't even use the expression "dream come true." Goals are accomplished through hard work. There's no magic to it.

I clear my throat.

"The square with Mercury, the planet of communication, ends on Monday," Rini says.

I don't try to hide my shock. Monday. That's three days to reveal a secret I've been hiding for three weeks. Maybe even three years, if I'm being honest with myself.

"And what does that mean?" I ask.

"It all depends what you're wrestling with."

I watch her. She likes this game. I'm so far forward in my seat, I'm practically leaning into her personal space. She's hooked me. I scoot back in the chair and say nothing. Rini breaks the silence.

"You can get a good telescope if you want to see the planetary transits. But if you want a truly tailored reading, you need to give me context," she says.

Yesterday I would have told you I didn't believe in astrology. Science is my life, not celestial mythology. And yet this morning I am aching for this stranger to tell me which feelings are real and which ones I should act on. For this reason, I spill my secret. The one more confusing than Beckett's behavior. The one I wouldn't dare hint at outside this room.

"There's a woman," I start. "But I'm married. And she's married."

"Which one is the bigger obstacle?" Rini asks without a hint of judgment. I'm sure these four walls have seen it all. I consider the factors.

"I value loyalty. My husband works in politics. He values appearances. Together we make a good team, but there's no love anymore. It wouldn't be easy, but our marriage has been unraveling for a long time. Meanwhile, she and her husband have always been toxic. She could do so much better, but she has no idea."

Even if I didn't name her, I cannot believe I admitted I have feelings for Aimee. Out loud. I shift my gaze up to the space between me and Rini, half imagining I can see the words floating above us. *There's a woman. I'm married. She's married.* Circling like smoke rings. Smoke rings that don't even feel real.

"I see a lot of hidden emotion here. Not in your birth chart, but in your current transits. A lot of shame. Does that ring true?" Rini asks.

I nod, unable to speak. As far as a generalization goes, that one cuts deep to the bone.

"The eighth house symbolizes things you need to let go of. Shame is all over that. In your current situation at home and your blossoming love for her."

It's not a leap to question whether I'm feeling shame, but the kindness in her tone forms a lump in my throat.

"So what am I supposed to do?"

"Follow the shame," Rini says.

I love an assignment, but this instruction goes against my every instinct to remain composed and in control. I don't wallow in shame, ever.

"You don't have to drown yourself in it, but use it as a guide to reflect on the deeper-seated feelings," she adds.

Rini announces our time is up and slides her papers into a folder. My mind freezes in panic. That's not enough information. What kind of shame signs am I looking for? And what if I don't have answers by the end of the weekend when the transit ends?

Rini stands and walks to the door. Her hand on the doorknob represents the last grains of sand slipping down an hourglass. Rini opens the door a crack, but I bolt over to slam it shut before she ushers me out.

"Wait, what will happen if I don't act before this transit period ends? Won't everything continue on as normal?"

Rini takes a large step back toward the bookshelves behind the desk, startled by my quick movements. Frightened even. After all, I'm a complete stranger to her. Despite my designer Veronica Beard slides, I might look unhinged. My entire body is blocking the door.

"I didn't mean to bombard you," I say.

"I don't scare easily, Farah," Rini says, her hands clasped behind her back.

"This part of the reading has been a surprise," I explain. "There has to be more you can tell me. What will happen if I miss the signs? Will everything still be normal?"

"Perhaps on the surface. But there will be many opportunities lost. What happens then?"

A rhetorical question. Indeed, what happens to lost opportunities? Do they come back around or are they gone forever?

"Your whole life is going to change this weekend, that much is certain. The changes have been set in motion and you cannot control them. You can fight it, try to salvage something of your old life, or you can let it happen, let the waves take you out to sea. There's knowledge out there."

This makes no sense. I don't let waves take me out to sea. Do I look like some kind of surfer? I don't know what she means when she says my whole life is going to change this weekend, but I do know she's wrong about something: there's nothing I can't control in the end.

ADAM

This is the best vacation ever.

Last night the weekend took a sharp detour from drown-my-sorrows-in-alcohol into dream-come-true-paradise.

"Writing early this morning?" Aimee asks when she returns from her morning run. She's slick with sweat, her face red.

"Huge breakthrough last night," I say. "Huge."

I keep my focus on the laptop screen, even though I've lost my train of thought. I wish I wasn't working in the bed. It sends the wrong message. I need to convey I'm in the "do not disturb" phase of writing. Which, unlike yesterday, is actually true. I'm inspired.

"No golf for you, then?" she asks.

I shake my head, reinforcing the point. But Aimee is relentless when she wants something. She used to be relentless when she wanted me.

She leans over me on the bed and kisses my ear. She slides her hand over my pants. My body responds automatically, the blood rushing away from my brain.

I scoot closer to the edge of the bed, forcing her off. I move my laptop to the desk. I was weak when she tempted me yesterday, but I'm not falling for it again. Definitely not after what happened last night.

"Well, I can't wait to read this draft when you're ready. I am already guessing the ways that Scarlett's arc might flourish," Aimee says.

This is a development. Aimee's finally read the last book and she's not-so-subtly letting me know. Too little, too late.

"I have to write," I say, pushing her away.

Thankfully, Aimee has an iron ego when she wants to brush off an insult. She playfully retreats to the bathroom, stripping her clothes off on the way.

I wait until I hear the shower water and I take advantage of what she started. I unzip my pants, close my eyes, and think about Eden.

Eden, my girl in the scarlet-red dress.

✦

Last night, my foot had barely touched the landing outside when Eden pounced, her hands and mouth all over me. The house behind us had gone completely dark, the caterers and cleaning crew gone, the guests drunk and passed out in bed.

I didn't ask any questions; we simply made love on the lawn, blades of grass tickling us in the weirdest places on our naked bodies. Afterward I found a discarded beach towel for us to cuddle on. It was risky, even at the late hour, but the whole scene would be perfect for my book. This is what I meant when I said I have to live the love I write.

Eden brought her face up toward mine. She looked like she was going to speak, but she turned her gaze down. Her cheek rested softly against my chest.

"What's up?" I asked. "I can tell you're holding back."

"That astrologer," Eden started tentatively. "She said some things. That maybe I'd made sacrifices that haven't proven to be exactly what I expected. Or maybe they were things I thought I wanted at the time, but now they aren't."

"I heard something similar in my reading," I shared. Old choices made by an old Adam.

After months of Eden insisting our current arrangement was fine while I was hungry for more, she and I were finally moving in the same direction.

Eden sat up and slipped on my T-shirt. Her expression turned serious. "I want us to be more than we are right now."

Right now?

Was there a comma in that sentence? It would change the meaning dramatically. Surely she didn't mean then and there, at midnight, naked in the grass on vacation. Eden watched me expectantly.

"I want more too," I said. "Soon."

I agreed, but I didn't appreciate her tone of urgency. I pushed her head down onto my shoulder and stroked her hair lovingly.

Big changes cannot be rushed. That's how mistakes are made.

AIMEE

Freshly showered with Alo leggings and a lightweight cropped hoodie, I meet Farah outside Rini's study after her reading.

"That's not what we're wearing for this," I say when Farah emerges with Rini behind her.

Farah and I coordinated all our outfits while we packed for Stars Harbor. We agreed that an exercise called Sun Worship at an astrological retreat did not call for swimsuits but for athleisure wear.

"What's wrong with this?" Farah asks, pulling at her Vuori joggers.

"Maybe change your top?"

"I'll meet you ladies on the back deck in five," Rini says.

"Were you listening in on my reading?" Farah asks.

"No, why, were you spilling your darkest secrets?"

Farah ignores me—about the outfit and the reading—and walks toward the back door.

"Oh my God, you were." I scramble to catch up with her. "You have deep dark secrets?"

She stonewalls me, but I'm confused. I thought she was simple; brilliant but totally straightforward. What could she be hiding?

There is no way she'd have an affair; she would end her marriage before crossing a line of impropriety. She's got an iron will. She's definitely not a gambler, and I cannot imagine her hooked on prescription pills. What other secrets are there at our stage of life? What kind of counseling would she want from an astrologer? I get no answers on the short walk from Rini's study to the back patio, where Margot and Eden wait.

"Rini said she would be right out," Farah reports.

"Sun Worship, anyone know what this is?" Eden asks. "I doubt it's about our favorite celebrity couples."

"Ah! That's why we say ship? As in worshipping," I say.

But Margot pipes up instead. "Reviews specifically say to go into this part of the weekend with no preconceived notions. There were a few people who included 'spoilers' and other guests had them taken down. I'm so intrigued I can't stand it."

Rini appears at the edge of our table, as if out of nowhere. That was quicker than five minutes. It reminds me of when she surprised us at arrival. I don't know if I'm not paying attention in this house or she's the stealthiest walker around.

"Follow me," she says.

I pull the sunglasses down from the top of my head over my eyes. Rini leads us along the edge of the property, which makes a sharp turn one hundred feet to the south. From our suites all we can see is the stunning, unobstructed view of the water. But here, over the beach grass, the steep drop to the beach below is evident.

Rini stops near the edge of a bluff and turns her back to the ocean. We form a semicircle around her.

"Bold. Blunt. Ambitious. Relentless," Rini says. "If you take these qualities and bestow them upon a man, he is a leader. He's a CEO of a Fortune 500 company, the head of a hedge fund, or a politician. These same exact qualities in a woman make her a bitch, someone to shun and shame. A psycho. A mean girl. A bad mother. No one aspirational or admirable. As a result, most women have learned to repress their masculinity."

Rini takes a step back, closer to the edge of the bluff. Beach grass wraps around her leg. I scratch my calf, imagining the tickle on my own leg.

"In the Western world, we confuse energetic qualities with gender. Men must be masculine, women must be feminine. We make them polarities and give them bodies to live in. But no man should be without femininity and no woman should be without masculinity. That's what I'm here to guide you through today."

Rini raises her hands to the sky—the sun. She then joins her palms together and takes a moment to look each of us in the eye. She begins with Margot, then Eden, Farah, and lastly, me. She doesn't break eye contact, holding it longer than is comfortable, longer than she did with any of the other women. My body sweats, trying to warn me of something.

As I'm on the verge of understanding her silent communication, Rini disappears over the cliff edge. The other women scream, snapping me out of my trance.

"What did you do, Aimee?" Margot says.

"Me? You were closer to her than I was," I say.

"But you two were staring at each other so intensely. Did you make her jump with your mind?"

"Margot, that's ridiculous, even for you."

Rini's head pops up inches to the left of where she fell with a dazzling smile and a ta-da.

"That was on purpose? Part of the act?" Eden asks.

"It was intentional, but it's not an act. I'm afraid of death, and trust me when I tell you it's more complicated than the average person's fear. I want you to do the same."

Eden turns abruptly, clearly angry. "I'm going back to the house. This is not for me," she says. I can't say I blame her. What is Rini playing at?

Rini waves the rest of us closer and points to a small shelf in the bluff three feet down where she must have landed.

"It's barely a jump," Farah says.

"I'm not falling off a cliff," Margot says. "She could have easily tumbled down way past that little ledge."

Rini steps between us and we fall back into our semicircle.

"You are missing the point. That was defiance of *my* fear. You have to identify your own act."

"I don't like that idea." Margot crosses her arms. "What if the universe interprets what you're doing to mean that you actually want to die?"

Rini walks over to Margot and takes both her hands. It's strangely intimate and I want to give them privacy, but I can't look away. Finally I search for Farah, who is already one step ahead in giving them their moment by staring at me.

"Margot, I don't want you to do anything you don't want to do, but I do need you to let go of your white-knuckle grip on life. It's paralyzing you," Rini says.

"I want that too. How can I do it?"

"Stand at the edge of that cliff. As close as you dare and shout out into the void."

"Scream?"

"If you don't want to defy your fears, then tell the Universe what you *do* want."

Assuming I'm next after Margot, I consider what it is I want. I want my husband to be back to his normal self. I want our perfect life to be as real as it feels to me when I post about it.

Margot does not appear to need to think at all. She carefully lines her toes up with the edge of the cliff.

Margot balls her fists up and thrusts them behind her as she leans over the edge with her torso.

"I want to be a mother," she yells.

Then she steps back and drops her head down. I notice a tear travel down her cheek, but it could have been conjured by the screaming wind at the edge of the cliff.

"I want to be the mother I never had," Margot whispers.

Rini steps closer to Margot, her arm straight, her hand reaching out. I think of the way Rini wouldn't break eye contact with me earlier, and the sickening feeling in my stomach returns. I can feel it, but I can't name it. Like she might push Margot.

"Margot," I say.

Rini touches Margot's shoulder and Margot flinches. She shakes Rini off and turns to the house.

"Margot?" I call out again.

She turns, but I don't know exactly what to say to her. I only know I have an urgent need to connect, one I haven't felt in years.

Let's get drunk together, without your brother.

Stay and talk to me.

And then the most pathetic:

Forgive me.

That is the most honest thing I could say.

My relationship with Margot can be divided into before and after. Before, Margot and I were on our way to being best friends. She was suspicious of my gregariousness at first because Adam needs to be the star of the show, but when she saw I was happy to let him shine, she backed off. After Adam and I got engaged, Margot threw herself into planning with me. She was dating Ted already and beginning to open up to the tradition and fun of a wedding. She was also happy to flex her super-organization skills outside the office. We had many deep conversations, largely revolving around love and life. But it was my bachelorette party that solidified our bond. We holed up in the corner of a midtown karaoke bar, whispering and laughing all night.

After, she had seen the monster in me.

I was an immature, damaged girl before I became a mother. And I acted like it, never more so than when I found out Adam was cheating on me during our first year of marriage. Adam let it go a long time ago, but it was mutual. We forgave each other. He had a choice. Margot didn't. And so Margot will never forget, like I'm her own personal tragedy.

I've changed, but I haven't had an opportunity to prove to her that becoming a mother healed me. It wasn't in the power of giving birth, nor did I hold Clara for the first time and have my psychic wounds close up like in a sci-fi movie. The tingle of healing first happened when Clara was a toddler, when we were beyond the excruciating boredom of babyhood. One day we were making strawberry jam. Clara dropped a chunk on the floor and I clucked at her, *No, no, don't eat that. DIRTY.*

Clara lifted up her dimpled hand to show me what she'd picked up. I saw her curiosity, her desire to explore. Not laziness and sloth, the way my mother the nurse treated messiness. That's when I did the impossible. I inspected the glob in her hand and told her it was fine. I didn't mention the microscopic viral particles as my own mother would have. I refused to think about the bacteria. Instead I told her she could eat it. She giggled as if I'd let her have cake.

As we continued to prepare, I got bolder. I rubbed the seeds and leftover jam on the counter with my hands. Bits dropped to the floor. Clara hoovered them up with her tongue. I licked chunks off my own fingers, off her fingers. The whole kitchen smelled sticky-sweet. My mother would have fallen over if she'd walked in. The mess. The germs. The bugs we'd attract. Everything would have to be sterilized. And yet I smiled at Clara like we were getting away with murder.

Clara's firsts became my own. First finger painting. First ice cream for breakfast and eggs for dinner. First middle-of-the-day dance party. First time she went to bed without cleaning up all her toys. As a mother I learned to loosen the reins. I no longer needed to be perfect, because now I was loved. And I never looked at my daughters like they were disgusting in any way. I knew the shame of that look all too well.

This is what becoming a mother did for me. It allowed me to reparent myself, alongside my girls. It healed me. But I can't tell Margot any of that without making her feel worse about what she doesn't yet have. And I don't need to give her another reason to hate me.

MARGOT

I walk away from Rini's Sun Worship, not to be rude, but because she made me realize I *have* been paralyzed. Even on this vacation. So I left to go inside, sit down with my brother and talk. Really talk.

But on the walk home from the cliff, I feel the telltale wetness of my period, and my dreams disappearing again with it. Month after month, year after year, the same cycle. Anxiously watching for signs of ovulation. Checking mucus: Is that thick or stringy? Cloudy or clear? Having sex every third day to optimize Ted's sperm without missing any potential fertilization days.

Then after sex, joking with Ted. *You put the best swimmers in there, right?* He wants kids as much as I do. I'm lucky to have a partner like him. He encourages me when I need support and gives me space when I have to shut down during two weeks between ovulation and testing. Ted and I don't talk about babies or family or logistics at all. I close myself in an emotionally sealed-off room. No fantasizing about a positive result. No mitigating a negative one. I pay very close attention to my body during this time, but the signs of pregnancy and period are deceitfully similar.

Inside the house, I grab a banana from the kitchen and head upstairs to our bathroom. I hear nothing but the thoughts in my head. What went wrong this month? Did I pick the wrong days? Tests found nothing wrong with my ovaries or fallopian tubes. I've resisted fertility drugs, but maybe it's time. Could Farah help me?

I open the door to our bedroom and root around in my suitcase for a fresh pair of underwear and a panty liner. For the first few months of trying to conceive, this spotting was an unexpected mind trick. Was it my period or was it the spotting common with implantation of the egg in the uterus? Spoiler alert: it's my period. Why would this month be different?

I take my phone out of my back pocket and see a text from Ted checking in on me. I type a sad-face emoji and that I likely have my period. Ted types back, *Too soon to say I'm looking forward to another month of trying? Too soon.*

I appreciate Ted's attempts to cheer me up, but it doesn't work as well as it did earlier in the process. For the first two years, I bounced back quickly and declared next month would be our time. Now I'm not so resilient. Sometimes I want to give up, but in reality I only want the pain to stop. Unless a doctor told me it was impossible, I could never stop trying to have a child of my own. Until then, I have to focus on the family I have.

After the bathroom, I leave the phone on my nightstand and make my way to Adam's room. I gently knock on his door.

"Hey, you in there?" I ask. His laptop sits on the small bedroom desk, but the chair is empty. On the nightstand, I see the flowers Rini must have set out from the dumbwaiter.

"Adam?" I call out.

I move out to the hallway. Through the windows over the staircase, I see Rini wrapping up with Aimee and Farah.

"Adam?" I yell louder.

I'm shuffling down the stairs when I hear a door on the other side of the hallway open. I reverse my downward momentum to investigate.

"Hey, there you are," I say. Adam keeps walking toward his room.

He tosses me a hasty "Hey" in return. I pursue him. "How's the writing going?"

"Pretty good," he says, opening his bedroom door.

I catch a sudden flash of color from the other wing, someone poking their head out into the hallway.

"No one is supposed to be in that wing. Is there someone here? Hello?" I call out. The shadowy figure ducks back into the bedroom and closes the door. I stop.

"What's happening?" I ask.

"Nothing, Margot."

I look at Adam. His untucked shirt, his tousled hair, and it clicks immediately. I want him to tell me I'm mistaken. Explain this all away.

"Adam, what is happening? I know this isn't nothing. Is someone here?"

"I've been writing."

I step closer to my brother and whisper.

"Adam, stop it. Are you having an affair? Is that possible?"

Adam shakes his head.

"It's so much more than that, Margot. I'm in love."

My stomach drops and I feel dizzy. None of this makes sense.

"How is she here?"

"She's been here the whole time," he says.

"Rini?" I ask. Adam shakes his head.

"You're the one that brought her," Adam adds.

I can't say if it takes me two seconds or ten minutes to process because my mind goes blank. I didn't bring anyone. That's when I fall forward into Adam, my legs weak.

Adam is having an affair with Eden. Ted's best friend's wife. Eden. A woman who is under this roof, sharing this house, invited on our vacation. The woman who was awful to me last night. Whom my brother defended when he told me to calm down as she attacked my infertility.

"You're so stupid," I cry. "So stupid."

"Margot, nothing has changed. This has been going on for months," Adam says. He tries to help me stand but my legs are jelly. I lean against the wall for balance.

"Is that supposed to make me feel better? This is insane."

"What's insane, Margot?"

"What isn't? The fact that you're cheating on Aimee, after what happened last time, and you brought your girlfriend on vacation with us?"

"Margot, you're overreacting."

"Please tell me that's because you're going back in that room and telling her it's over. Effective immediately. Then we can go to a winery and pray Aimee never gets wind of this."

Adam says nothing. He's not going to end things with Eden. He's going to break up our family over this.

Looking away, I stare at the wall behind him. The betrayal feels like my heart is being ripped out of my chest. I turn on my heel and sprint down the long hallway to the back staircase as fast as my legs will take me.

Most people wouldn't react this way if they learned their brother was having an affair; I know this. They'd be disappointed. Upset. Feel sad that Christmas celebrations will be affected by his custody arrangements.

To me, this news is devastating. And it hurts more because I cannot get pregnant no matter how hard I try. Plus I have a sister-in-law who flew into a murderous rage when my brother cheated years earlier, before they had three daughters, and I can't imagine all the ways she'll lose it now that the stakes are even higher. I hold on to the railing and run down the back stairs at Stars Harbor. With every step, a new vision flashes in my mind.

Adam at the bottom of the stairs in a pool of blood, Aimee smirking from the top.

Adam with half of his face missing, Aimee holding a gun.

At the bottom of the back staircase, I search for the door I sought out earlier this morning. I slam it with urgency and it pops open. As a child, even as a teenager, I'd grab my big brother and scoot into the dark where we felt safe to spill our secrets, or where I solved problems that were too big for me. I even have a small tattoo of the outline of a staircase on my side ribs, the same one Adam has on his calf. I always feel safe when I find the cupboard under the stairs. I need to feel safe right now.

I crouch down and hide in the oddly shaped triangular storage space underneath the stairs. This small space contains me. Calms me. I will figure out how to save us.

✦

I close my eyes and rest my head on the cedar walls of the storage space. It smells like Nana's attic, a place where costumes and mementos of past lives were lovingly kept.

Adam pounds down the stairs above me. He calls out. I hold my breath. I hear a door open. Adam shouts my name a second time, the sound of his voice muffled with distance as he retreats away from the house, searching for me.

I burst out of hiding and race up the stairs to the room he's abandoned. Eden stands outside on the balcony, watching for Adam to come around the house.

"Do you see her?" Eden calls down.

I scream at the top of my lungs. "I need to make this stop. You're going to ruin everything."

Eden steps inside the bedroom, leaving the balcony doors wide open.

"Ruin everything? Nothing in my life made sense until Adam and I found each other."

Eden smiles. It's not the evil smile of the night before when she needled me about a baby. It's the satisfied grin of someone who has met their destiny.

Next to her, the sheer white curtains blow in the wind, adding to the ethereal scene. The view of the water is serene. Outside promises the easiest way out of this mess.

Gathering up my courage, I run toward the balcony and shove Eden with superhuman force. She whips around and tries to grab hold of me, but I have momentum on my side. I grab Eden low on her body and lift her up.

"Margot! What are you doing?" she screams. She tips her weight in my direction, and I have her draped over my shoulder in a fireman's hold.

"ADAM!" she yells.

"Margot," Adam shouts. "Put her down right now."

I spin around and push Eden off me. She dangles over the balcony railing, headfirst. I give her one more shove.

Her body falls in slow motion. Her long blond hair floats around her face. Her limbs spiral as if she's trying to regain her balance without solid ground beneath her. Adam runs toward her but not fast enough. Her body crashes at his feet. Her head explodes upon impact with the flagstone patio.

My problem is taken care of.

But is it really? This is too messy. Who is going to clean that up? Not the local cops. Rini? Cruel. But also, going to jail would negate the goal of keeping the family together and seeing my nieces every day.

I startle when I hear Adam calling my name. I hold my breath. A minute goes by. Then another.

The storage-space door under the stairs opens. Adam crouches and shuffles in. I scoot over to let him sit.

"I'm trying to figure out how to fix this," I say.

"How about a story?" he asks.

Instead of growing more anxious because I haven't figured out my solution yet, I feel calm blanket me. Adam can make me insane with frustration, he can make me crazy with worry, but when I'm at the edge and about to lose it, his mere presence can soothe me.

That's it. It's not a quick fix, but it's the right one. A moment of vulnerability. I want action and resolution, but this is more important. This is connection.

ADAM

We used to do this all the time as kids. Whenever Margot was scared, which was a lot, or I was bored, which was often, we would scurry into the small triangular space under our stairs. We sat shoulder to shoulder and talked. Sometimes we'd rehash what had frightened her; other times we'd pretend it never happened and discuss our school crushes.

Margot would then endure a maximum of thirty seconds of silence before she'd press her knee into my thigh. She wanted me to tell a story, but she never liked to ask for what she needed.

One morning she'd found Dad passed out on the couch with a bloody gash on his head. Margot came crying to me, insisting he was dead. I held my hand on his chest, his heart beating under my palm. I assured her he was still alive, without commenting on whether I thought that was a good thing. Mom caught us hovering over him and shooed us away. Her tone was a mixture of disgust and annoyance, and it came off like she was directing those emotions at us when the source of her anger was Dad.

Margot took every one of those careless comments to heart, and that day she was shattered. She believed Dad was dead and in the face of that emotion, Mom belittled her. *Don't be so stupid,* she'd said.

That day, I found Margot under the stairs in the dark. She wiped her runny nose and wet cheeks on her sleeve, trying to hide her tears.

Today in Stars Harbor, she wasn't crying, only because she'd learned to keep that inside. But I could see the same shattered Margot. She took my failed marriage too personally. I don't expect her to ask; I simply launch into the fantasy.

"Once upon a time, there was a girl named Margot. She was sensitive but strong. Easily overwhelmed emotionally, but relentless in her actions. One day she was feeling so misunderstood that she hid in the crawl space under the stairs. There, she found a portal to a world where it was forever autumn with brightly colored leaves and sweater weather. Margot couldn't retrace her steps to see how she ended up there, but the townspeople knew the how didn't matter. She was their queen and her brother their king. Their royal family. The prophecy had told them all about this brother and sister. They had been waiting for us."

Every time Margot's heart broke, I was there to heal it. At Nana's townhouse the space was smaller and more narrow than in our childhood home, and we were bigger. Nana kept the space jammed with toilet paper and paper towels, but we wriggled in anyway. After Mom and Dad died, Margot made me scrub the mean parts about our parents from my stories. She was content with the place that looked beautiful but strange, where we were in control and we decided that nothing could hurt us as long as we ruled together.

In this astrology house, Margot rests her head on my shoulder and remembers who we are. The invincible brother and sister. When I'm done, something inside her opens up.

"I'm so scared," she says.

"Of what?"

"That someone's gonna die."

"You think Aimee's going to kill me?"

"Remember what she did when she caught you cheating years ago? Now you have three kids and you're with another woman in the same house. I'd say that's next-level all around."

"It's not a terrible point. How is she going to kill me?"

"With a gun? Or a knife. I bet she has the guts to do it with a knife. Slice you up."

I ruffle her hair and shift my seat. "This isn't as easy as it used to be," I say.

"She is still postpartum from the baby. Good mothers can snap too."

I shake my head, her ear bobbing on my shoulder from the way we're connected.

"Not Aimee," I say.

"Then you're going to end up in a sad two-bedroom apartment in Kips Bay, and I'm going to have to live with you every other weekend to help you take care of the girls," she says. "I'm not sure that's much less of a nightmare."

"Oh shit, Margot, that's bleak."

Margot starts laughing so hard that a single tear escapes. I feel her arm move to wipe her face.

"Where did you come up with that scenario?" I ask.

"I was sure it was coming for us," she says. "Real as the day before us."

I'm both disturbed and impressed. I always think of Margot as the practical one, while I'm the creative one. For the first time, I realize with all the damage in our past, Margot could have been a writer too. A dismal divorcé's apartment and her as my pseudo-coparent. That's the work of a wild imagination.

My story will have a happy ending; it's the only way things end for me.

RINI

t's a day of lasts. My last Sun Worship event ended after fifteen minutes. Cut short. Ahead, my last dinner at Stars Harbor awaits. Will I die at midnight? Will I make it through the whole day tomorrow? There's no way of knowing. The only thing guaranteed is today, my last full day alive.

Walking through the farmers' market in town, I glance down at my phone. Still no word from Eric. I don't regret texting him last night, but I won't badger him either. I'd love one last conversation, but I leave that detail in the hands of the Universe. Instead, I gather up the courage to dial my mom, crossing another goodbye off my final-day to-do list.

"Who's this?" she says by way of greeting.

"Ha, ha, it hasn't been that long," I say.

Of course, that's a lie. It's been nearly six months.

I had called my mother as soon as I hung up with the psychic and found out my date of death. It was instinctual. I was scared and wanted my mother. But as soon as she said hello, I couldn't bring myself to tell her. She had enough pain from one daughter. I was supposed to be her relief.

Andi and Mom had always butted heads. Two Tauruses, stubborn in different ways. My mother's insistence that Andi change was matched

140

only by Andi's will to stay the same. I always loved my big sister, but I knew she was difficult. Stories cast her as a colicky baby. A tantrum-prone toddler. Those could have been normal developmental milestones, and her rift with my mother resolved by her sweet elementary-school years, but my father upended that.

Andi's first nosedive happened when Dad left our family for another woman. She took it the hardest of the three of us. Mom wanted someone new, I wanted to forget him, but Andi wanted her daddy. It was unfortunate timing, as Andi was facing down the new hormones of puberty; she struggled with anorexia and bulimia through her teenage years. And then it got worse.

Andi's second nosedive came in college. Even now, I have nightmares of the day she dropped out. She shook with fright in our apartment doorway with two trash bags of clothes, having moved out of her student housing. *I will never feel safe again*, she said. She repeated it over and over like a mantra. Even though I was barely sixteen, I knew that in a way Andi died that night when she came home from college. She lost her will. Her joy. Her spirit. A shell of my sister returned to us.

Mom thought she needed a break. *Time heals all wounds,* she'd said. Andi didn't get out of bed for days. Days became weeks, weeks became months. We knew Andi was depressed, but we didn't know why she was afraid to go to a doctor for help. As soon as I saved up enough money for a visit, I went to a clinic and gave them all of Andi's symptoms as my own. I left with a prescription for an antidepressant.

The pills kept her from getting kicked out of the house, a threat my mother had leveled when it was clear Andi wasn't going back to school. She said Andi was an adult and needed a job to help pay some bills. Andi secured an at-home position as a customer service phone rep for a department store, but when someone would yell at her, which inevitably happened, she would shame-spiral. That job didn't last long, Andi stopped taking her meds, and my mother made good on her promise. She told Andi she was no longer welcome under her roof. I thought my mother was too harsh, but when our father's gift of the property came through, I didn't need to fight about it. Andi and I left, with whatever thin thread of a relationship we had with our mother intact.

During that first winter in Greenport, Andi and I felt like two little kids whose parents had left them home alone for the first time. Except it was our house. We layered on all the clothes we brought from Queens and warmed ourselves by the fire day and night. We dreamed of what the house could be. Andi wanted some place she could be safe: a home. I wanted some place that could be my legacy: a business. With Eric, we designed both.

I expected Andi would slowly reveal more of what had happened that night, things she couldn't tell her baby sister. Then my eighteenth birthday passed, and my twentieth, and I was a successful business-woman, but I never found out the whole story. Over the years I'd pieced together that she'd had an inappropriate relationship with her professor that ended badly. But I didn't feel the need to drag out the horrid details of the past as long as we were together and moving forward. I didn't expect that things would grow worse than ever when we left the city.

"You need something, Rini?" my mom asks. A bee buzzes around a bouquet of sunflowers at the farmers' market.

"No, I'm just checking in. Where in the world are you?" I ask.

"It's summer, so I'm in Hawaii. You caught me before my shift."

"Hanalei Bay?"

"I'm checking out Maui this year."

"I miss your hospitality tips."

Mom sighs. "I know our last conversation didn't end how you wanted it to," she says.

"You get what you get," I say.

I had called my mom again a few weeks after the psychic's death-date delivery, this time with a request for help, which was foolish in hindsight. My mom was still her Taurean self. Back then I hung up and resolved to not call for a while, not because I was mad but because I wanted to let her get used to not hearing from me. I realize how misguided that was. I can't prepare her for my sudden death by ignoring her.

"Well, if you're really calling for ideas, I have lots for you. Is business slow?" my mother asks.

"No, not at all. Business is great," I say.

I feel slightly guilty, but it's not hard to hold back the psychic's prediction from my mother. It would be sadistic to say, *Hey, Mom, guess what? I'm gonna die tomorrow.* Especially if she refused to hear it for the second time. Instead we chat about hospitality for a few minutes, and it's nice to forget death and my plans.

"Well, baby girl, it's always good to hear your voice. I've got to head across the island for my shift."

"It was great to catch up," I say.

"It was. How about you don't let another few months go by?"

"Sure," I lie, grief gripping me by the throat. "Goodbye, Mom."

I fight the urge to say something—anything—to keep her on the phone. Instead I wait for her to hang up, knowing I can't do it myself. I put my phone away and gather my flower purchases to take up to the cashier stand. Still nothing from Eric.

"End of those pretty pink begonias," the owner says. "You sure you don't want to grab some more? They're gonna die in this heat here."

"Why not?"

If I can't save myself, maybe I can save some begonias.

For a long time, when I thought about death, I thought of my sister. During a trip to the Southold Book Cottage to pick up new stock for the Stars Harbor library, I spotted a nonfiction book about the afterlife. I devoured it in one night. It made me laugh out loud, in the dark, alone in my bed. And that was better than crying.

It also made me curious. Since it was unlikely I would see death coming, what might I expect in the moments after it took hold of me? A computer doesn't shut down in an instant, and if you think it does, try shutting down with thirty-five tabs open and ten apps running. It takes longer to shut every process down, one by one.

I found other nonfiction titles about the afterlife as told by those lucky enough to come back to detail the journey for the uninitiated. Their accounts were astonishingly similar, as well as incredibly personal. The most common theme was being reunited with a beloved family member in a serene setting. If I imagine my crossover scenario, I expect to see Andi by the water as we have a conversation that's open and honest and leads to a beautiful connection while watching the sunset.

At home, I wait for the gate to open and watch the Victorian house that Andi, Eric, and I built appear on the horizon. I admit it isn't just the begonias that help me cheat death. Stars Harbor is my refusal to die, at least in one sense of the word. I accept that my body will expire tomorrow, and yet I will also live on with this business I created. To ensure that, I need one thing. One final piece of the puzzle.

FARAH

I have never been so terrified to be alone with Aimee—never felt anything but excited—yet after my reading and the threat of having to yell out my deepest desire over a bluff, I'm on edge. My secret is already out in the universe in some sense, and although Rini would never tell anyone, there's no way to take it back. *Maybe that's a good thing*, I think now as Aimee and I walk side by side along the bluff after the failed Sun Worship exercise. It will force me back to myself.

An ugly flower of doubt bloomed weeks ago, and since then I've been carrying a level of uncertainty I've never experienced in my life. I knew I would be a doctor in elementary school and never veered from the course. Within a month of meeting Joe, it became inevitable that we'd hit the appropriate dating milestones before getting married in three to five years. I've always been able to lock in on the long road ahead. Now all I see is what's right in front of me and that's Aimee. It's disorienting.

"Should we go back?" Aimee asks.

"No, let's keep going. Walk a little farther along the bluff."

The force of my own assertion surprises me. It sounds like the old Farah, clear and direct. Not the waffling one who has been off-kilter for the last few weeks, since the dream. Rini called it a vision, but I still blush at the obscenity of it.

While I slept one night, I imagined Aimee in my office. She was laid bare in a thin paper gown on my exam table. Like a good doctor, I told her everything I was going to do before I did it, but my words sounded like a phone-sex operator, not a seasoned OB. For her part, Aimee consented with small nods and soft moans. Her body melted under my fingers. When I woke up, I still ached for her, but it was Joe next to me. He was happy to finish the job.

The next time I saw Aimee after that night, I flushed with shame. Fifteen minutes into the playdate that day, I pretended I'd been called to the hospital for an emergency. At home I locked myself in the bathroom and cried until my three-year-old shrieked because the stinky in his diaper was burning.

While I smeared diaper cream on him, I reminded myself the dream wasn't real. I'd never once had a thought that crossed the line at work, let alone taken an action that was questionable. Aimee hadn't been a patient in eight years, not since she became my friend in our postpartum Baby Yoga class. I drew that line even though technically there was no conflict. It would have been weird, and I don't come anywhere near "weird."

Defending my reputation as a doctor as a result of this fantasy had been much easier than looking at what my marriage might be lacking. Joe and I were great partners, but we'd lost a deeper connection years ago. We weren't even best friends like we'd been when we dated. Aimee had taken that spot. And now she was igniting the passion Joe and I had lost too.

Unlike Aimee, who had divulged some of her same-sexcapades, I'd never kissed a girl in my whole life. Never felt that kind of desire.

Rini suggested my whole world was about to change this weekend, but she was wrong. My whole world changed weeks ago, when I had that dream, but now Rini warned that the planet of communication would push me to tell Aimee. Even though I don't believe in astrology I swear that, post–Sun Worship, I can feel the planetary pull.

"I want to walk and talk," I say to Aimee.

"Okay, we can FaceTime the kids when we get back."

At her prompting, I check my phone. There's a text message from my husband.

"Joe's on the road," I say absentmindedly.

Aimee links her arm in mine. "Our time alone is limited," she laughs.

She doesn't know it's not a joke for me and that now there's a clock ticking in my head. Following my feelings would lead me away from the trappings of the nice life I have with my family—a penthouse apartment, a summer home in Southampton, two kids in great private schools.

In the hospital, impossible choices are decided in a split second, but in my life I seem to do nothing but delay. I can feel patience being sucked out of the air around me, like when I say I'm bored hanging around the nurses' station waiting for mothers to progress in labor and the universe retaliates by having them dilate to ten centimeters in the same hour.

I try to break down my mental block to envisioning life with Aimee. It wouldn't be all that different from now. I would go to work every day, and Aimee would have more kids to play with. I could take the financial hit of divorce; my practice is flourishing. Aimee would have the support of my nanny too. We'd coordinate custody to arrange weekly date nights, and regular carefree weekends to go on adventures (for her), or stay in and binge trashy television (for me).

The details come together a little in my mind, and I start to feel happy, but the big picture worries me. Will the neighbors accept us or ostracize us? How will the kids react? Lurking deeper in my subconscious is the question I don't dare ask even myself: Would Aimee actually choose me? It's too scary to think about.

"I guess this means you're ready to tell me what's really going on with Beckett," Aimee says.

"What?" I ask, confused.

"You said you wanted to talk, and I've been waiting for you to come back to it since the car ride out here."

I take a beat and Aimee gives me space. We walk in silence, alternating between looking out at the vast ocean on the horizon and the beautiful, varied homes along the walk. After Rini's reading, it almost feels like a relief to talk about the logistics of this.

"Have you ever thought something was wrong with him?" I ask.

"Wrong with Beckett?"

I'm messing this all up, as I knew I would. "Not wrong. That perhaps he might need some medical intervention or support," I clarify.

"No, I've never thought that," Aimee says.

If Aimee's never noticed, then maybe this line of thinking is a mistake.

"I could see you holding him to a standard that's too high for an eight-year-old. Is that what's happening?" she adds.

I shake my head. "There are some patterns. Things I don't see in Clara."

"Clara is an old soul. She's not a fair measurement."

It's tempting to defer to mommy expert Aimee, but no, I can't ignore my suspicions on this. I've witnessed it with my own eyes and ears. "I might have him evaluated."

Aimee shrugs. "Sure, why not ask some questions? Will you take him to his pediatrician or a child psychologist?"

"I don't know. I don't know if I can handle this, Aimee."

My voice cracks unexpectedly. Aimee stops and turns to face me.

"We'll get through it together," she says, holding my shoulders.

She doesn't say "as a couple," but I hear "together" and my confidence creeps back. At work people expect me to have answers because I'm a doctor. But I don't have to wear my doctor hat for my son. I'm a regular mom who has questions. That doesn't mean I'm failing—not yet anyway.

"Are you okay?" a woman's voice asks. "Are you okay? Can you talk?"

On the lawn of a small cottage, a woman is frantic as her companion doubles over in pain on the grass. I pull Aimee off our walk and toward the couple.

"What's happening?" I ask.

"I don't know. We were walking and all of a sudden he froze."

The man claws at his throat.

"Do you have allergies?" I ask. "Did you eat something?"

He shakes his head no. I scan his body and notice the hives on his legs, arms and neck.

"Is he allergic to beestings?"

The woman shrugs. "It's never come up."

"I'm a doctor. I think you're having an anaphylactic reaction."

The man nods.

A few other people have come out of the house to check on the commotion. I direct them to lay their friend down flat and check for a stinger. Someone calls out that they found it; another runs inside for some tweezers.

"No, that will push more venom in," I warn. "Scrape it with your fingernail or a key."

I rummage in my purse and dig through to find my EpiPen. Beckett has a severe tree-nut allergy, and though he's not with us on this trip, I no longer leave home without several medical-grade epinephrine injectors. It's a doctor perk that comes in handy. Last summer, I saved a neighbor from an unknown shellfish allergy after eating shrimp at a kindergarten graduation party.

"I need clear access to his outer thigh."

"His eyes rolled back in his head," the woman explains.

"Farah, he's fainted," Aimee says.

"It's okay. That's why I had you put him down."

I lunge toward the man with the injector in hand, but pause to sweep in a deep, calming breath.

"What are you doing? Don't wait," the woman shouts. "He's dying."

I ignore the panic. Careless mistakes are more costly than the seconds it takes to center myself. I open my eyes and jab him in the thigh. I press down steadily on the plunger and count.

"It's not working," the woman cries.

I remove the empty needle and set it down next to me. I take his wrist and check his pulse.

"Just because you can't see it, doesn't mean it's not working. His heart rate is getting faster and stronger."

"That's good, right?" Aimee asks. She watches me, waiting for my command. A crowd has gathered from the cottage. I have an audience.

"Give him some space. He needs oxygen," I say with authority.

His eyes begin to flutter. I lean down to explain that he's had an allergic reaction, I've administered epinephrine, and he's going to be all right. His fingers tighten around my wrist.

"You're welcome," I whisper.

We move through the house to the front while we wait for the ambulance to arrive, and I give his wife some information. "Expect the ER doctors to give him Benadryl, Pepcid, and an IV of steroids. That's the anaphylactic-shock cocktail."

I make the EMTs take note of the time the patient received epinephrine and tell his wife they're going to have to monitor him for four to six hours. When the ambulance pulls away, the cottage crew erupts in applause. I'm embarrassed, more for them than for me. This is my job.

Aimee and I return to our place on the walk, but this time we agree to head back toward the astrology house.

"Farah, you gave that man life," Aimee says. "Right here. Gave him life."

"I stopped his body from going into full anaphylactic shock."

"And what happens if someone goes into full anaphylactic shock?"

I skip over the technical medical analysis to the drama she wants.

"They can die," I say.

"But he didn't. Because you gave him life."

"Saved his life, maybe."

"That's hot."

I blush then, my neck red and burning with shame.

"Stop," I say to Aimee, but I'm also talking to myself. She's using the word *hot* like Paris Hilton in the 2000s. She's not saying I'm appealing to her. Or is she? There's a twinkle in her eye that I cannot deny.

"Wanna have some lunch on the back deck?" Aimee asks.

"I snuck in some Veuve," I say.

Aimee wraps her arm around me and puts her head on my shoulder. "Goat cheese salads and champagne. That's why I love you," she says.

I smile, no longer mortified by the way I read into everything she says. I can choose to have fun with it, especially while the fantasy lives in my mind.

Rini said the transit is coming to its end, that the energy will shift. A door will close. It occurs to me that the practice of astrology foretells something acting upon us. That's a foreign concept for me as a doctor who plays God. But maybe here, unlike in a delivery room, I don't have to do anything. Perhaps my future with Aimee has already been set in motion and all I need to do is wait for it to play out.

Or at the very least I should have the confidence to believe that when the opportunity arises, I'll spring to action without a moment's hesitation. Just like I did today, like I do every day. I've put too much weight on matters of love versus matters of work. The truth is I am who I am. I'm a person who knows how to take action when the moment arrives.

AIMEE

Farah and I finish lunch and our bottle of champagne on the deck and head inside to check on the busted itinerary. Ted, Rick, and Eden are sipping cocktails in the living room. Adam and Margot appear, Margot with her arms crossed over her chest, Adam with a beer in hand.

"Farah saved someone's life an hour ago," I say, feeling warm and floaty from the champagne.

Ted and Rick each lob a question at Farah for more details. Instead of the big reactions I had expected, Adam remains quiet, and Margot looks uneasy, shifting her weight from foot to foot. Eden drains her cocktail in silence. A dark mood hangs in the air, and it sets me on edge.

"That was after the two of you ruined the Sun Worship," I say. Neither Margot nor Eden acknowledges that I'm speaking to them.

"What are you talking about?" Adam asks.

"Margot and Eden walked out without a word to us or Rini."

"I don't have to explain myself to anyone, let alone you," Eden says.

I shake my head with disappointment. So rude.

"You should apologize," I say.

Rini emerges from her study then.

"Can I have everyone's attention to discuss the changes to the schedule?" she asks. "It's two p.m. now, and we're well into the time for the

152

compatibility reading for Farah and Joe, but Joe is not here yet. I could have swapped their slot with Margot and Ted, but they went yesterday. Adam and Aimee, are you ready to go today?"

"I'll pass," Adam says.

"You'll pass?" Rini says.

"Can we do it tomorrow?" I ask.

"No, we're skipping it. I don't need someone to tell me how compatible I am with my wife. We've been together for a decade," Adam says.

"Same here," Farah says. "Joe and I will probably opt out as well."

"Oh, well then. That leaves individual readings for Margot and Aimee," Rini says.

"Right now isn't a good time," Margot snaps. "Can I do mine after dinner?"

"I'd be happy to go now," I offer.

"All right," Rini says. "I'll see the rest of you for dinner at seven p.m."

I follow Rini into her study, but as she disappears into the room ahead of me, I recall the feeling I had as she slid off the edge of the cliff this morning.

"I'm a thrill seeker too, but what you pulled earlier? That was insane," I say.

Rini tilts her head at me. "What do you mean?"

"Falling from the cliff like that. We all thought you were dead."

"I am sorry the exercise frightened you. It's meant to jolt you into action. That's masculine energy."

I take the seat across from Rini at her desk, the same chair I sat in with Farah yesterday. "I wasn't looking for an apology. And that woo-woo stuff sounds good, but what's really going on here?"

The foul mood I saw in Adam and Margot seems to have seeped its way into me. I don't know if it's this house or Rini that sets it off. Which reminds me of another question that's been hanging over my head. "Do I know you?"

"No, we've never met."

That feels like an answer that's not really an answer.

"Are you hiding something from us? You are. I can feel it."

Rini looks unnerved by my rapid-fire accusations. She wanted masculine energy, but even I'm surprised. My normal impulsiveness has taken a dark turn. She glances over her shoulder at the bookcase behind her. My gaze lands on a trio of books that appear out of place among the leather-bound rows. My grandmother had shelves like that, but the third one was a dummy where she hid jewelry and the occasional box of Mallomars. Alone in this big house, entertaining all sorts of strangers, Rini might have protection in there, like pepper spray, or something stronger.

"This sounds like classic projection," Rini says. "Are *you* hiding something?"

I read her reaction wrong. She's not defensive—she's attacking me. "Me hiding something from you?"

"From me, from everyone, from yourself?"

Rini's right. I sigh. She's not an evil mastermind, she's got a reputation to uphold. Her astrology brand is expected to be a little witchy. "I've been feeling off since we left the city. I can't shake some things I'd rather not remember."

"Ah, well, that sounds like the emotions conjured up by the Mercury Retrograde we're experiencing."

"Isn't that an excuse people use when their Insta live feeds glitch?"

"I'm talking about the impulse to go within, to revisit the past. Most people ignore that to plow ahead, but you seem tuned in."

I shake my head, resisting the urge to overshare. That type of influencer annoys me. Why put that kind of bad energy out onto the internet? Even though this is a private reading, and some people would see it as the perfect opportunity to unload their darkest secrets and their innermost desires, I believe that as soon as you speak the words, they are released into the world. They are out there for someone else to intercept, to hear, to know, even if you don't tell them directly. And yet, I don't want to sleep on this opportunity to get clarity.

"It's not a good feeling. It feels like I could lose everything, or that maybe I already have and I don't know it yet."

"Every loss makes space to gain something new, different, or better. The scales always balance," Rini says.

She begins to describe my Libra Moon and the scales of justice, but I can't absorb a word she's saying.

Abruptly, I stand from the green leather chair and collapse onto the couch against the wall. The champagne and goat cheese sour in my stomach, and I feel like I might get sick. I throw my arm over my face and stare into the darkness of the crook of my elbow, knowing I'm going to lose control of this impulse.

"Ten years ago there was a girl I wanted gone, and I haven't seen or heard from her since," I confess.

To prove my earlier point, as soon as the words are out of my mouth, something is unleashed. A heaviness in my chest. A weight that makes it hard to breathe. *What have I done?*

I had stopped thinking about her for a long time. Adam and I forgave each other and moved on completely. She never entered my mind. She was a mere blip in our story. But when my third daughter was born, I found myself replaying those days in the moments before I fell asleep from exhaustion. She took on a lead role in my recast memories. So I started looking for her. I wanted to forget her, not stalk her. To update my visions in hopes the old ones would be replaced if I had a picture of her now. But I found nothing. Nothing on Google. Nothing on social media. Maybe she'd blocked me, but it felt like something worse.

"Did you—?" Rini stutters.

"No, no! I barely laid a hand on her. But it's possible I willed something bad into happening."

"Do you really believe that?"

I shrug. I don't know what to believe anymore. But I suspect I'm stronger than I give myself credit for sometimes.

I feel a whoosh of air as Rini takes the seat next to the couch. Then she takes me by the shoulders, her thumbs pressing into the soft parts of my neck. This is more intense than the baby crying in the shower. I can feel this. The room closes in around me.

I open my eyes and sit up, ready to defend myself. Rini is next to me in her chair, one leg crossed over the other. The haunting strikes again.

"I'm sorry, but I need to leave. It's nothing you've done; I respect your hustle. But this talking to a stranger and confessing bad acts, it isn't me. I need to think good thoughts. I'm calling only positive vibes into my life right now."

I hop up from the couch and leave Rini with her preparation for my reading untouched. I was not rude like Eden or Margot; I explained myself, at least partially. I don't need to hear anything she was planning to tell me because I know exactly what to do.

I step out of the study and go upstairs to our suite with a cocktail. I pick out the perfect outfit, shower, and do my hair and makeup, sipping my drink and listening to my favorite love songs. When I'm camera-ready, I head out to the back lawn. I arrange the Adirondack chairs side by side, looking out over the dock in the water. My timing is perfect. It's magic hour and the Stars Harbor lawn is bathed in glowing light like fields of gold. I return inside for a bottle of wine and two glasses. Now, I find Adam.

I know how to keep this life I love. I've been doing it for years; it's called manifesting. My Instagram will prove it.

ADAM

sink the eight ball in the left corner pocket. Margot is about to cry about her second loss when I hear Aimee call my name. Margot stands straight, her pool cue erect like a weapon in waiting.

"Settle down, will you?" I say, reading Margot's nervous energy.

"What does she want?"

"I am still her husband. It's not a sign of insanity for her to look for me."

"Do you think she knows?" Margot whispers.

"Seriously, this has to stop. I cannot survive this weekend with you jumping every time Aimee says my name."

As if on prompt, Aimee calls out again. This time her voice is playful. I can tell she's been drinking. Margot's shoulders relax.

"What?" I shout back.

Aimee follows my voice until she appears in the game room doorway. Her hands press on either side of the frame.

"There you are," she says.

Her sweater rides up to show a sliver of her midsection. Her face is flush, but not blotchy like after a run. The alcohol sends the blood to her cheeks, like makeup. When she drinks, she licks her lips until they're dark pink. This is my favorite Aimee.

Was my favorite Aimee. Before I recognized her love was all smoke and mirrors.

"Can you come outside?" she asks.

"Me and Margot are in the middle of a game."

Margot sets her cue against the wall in a reluctant gesture of surrender. She probably wants us to talk. Or at least it's better than me being around Eden in her mind.

"Can you come outside now?" Aimee asks.

She laces her fingers through mine and leads me down the hallway, but I drop her hand as we walk through the dining room. Aimee glances back at me when I let go. I point to the bar cart but Joe walks in the door, looking for Farah.

"No, no, I've got wine outside waiting for us," Aimee says to me. She doesn't want Joe to distract me, I'm sure.

Outside I turn back toward the house and spot Eden sitting on Rick's lap in the sunroom with the screened-in porch. He's looking at his phone and hands her one of his earbuds. Eden notices me catch her, but she doesn't move.

Is this what she's like with Rick when I'm not around? It makes me feel sick seeing her so close and intimate with anyone else, even her husband. I look away quickly and block them out of my mind.

"What are we looking at?" I ask Aimee.

"I need to do a post."

She waves her hands with a flourish and I notice her romantic setup. Magic hour over the water, the Adirondack chairs, the glasses on the small table between them.

"With us?" I ask, caught off guard.

Aimee's online persona as a momfluencer typically has nothing to do with me. She does her work with the girls, her ring-light tripod, and a self-timer. It occurs to me she's never once asked me for help, not even in the beginning.

"Can't be a mommy without a baby daddy. Or that's what the advertisers who have turned me down said. They need to see more couple shots," she says.

Now this makes sense. She doesn't want me involved, but she knows how to take a note from the guys with the money.

"Sit," she says.

Aimee takes the seat next to me and props her phone on the table between us. She positions our hands together on my armrest with her engagement ring shining in the setting sun. After a few seconds she leans over and makes a kissy face.

"No," I object.

"Come on, meet me halfway," she says.

"This is so contrived."

"And your novels are real?"

In another time and place I would have volleyed her banter. My novels are fake in a different sense, but an essential element of truth has to shine through or the book will flop. Aimee knows that, and that's what bothers me. She doesn't see that there's nothing real left between us. We're already dead in the water.

I don't say any of this. Instead, for some reason I can't explain, I try. I sit up and lean slightly toward her while keeping my eyes on the view ahead. Aimee leans in and kisses me on the cheek. Behind us her phone silently captures it all. I'm annoyed that she's dragged me into this, but I can't argue with Aimee taking her career seriously.

"Okay, one more," she says.

I look to her for a cue and she grabs my face with her hands. She kisses me full on the lips, slipping her tongue into my mouth. Without even trying, I lose myself in the kiss, so sweet and soft and lovely.

I pull away sharply and glance over my shoulder at Eden. She's still sitting in Rick's lap, keeping up her part of the charade.

"Let's see if I got my shot," Aimee says, scrolling through her phone. That's her signal that she's done with me.

"I'm heading back in," I say. I stand and take my untouched prop wine, resentful of the surge of power Aimee exerted over me. The power to make me forget the cruel side of her. Power I want to take back.

"Oh no, you have to see this." She grabs my hand and pulls me back into her orbit. "It's perfect."

Aimee holds out her phone, and my eyes are drawn to our picture. She wasn't exaggerating, using the term *perfect*. The light is stunning. Our silhouettes are black against the brilliant sun. A single ray shines through the outline of Aimee's plump lips, subtly sensual but still G-rated. Her hand cupping my face is the jewel in the crown of intimacy.

"Let the love shine through," she says. "That's the caption."

"Yeah, that's it," I agree.

My medium is the written word, but Aimee tells visual stories. And this one portrays nothing short of a fairy tale. She looks up at me and the ice between us cracks. I smile with pride.

What can I say? When she's good, she's good.

If this was us—the way it used to be us—I would have never fallen in love with Eden. But I can't trust Aimee. This photograph. This moment. It's nothing more than a setup snapshot.

RINI

Part of me seethes at Aimee's implication during her reading that she could make things happen that are entirely outside her control. That she can defy her own fate . . . by what? Ignoring it? Sticking her fingers in her ears and singing "La la la la"? But the truth is, I'm more angry she might be onto something. She must be a good social media influencer, because I'm desperate to follow her lead. Could I have altered my fate before I called the psychic six months ago? Is it too late now that my death date has been issued?

Aimee would say it's never too late. I set aside my pride and protectiveness and call Eric on the phone. He answers and I don't hesitate.

"Please come over," I say. "It's not about floor joists."

"I'm actually finishing a job down the road," he says simply. "I'll be there soon."

This time, I want to tell him everything. If anyone can change my fate, it's my soulmate.

The moment I first laid eyes on Eric, time stopped. I spotted his laughing face from ten feet away on a Sunday afternoon at the local outdoor concert series on the wharf. I don't know if he sensed me or not, but he looked at me from his spot at the table. He was with a bunch of his guy friends while I stood in the entrance with a wine vendor I'd met to discuss discounts. Eric and I locked eyes. You don't have to know anything about astrology to know that soulmates are all in the eyes. I saw it and I felt it. There was a connection between us that transcended that day, this life, these bodies.

When the wine vendor left, I sat at the bar alone collecting my thoughts. Eric had volunteered to get the next round for his buddies and parked himself at the stool next to me. We chatted and laughed until the sun sank into the Peconic Bay, and then our conversation got deeper and the large outdoor deck felt as small as a table for two. After the band packed up, his friends wanted to go to a dive bar, but I was ready to go home. I wasn't much of a drinker or partier, and the night out had been Andi's idea. I wasn't even twenty-one yet—I'd used her ID to get in—but our plans for the house and the business were struggling, and Andi thought it would be good for me to meet people around town who could help us renovate and grow.

"I have something to tell you, but I don't want you to get mad," Eric had said.

"Whether I get mad or not has nothing to do with what you tell me. It has to do with what you've done."

"So maybe I shouldn't tell you."

"Maybe you shouldn't have done it."

"Too late. How do you know it's bad?"

"The guilty look on your face gives you away."

"I have a girlfriend."

He was right—I was furious. But instead of venting, I said, "You did nothing wrong. You didn't touch me; you didn't ask to see me again. It's okay."

But it wasn't okay. Not at all.

He leaned in for a hug, but I practically ran away. My disappointment grew to anger as the days moved on. I ranted to Andi that there were no good men, that they were all scum. But she wouldn't tolerate that kind of talk from me. Andi had long ago decided that her fate was to attract all the wrong men, but she got mad at me for suggesting it might be mine too. She wanted more for me.

Meanwhile, I wanted to pursue Eric. I wanted to dive into the feeling I had around him. I wouldn't reduce it to lust, though I couldn't call it love yet. Even without a definition, I'd never felt that way before. I knew from my mom and Andi, and even my own teenage interactions, that what Eric and I had experienced wasn't easy to come by. And so if *we* were supposed to be together, then it seemed clear he was with the wrong woman. But that was his choice and I wanted to respect it, even though it took everything I had not to creep. Stalk him on Instagram. To stop myself from dropping by Claudio's every Sunday for the chance to see him and to call it fate.

As my urges grew and my moral compass went haywire, I wondered if infidelity was genetic. My dad had cheated and left my family devastated. Andi had hooked up with a married man and it ruined her. And now I wanted to pursue Eric despite his good boundaries. I thought it was in our DNA to ruin lives.

Nineteen days later, Eric showed up at the house where Andi and I were camped out in sleeping bags and futon mattresses on the floor. I slammed the door in his face, less out of commitment to my stance and more because I didn't trust myself face-to-face with him. In the five seconds it took me to register he was at my door, a karmic pull made me want to kiss him.

He rang the bell again.

"I broke up with her," he shouted.

I flung open the door and he leaned down to kiss me, his shoulders rounding with the promise that he would hold me and protect me. It was a dream I didn't know I had, come true.

Six years after that first meeting, and six months after we broke up, Eric is at my door again. This time my doorbell camera picks him up, first at the main gate, then as he approaches my cottage. After walking slowly from his pickup truck to my door, he pauses outside. He's dressed in khaki shorts and a navy blue shirt, my favorite color because it matches his eyes.

Those eyes. The ones that see through to the core of me. The ones that transport me to a place where I feel safe and loved. Even the thought of looking into his eyes in this very moment sends me into a panic. What am I doing? Why did I ask him here? What's the plan? Should I really tell him about the psychic prediction? Or is that selfish?

Eric finally works up the nerve to knock on my door. I open it even though I'm not ready.

"Hey," he says, sexy without even trying. What is it about a slyly spoken "Hey" that can turn your insides into goo? From that moment, my plans fly out the window. I pull Eric into my cottage, and with hungry kisses we tumble into the comfort of each other's body. We don't talk—we just know.

Later, wrapped in my bedsheets, he combs his fingers through my hair. "Not that I'm complaining, but what was this?" he asks.

"I'm sorry," I say. All my repressed emotions break through the surface, and I'm crying without my own consent.

"For what? That was amazing. It was everything I've wanted since the day you broke up with me. I just want to know if it was a one-time thing or if it's the beginning of another chapter for us. Either way, I have no regrets," he says.

I look up at him, a new idea on the horizon.

"What if we could take off? Run away together and disappear?" I ask, wondering if there is a way to physically escape my death.

Eric's face softens a bit. "You would never leave this place."

"Maybe this is the time."

"I would never let you," he counters.

"You're right," I say.

At the end of an era, nostalgia brings us back to the beginning. Graduation, divorce, moving house, these life events tempt us to reminisce about the journey. To marvel at the strength we've gathered over all the bumps in the road. On that day after our first kiss, Eric and I sat at the kitchen table for three hours chatting about old-home renovation. He walked around the first floor pointing out the original features I should never touch and the ones that should be modernized. He assigned me renovation shows on HGTV. By the time he left I was impossibly in love with him, and he was in love with Stars Harbor. Abandoning this place isn't the answer either. It was a bad last-ditch effort to quell my fear and anger.

Eric and I have come so far, and yet we should be just beginning. What if this was the beginning? I let myself imagine that as I kiss Eric again. This might be the start of a new chapter for us, one I can't yet comprehend.

"We will talk tomorrow. If you're interested in hearing me out, I'll have a lot to explain," I say.

"Why not now?" he asks.

"I have guests, and this little detour ate up all my time. I'll call you tomorrow night, after they leave."

It's not a lie; it's a wish.

After we're dressed and ready to say goodbye, Eric stands by his truck. I can't hold back from running to him. He catches me in his arms and we kiss. If it's the last kiss, it will have been worth it.

I change my clothes and check myself in the mirror before heading back to the main house to make sure the Dinner under the Stars is moving along smoothly. I swipe on some red lipstick, like the shade Aimee was wearing last night.

I've done a lot of good in the six months since I spoke to that psychic. I've gained so much momentum for plans long delayed. But I've also made mistakes, none as terrible as cutting off the only man I'd ever loved. If I can promise him tomorrow, I will. Even with the knowledge that the Universe will make a liar out of me.

MARGOT

The bonfire dinner transforms the bucolic backyard of Stars Harbor into a cover of *Martha Stewart Living* magazine. White fairy lights twinkle over the long table and benches. Brightly colored flowers decorate the table. The air smells of wood and the sweet smoke of barbecue. The sun hovers over the horizon, casting pink and lavender cotton candy clouds while the half-moon illuminates the same sky. This sunset is magic.

"Good news," Rini announces. "Weather forecasts put Tropical Storm Clementine two hundred miles off the coast of South Carolina tonight and moving east. The wineries won't close even for heavy rains, if it comes to that. So tomorrow's plans are intact."

I should be glowing in the execution of my vision come true, and yet all I see are the cracks, unable to gloss over them for the first time in my life.

Adam continues to rebuff Aimee's simple gestures of affection. Farah and Joe aren't even looking at each other. At least Ted is distracting Eden, and Joe is talking Rick's ear off about the Fed.

And Rini. She's been here with us, but at the same time, not here at all. Not engaged with us, but not ignoring us. She's been watching. Cataloging and storing information. I know because I've been doing the same thing, keeping an eye out for danger lurking in the dark. And even though I know why I'm doing it, the behavior looks ominous when I watch Rini. Good staff should be both attentive and invisible, but this feels wrong. She catches me tracking her and approaches with fierce eye contact. I look away nervously as she approaches.

"I know what you want," Rini says.

"You do?"

Rini nods. "Your reading. It looks like you're finished with dinner. If not, I can come back."

"No, I am done."

"Good. Let's sit." She gestures to the Adirondack chairs around the firepit, away from the main stage of dinner.

"I thought you meant something else," I say. "When you said you knew what I wanted."

"I know that too. You want to protect and grow your family. It's all over your chart. Up and down. The generation before you and the generation after you."

"The generation after me? Is that Adam's kids, or—"

"I'm talking about your child too," Rini says.

Her tone is ominous, a stark contrast to the heart-exploding joy I feel. "She—or he—is coming soon? Your website says you can see eighteen months out in our charts."

"Yes, the baby is coming much sooner than that."

My hands quiver with excitement. I tuck them under my thighs. "You've been dropping hints all weekend, but I'm still shocked to hear this."

"Hints?" Rini asks.

"Like me changing my last name, and the tarot card you left."

Rini's head tilts to the side as if she's trying to recall something.

"Tarot card? I don't work with them in my readings anymore. They were more of my sister's thing," Rini says.

"It was the Empress. I found it in the dumbwaiter."

"The dumbwaiters aren't for guest use. I use those for housekeeping. To deliver the flowers and horoscope cards to each of the rooms without anyone seeing me move through the hallways upstairs. I feel my cover is blown," Rini says with a tentative half smile.

"Your secret's safe with me. Besides, I'm used to old homes. And the tarot card? Does it mean what I think?"

"The Empress is the number-one card to predict pregnancy. Was it right side up or upside down when you found it?"

"I can't remember."

"It doesn't matter. Let's look at your chart." Rini pulls out her phone and shows me her screen, but all I see is a bunch of dots and lines and symbols. "Jupiter will be transiting through Pisces in conjunction with the Moon in your fifth house in nine months. It could be a metaphorical birth, but given that Saturn is transiting through Ted's ninth house at the same time, the context tells me it's literal. I see it plain as day."

I share with Rini that we've been trying to conceive for five years, unsuccessfully. "I'm so relieved to hear I didn't mess up by waiting to make partner at my law firm before trying to get pregnant."

"The law is an important part of your journey. You had to choose to be an advocate for others. Your chart is deficient in air signs, which means you have difficulties expressing yourself verbally. Your experiences in speaking up in conflict have often ended in devastating miscommunication."

Logically, what Rini's saying doesn't land, but emotionally, it hits hard. Like a lump in my throat.

"Sometimes it feels like I'm choking on what I can't figure out how to say. So I just swallow it all down."

"These issues began way before you were born," Rini says. "They have been passed down in your family lineage. With every generation, more lessons are learned, more healing occurs. You're going in the right direction."

My parents fought when I was a kid, and of course it upset me. But it was scarier when I knew they were mad and they ignored each other. The tension was so thick I couldn't breathe. Any terse words passed back and forth were communication, clues for me, and I could track the progress of their resolution until I felt safe again.

I pick my head up to check on my brother and the rest of the crew, chewing the tiny piece of skin I've ripped off from my thumb.

"If you stop ignoring what you don't want to see, you could find more confidence to speak your truth," Rini says. "Margot, your family is figuring out a lot karmically. And even though your baby is coming, there's much work to do."

My stomach drops. She must be able to see Adam's troubled marriage. I'll have a child, but the rest of us will fall apart. Adam and Aimee will get a divorce, I'll have to coordinate visits, Christmas will be broken up, school events will be tense. It will be a juggling act that I can't manage. I'll drop every ball.

"I feel like everything falls on my shoulders," I admit.

Rini scrolls through her phone again before turning the screen to me. "This is Saturn. Saturn takes about twenty-seven years to orbit the Earth. Does that time frame mean anything to you?"

"My parents died in a car accident twenty-seven years ago tomorrow."

Rini nods as if it all makes sense, but I'm not seeing the big picture.

"There's something big coming to you around their death. Some new information, or a new perspective. It's going to be a life-altering realization. Maybe a story that's different from the one you've been telling yourself."

"For that, I'll have to ask Adam. He's the storyteller," I say.

"You are too, Margot. You tell yourself stories all the time. It's what makes you a survivor. Maybe you've neglected the creativity of your Pisces stellium in favor of your hardworking, practical Capricorn Moon, but it's there."

The story I hear loud and clear is how I need to keep my brother's marriage intact so I can bring my baby into a solid extended family.

Rini puts her hand on my forearm, her grasp damp and heavy. With her touch, I'm grounded in this very moment.

"Be careful what you wish for," Rini says, her brown eyes shining black as night. "Getting what you want isn't the same as getting what you need."

Out of the corner of my eye I catch a glimpse of a shooting star, and all the dots connect. I would have missed it if Rini hadn't laid her hand on me.

In third grade, we read a poem in which the author reimagines stars as openings in the sky where loved ones shine down to let us know they're happy. After I heard that, I would make Nana bring us out to her country house in Southold a few times a year so I could see Mom and Dad. There were no stars at all in the city, and I hated to think that meant they weren't happy. Or worse, that they were happy and they forgot to shine down to tell me.

Nana, Adam, and I would lie on Nana's lawn bundled up in our winter coats and hats. Nana would point to different constellations and name all the people she'd lost. Back then I would talk to my parents in my head all the time, but I've stopped. I thought it was a child's game, but I can do that anytime I need. Tears spring to my eyes.

"I should get back to the kitchen. S'mores in a few," Rini says.

I nod. Rini taps the arm of my chair as she walks by me.

"Serena is a beautiful name," I say, remembering the moment we met and she introduced herself. "Why don't you use it?"

"It's not me. Serena is a girl for whom the world is her oyster. That's what my parents wanted for me when I was born. But that wasn't my life in the end."

Rini disappears across the lawn and inside the house. I turn my face up to the night sky and take in everything she said.

It occurs to me that if my parents are souls dancing among the stars, my future child might be up there waiting. I search the sky and point to the one that might be Serena Dylan Flynn. In the distance, not at all where I was looking, a light zooms across the sky. Another shooting star. It's her.

"Serena," I whisper, touching my belly.

My arrival-day fears were both right and wrong. Everything is changing, but nothing bad is going to happen. My family is coming.

FARAH

After dinner, Eden refills her wine and moves to the seat next to me. Eden and I have an unspoken pact to not discuss kids, motherhood, or anything tangential to either. It started the first time I met her. She asked me what I did for a living, and after I answered, she declared she was not having children. Clearly, she was set off by my work, as if I was going to force her into becoming a mother because I deliver babies for a living. She was still wrestling with the consequences of being open about her child-free status and expected me to preach and persuade her to change her mind. Quite the opposite, I revealed why I chose to become an obstetrician and how it had nothing to do with mothers as a whole, but instead, *my* mother.

My mother is a breast cancer survivor and when I went to med school I started with a mind toward oncology. Though she beat the cancer when I was too young to remember, I thought of her as a warrior. I could help other women be warriors too. But when I did my rotation in med school, I knew the field was not for me. Giving people bad news, counseling women through their lowest points, having patients look at me like I was the problem and not their source of wisdom—it was a far cry from my mother's hindsight warrior story. I broadened my search to any practice that focused on women's health, as it was consistently underfunded, under-researched, and largely ignored by old-school medicine. That's when I found my calling. Being an OB-GYN meant caring for women through their reproductive life from the ages of fifteen to fifty-five. Dozens of stages of life. Long periods of slow changes. There was nothing better suited to me.

After I shared that, Eden relaxed, and when we saw each other, we often chatted about our favorite dark psychological TV dramas. But tonight, she has something else on her mind.

"Was I too hard on Margot last night?" she whispers.

"Yes," I say plainly.

Eden sips her wine. I can tell she's fighting off the feeling of defensiveness that's curled in her chest. The topic of motherhood, even if it's not a fit, can peel away every nerve protection we have. It's something society pressures every woman to reckon with, and answer to in some capacity. Nuanced conversations are by and large unwelcome. Even when we find a safe space, none of us know how to say the things we've been taught to never admit.

"I don't think that the world needs more of her kind of mother," she says.

"You don't even know what kind of mother she will be yet," I say. "She doesn't even know. Before children, we think we know so much about what we want to do, how we want to do things, but I've seen women turn complete one-eighties as soon as they give birth."

Aimee approaches with a full bottle of red wine, eager to join the motherhood conversation.

"Being a mother is the first thing I was ever bad at," she says.

"And you have three kids? That might be something you want to keep to yourself," Eden says.

"She's lying. I've known her since her first day as a mother, and she's always been flawless," I tell Eden.

"No way, not even close, but that's the best part. Having to learn and struggle. Most things in life came pretty easily for me, but I've had to work at getting motherhood right. When the effort pays off and it finally clicks in some small way, it's incredibly rewarding."

I've never heard Aimee say anything like this before. That being a mother *isn't* completely natural for her. It sounds like she's had doubts. She's made mistakes. She's relied on trial and error. Could I really not know this? It's possible. When we connect, it's rarely over parenting. Maybe all I see of her as a mother is the highlight reel, not the behind-the-scenes struggles.

Aimee pushes her wineglass away and rubs her finger around the water ring left on the table. "It gets easier and it doesn't. Every kid is different; every parent-child dynamic is its own thing. It's like my husband says: everything he writes teaches him a new lesson. He feels like he's starting over from scratch every single time. Like delivering babies."

"What about it?" I ask, not seeing the parallel.

"Is every birth experience the same? Every labor, every C-section, every pregnant woman?"

"Of course not," I say.

"You have pride in the knowledge and experience you've gained from the past, but also find daily self-esteem from knowing what situation calls for, say, forceps or an episiotomy, and which delivery can push without it."

"The small things matter," I say. I'd never thought of mothering as deeply as my work. How could something so fascinating to her be so utterly pedestrian to me?

Aimee pulls her wine closer and takes a sip. We look away from each other, reminded that we shouldn't exclude Eden from our conversation.

"How do you know you don't want kids?" Aimee asks Eden.

"How did you know you did?" Eden returns the question.

"I just knew," Aimee says.

"And were you right?" Eden continues.

"I was."

"You haven't changed your mind like everyone assumes I will?" Eden asks.

"I haven't," Aimee says.

"It's the same for me. I just know," Eden says.

Neither Eden nor Aimee regrets her choice, despite landing on different sides of the child question, but what if I have some? I could never say that out loud. Ever. Even thinking it feels disloyal.

Besides, it's not accurate. It's not like I wanted kids, had them, and then decided I didn't want them. I never felt that desperate need to procreate in the first place, but I didn't think that was a requirement. My family expected it, Joe wanted them, and it didn't occur to me to wonder one way or the other. I didn't "just know" anything the way both Eden and Aimee declare. It sort of happened. But I resent the idea that now that I have them, my whole world should be different.

"They don't have to change everything if you don't want them to," I say.

Eden and Aimee both look horrified by my statement. Now that it's out of my mouth I realize that it could be interpreted as pushing Eden to have children, when it's really a defense of my own stance. Still, it's disturbing to see them react identically.

"What?" I ask. "Why are you both looking at me like that?"

"My whole identity was turned upside down. I left my job in magazines, I moved apartments, my body was split open," Aimee says. "I know that was extreme, but I didn't think upheaval was a choice."

"I'm with Aimee on this one," Eden says. "Drastic change shouldn't be optional. Why have them if you won't let them transform you? That should be part of the deal."

In my practice, I saw women change in all kinds of ways. The practical woman suddenly cried at every visit. The ones who thought they'd be a stay-at-home-mom couldn't wait to get back to work. The ambivalent woman fell hard during pregnancy. The consummate caretaker couldn't bond with her infant. The list went on in every direction.

There was no way to predict what would change, only that change was inevitable—and that was exactly what I inoculated myself against. I didn't care if it was good change or bad change; I didn't want anything to be different once I became a mother. I loved my life, and I'd carefully constructed it. No eight-pound wrecking ball was going to threaten that.

No hormones were going to convince me otherwise. By not succumbing to the emotional journey, I could keep the ship straight.

I drain my wineglass and stand, in search of water. "I'm off to find some of the fathers on this trip, to hear how drastically their lives changed after having kids."

I walk past Rini and Margot deep in conversation.

"Ten minutes until s'mores," Rini calls out to me in passing.

"I'll be back by then."

There are carafes full of ice water on the table outside, but I need a moment of peace as much as I need hydration. Inside I take a drinking glass from the cabinet and set it under the faucet until it turns cold. I gulp down half the glass in one sip.

In the distance I hear Joe. I turn off the tap and follow the sound of his voice.

"No, I'm not bluffing. I think you're making this a bigger deal than it needs to be. He's on our side. It's only a matter of timing," Joe says. I spot him pacing the foyer and glancing out the front window every few rotations.

Objectively, Joe is good-looking. He has a thick head of hair and one of the brightest smiles I've ever seen. But lately, his grin doesn't move me as it once did. I feel different inside.

"Tell him that will not be necessary. He's here. Yes, right now. And I will take care of it. Give me twenty-four hours," Joe says.

Uncomfortable with his conversation and my unintentional snooping, I step out of the shadows and announce myself with a wave. Joe nods at me.

"I'll call you tomorrow," Joe says before he hangs up. "Work," he says to me while slipping his phone into his pocket.

I nod. The conversation isn't necessarily out of the ordinary, but something is off. Whether it's Joe's demeanor or my suspicion is unclear at this point.

"Everything okay?" I ask.

"We have a new donor who hasn't delivered his pledge. He's off in

Europe on holiday and doesn't want to be bothered. Pam's working on his CPA while I'm looking at a money bridge."

"Is there someone outside there?" I gesture to the window he's been diligently watching.

Joe shrugs. "I didn't even realize I was looking."

I'm not sure I believe Joe about work or the window, but there's enough history there to let it lie. "Rini's serving s'mores in a few minutes."

"I hope there's another option besides s'mores. You know, for the adults," Joe says.

I smile. "I had the same thought, but as a woman I know to keep that inside."

"I won't tell if you don't," Joe says. He places his hand on the small of my back, directing me away from the dark foyer. Joe's phone vibrates in the silence between us. I step outside his reach and fall in line next to him.

"Do you need to get that?" I ask.

"Probably." Joe turns around, back to his spot in the foyer. He swipes his phone open but doesn't speak. A muffled voice yells on the other end. Joe catches me watching him and waves me on. His impatience suggests *It's fine*, but I'm not sure it is. I'm not sure anything is fine.

I've always safeguarded myself against obvious emotional shifts. Our first year of marriage was unremarkable, and I kept my work pace during pregnancy and my first year as a mother. My schedule stayed the same, my career path stayed the same, and I was completely unchanged. And yet, maybe I was wrong to think I could stave it off forever. Maybe all I really did was hold off for Aimee to rip me open and turn my world up-side down. Her influence has been a slow burn—from patient to fellow mom to best friend and beyond—yet all of a sudden, everything in my life is out on the table for evaluation. It's up to me to figure out what I want and what I'm willing to do to get it.

ADAM

This evening is nothing like what I expected. Eden and I stole away for some alone time earlier and now I have Aimee by my side, playing the role of doting wife in front of our dinner party audience. I have two women fawning over me, one in public, the other in private. Enjoying it is only a matter of keeping good boundaries.

Monogamy runs deep in my romance writer's roots. I include characters across the spectrum of sexuality in my novels, but their relationships remain very traditional. One soulmate, one right person. Anything less than full, modern partnership is settling for less than they deserve. But what if it's actually more? Having my cake and eating it too sounds delicious. Granted, it's been a dangerous juggle in the same house, but under normal circumstances, this arrangement could be ideal. Maybe Eden was onto something I too quickly dismissed.

I pat Aimee's hand and plant a kiss on her cheek while I make eye contact with Eden. She flashes me a small nod as I excuse myself from the dinner table, explaining that while it's been a wonderful night, a writer has no days off when there's a deadline to meet.

Inside the house I wait for Eden in the back stairwell. A few minutes later, she hops up to me with a grin and a kiss. I whirl her around and place her on the step above me.

"There's something I have to tell you," she says. She hooks her arms over my shoulders while I snake my arms around her ribs and down her back. She leans in, pressing her whole body up against me. I breathe in her hair.

"I love you," she says in a raspy whisper.

It's a good thing she can't see my face because there's no way to hide my shock.

I convince myself the queasiness is a sudden wave of guilt about having sex with Aimee yesterday and not telling Eden. That's strictly against the rules; Eden's rules. I certainly never wanted to hear when or if she had sex with her husband, and it was a thought I never allowed myself to have. But Eden had told me right off the bat that she expected to be informed when Aimee and I were intimate. To this point, it had never happened and thus I'd never had to own up to it. I didn't know how to do it, but I was sure it wasn't the right time after she said she loved me for the first time. And she's kissing my neck.

For Eden, saying "I love you" is a step toward the traditional. Toward monogamy. Toward everything I'd been arguing for.

I told Eden that I loved her weeks ago. We sat at on a sidewalk patio alongside a cobblestone street in the city. The day had been muggy, but as the sun set brilliantly in the sky, the air settled to the perfect evening temperature. The air smelled of rosemary focaccia, sharp and sweet. Eden looked gorgeous in an emerald-green dress that made her eyes sparkle like the Caribbean Sea; her blond waves, the sandy shoreline. I was unable to hold back after the first bottle of wine. I told her I was in love with her. Without hesitation, she laughed at me.

What does that mean? she said. *People say it all the time and they don't have the first clue what they're trying to convey. Do you?*

Eden was someone who liked to buck convention, whether that was marriage, monogamy, or the basic phrase "I love you." She wasn't actually laughing at me, but the silly idea. She wasn't saying she didn't love me. She was simply being herself.

I told her I loved her again a few times after that night, but never absentmindedly like Aimee, who tossed the words to me like car keys every time I left the house. I said it to Eden only when I felt an overwhelming moment of connection. She never said it back, but she returned the sentiment with a look or a touch, an act of intimacy that felt bigger than my words.

I am gobsmacked to hear her say it back to me now, but it doesn't feel like the victory I anticipated. Instead, unease brews in my chest.

"So what's the plan?" Eden asks.

"For what?"

"Us. Like I said the first night, I'm ready now," she says. "When are we going to tell Rick and Aimee the bad news?"

"What's the rush?" I ask.

"It might make sense to act like it all came up at this retreat. Like the astrologer made us do it."

I remove her arms from around my neck and step down to back away from her. "I don't know about that. Aimee will have a lot of questions."

"There's nothing I can't answer," she says.

I'm surprised to hear her even suggest that she could answer Aimee's questions.

"That's my job," I say. Eden pulls back slightly. She places a hand on her hip and looks away. I don't understand the confusion. I never imagined her talking to Aimee about us, not even with me. In fact, I'd prefer to keep them as far apart as possible. One long weekend together is quite enough flying in the danger zone.

"I wouldn't talk to Rick without you," I say, waiting for her to reciprocate. A beat goes by. Then another. "You wouldn't talk to Aimee without me, right?"

"Are you afraid of her?" Eden asks.

She's missing the point, but I know the time is not ripe to push my new thinking on her.

"No," I say.

"Then explain this to me. Because every time we've done something risky or blatant, you're the one who has been saying you want to get caught. Suddenly you're worried about her finding out?"

"No, but I want to do it right. I don't need her becoming vindictive or using the girls as pawns."

Eden considers this and gives the idea some weight. She seems to realize I'm being strategic rather than acting like some lovesick teenager. Unfortunately for her, I'm being strategic about admitting that I'm having second thoughts.

"You know I would never want to harm your family," she says.

"I do know that. And that includes Aimee."

"I'll hold off for now, but we've got to get on the same page."

Eden kisses me, but I'm not feeling it. Something has soured. The confrontation with Margot earlier might have set me on edge more than I'd like to admit. At the first sign of strife, I'm fending off intrusive visions of a sad divorce and a sister-coparent rather than a sister-wife.

"Adam?" As if summoned, Margot's stage whisper hisses through the dark house. I push Eden away as a reflex. She slips off the stair ledge, but I catch her before she falls.

"I should go see what she wants," I say, relieved to escape the pressure of Eden's change of heart.

"Fine," she says, though I know by her tone that it's anything but fine. She frowns as I slip away.

MARGOT

After my reading with Rini, I steer Ted upstairs and away from the game room with Rick to tell him the good news.

"She said she sees a birth. In nine or ten months," I say. I rub my wrist while I tap open the Ava app on my phone. All my data points are normal. "This thing really should tell you when you're pregnant, not just peak fertility."

"What? Who?" Ted asks, confused that I've launched into a conversation without context. He takes a seat on the bed while I close the app, slide off the gold bangle I wore to dinner, and place it on the desk.

"Rini. She did my reading by the firepit. She basically said I'm pregnant."

"Wait, I thought you got your period earlier?"

"Remember how I've told you that spotting is normal with implantation?"

"Yeah, but you also told me that never happens to you."

"Well, I've never actually experienced implantation before. But it could be next month too. Why are you fighting with me about this? I thought you'd be more excited."

"I just don't want you to get your hopes up because of what some witch lady pointed out in the stars."

And there's the real issue. When I booked this trip, Ted had focused on the luxury, the golf, and the time to recharge. He didn't care about the astrologer. But over the weekend he's grown more agitated with the chaos she's creating.

"Why won't you let me have a little hope? Is it hurting anyone?" I cross my arms. "Why do you seem so on edge?"

Ted drops his head into his hands. "I've done something terrible. I've kept something from you," he says.

Affair, affair, affair is the drumbeat in my head. Not because I'd ever suspect Ted, but because I've already been blindsided by an affair today. I lean against the back of the desk chair for support. I almost stop Ted and say, *Whatever it is, I don't want to know.*

"It's about getting pregnant," he adds. "I know we've both been getting tested and they can't find anything wrong with either of us. There's no clear medical reason why we haven't gotten pregnant."

"Right," I say.

"And I know the doctor asked if you'd even been pregnant before, but she didn't ask me. No one asked me. That's not an excuse for me not telling you."

"I'm confused. I said no and that's right. I would know if I was pregnant before."

"I'm trying to say that I have."

"You've gotten someone else pregnant?"

My heart sinks when Ted hangs his head and nods.

"How? When?" I ask.

"At Yale. It was almost twenty years ago. I'm sure it has no bearing on what's happening now."

"Do you have a child somewhere out there?"

"No, no, we went to a clinic."

I'm both relieved and disappointed, and the latter surprises me.

"Was that what you wanted?" I ask.

"Oh yeah. We were too young to raise a child. It would have been a disaster for so many reasons. I don't regret it; this isn't some big confession. But I am sorry I didn't say something sooner."

"Why are you telling me now?"

"Something that stupid astrologer said last night about intimacy and how I work things out."

"That makes you a bit of a hypocrite. Telling me not to believe Rini's pregnancy prediction but acting on what she said to you."

"This isn't about the astrologer, or my old girlfriend; this is about us. I have a new perspective, to consider whether me withholding this information might be holding us back."

"Karmically? You don't believe in that stuff."

"But you seem to. And I believe in you. More than anything else."

Ted hooks his hand on the back of my neck and kisses me on the forehead. He leans down to catch my eye, but I keep my gaze trained on the floor. He kisses me on the nose, the cheek, the other cheek.

"Ted." I pull away before he makes it to my lips and I forget about being upset.

"You're mad," he says.

"I'm upset."

Something about this information is really bothering me, but I don't know if it's the abortion itself, the fact that he withheld it, or something else. It's a lot to take in at one time.

I walk out and Ted stays. He knows I need my space. I search for Adam.

"Can we go for a ride?" I ask when I find my brother.

"Where are we going?"

"Anywhere. 7-Eleven? You can get cigarettes."

"I quit."

"Good, then you can do it again tomorrow."

Adam gives in, knowing I need this. He grabs his keys and smiles. Maybe he even wants to be alone with me too.

"So what's up?" he asks as he turns the engine in his car.

"Are you actually thinking about getting a divorce?" I ask. *Divorce*. The word expands like cotton in my mouth. I want to talk to my brother, my calming force, but the first thing that popped into my head might not have been the best topic. All I know is I'm not ready to share the new information Ted gave me.

"Divorce is a thing, Margot. Lots of couples do it. And it can make a family stronger."

"You didn't answer my question."

"I've thought about it a lot, yes. Even before Eden."

"Why?"

The one-word question is basically my cry for help, but Adam pauses as if he's trying to find the right words to give me a real answer.

"Because I deserve better than the defunct marriage Aimee and I have. My girls deserve to grow up with a better model of love than our parents gave us. I'm doing the right thing, Margot. The hard thing, the sad thing, the painful thing—but the right thing."

Knowing my brother the writer, he's rehearsed this several times. It might even be in his newest novel.

"That sounds wonderful in theory, but in practice this will be a nightmare. Is Aimee going to invite me to every ballet recital, or it'll be on you? Because you didn't even show up to the last one."

"I'll be a better dad if I'm not avoiding Aimee."

"You could stop avoiding her now and work this out."

"I'm in love," Adam says.

"That's the second time you've mentioned that and it doesn't sound as compelling as you think. What about the girls? They need both of you."

"No one is abandoning the girls. Even with divorced parents, they'll be better off than we were. At least Aimee and I will be alive."

There's no way to argue that point, and even if I could, this distraction isn't working. It's only making me more agitated. I still can't shake my conversation with Ted.

"Ted just told me he got a girl pregnant in college," I say.

"He did?" Adam asks without missing a beat despite the abrupt change in topic. "Who was it? Avery?"

"Adam, that's not the point."

"Which is?"

"He never told me."

"Until today. When he told you. Voluntarily."

"I guess," I say, considering how much weight that should have. Probably more than I'm giving it now.

"I don't remember that happening in college," Adam adds.

"You weren't friends," I say. "You barely knew each other."

"Whatever, it's not a big deal."

"What do you mean?"

"It's ancient history. You've been together for a decade. What, are you thinking your whole relationship is a lie or some crap? Why are you upset with him?"

"We've been trying to get pregnant for years. Perhaps this was relevant before."

"Why? It happens. Teenagers aren't the bastion of impulse control and good practices."

"Well, it never happened to me," I say as we pull in to 7-Eleven.

Inside the store, Adam heads straight to the counter for cigarettes while I move to that weird aisle in the back where pregnancy tests sit next to infant pain relief and geriatric fiber pills. I stare at the two types of pregnancy tests, the expensive one and the store brand, until the packages blur. I stand there for a minute, maybe two or three, while tears stream down my face and my nose runs. I don't have the nerve to buy them, not after what Ted told me.

I go back empty-handed to the car, where Adam's already puffing on his cigarette. I can tell from his double take that Adam has noticed I'm upset. He stares ahead, quiet.

"What happened?" he asks.

"I couldn't do it."

"It must be painful, month after month."

He's right, but it's different this time. "If I'm not pregnant, I'll know exactly who is to blame."

Adam shakes his head and starts the ignition. We drive in silence for a few minutes until we turn onto the north road. I stare out the window, not noticing anything we pass, and it's not because of the lack of streetlamps. I'm lost in my anxiety.

"You can't be solely responsible for something that requires two people. Just like I'm not solely responsible for my marriage falling apart," Adam says.

"The affair doesn't help."

"It didn't hurt either. I'm telling you, we were already broken."

"Adam—"

"Stop, Margot. This is about you. If you keep taking on so much of other people's stuff, one day you're going to get fed up and lose it. Just like Mom did."

"You're comparing me to Mom right now?"

"You're becoming her," he says. "You take responsibility for everything."

"You say that like it's a bad thing."

"It is."

"It's better than acting like a victim," I retort.

"She was no victim. In fact, I think she's the one who crashed the car while Dad was driving."

On one hand I'm not surprised we're talking about Mom and Dad, given Rini told me less than an hour ago that I might form a new story around their deaths. But on the other hand, this conversation feels like a fantasy. In over two decades, Adam and I haven't spoken about our parents' car accident. I'm shocked, not only by his twisted theory that Mom killed Dad, but by the mere suggestion that it was anything other than an accident. The police report was straightforward.

They were driving along the Saw Mill River Parkway, a narrow and treacherous strip of road. If you've ever had a car zoom by you in the right lane while you frantically try to hold the ground between the median guardrail and the two-lane highway's center dotted line, the fact that there aren't more fatal accidents is surprising. It was the middle of the day. My father was sober behind the wheel. They were both wearing seatbelts.

The car crashed into the median at a high rate of speed. It flipped an estimated one to three times to where it lay, unmoving, until an SUV came barreling around the sharp curve and crushed their BMW. Both were pronounced dead at the scene. Time of death put the proximate cause in the hands of the speeding SUV, and there was no evidence of foul play. Nana told us so. We had no reason not to believe her.

"It was an accident," I insist.

"What if it wasn't?"

I want to tell him he is sick. I want to tell him he is wrong. But I spot a light brown mass emerge from the thick trees, illuminated by the headlights of an oncoming car.

"Adam! There! A family of deer."

In my mind, I'm yelling, but I can barely hear my own voice. I'm captivated by their presence. As if we're the ones intruding on their space rather than them encroaching on this narrow highway.

"I can beat them. Let them cross behind us," Adam says.

The deer are moving quickly. They are so beautiful.

"No, Adam. Slow down."

The deer halt their gallop at the edge of our lane as a white pickup truck zooms by in the other direction. The biggest one steps out, creeping into the lane. He darts backward when a beige minivan honks.

I watch the speedometer move from thirty-five to forty to fifty.

"Adam, please."

The family of deer takes off across the road in front of us. Adam stops in time.

"That was close," I say, relieved.

I never see the Subaru from the westbound lane swerve to avoid hitting a single baby deer that darted out at the last minute, frantic to join her family. I only understand what's happened behind us when Adam's Acura bucks forward. The car clips our rear quarter panel and sends us into a tailspin.

"Hold on," Adam shouts, though I don't know what to hold on to. He turns the steering wheel hand over hand.

One rotation, two rotations, spinning like we're on a ride at the Suffolk County Fair. Just like when I was a kid, I want off.

✦

The first thing I see when I wake again is the deer. The family of deer that were on the side of the road. But that cannot be right. The deer were there before the crash, not after. And I should be in the car, but I'm walking in the grass next to them. It's a hazy shade of daylight, like winter.

There are four grown deer, and four fawns in various sizes. Strange as it sounds, I recognize them all. There's Adam and Aimee, my three nieces, me and Ted, and our child. Our baby.

I saved your lives, I say. *I'm so glad.*

But it wasn't enough to save yours, a buck says.

Look at the sky—the world is ending, one of the does says.

I reach my hands out, palms up. The rain turns to blood. It pours down from the black clouds.

What will you do? they ask.

Will you save me, Mommy? the littlest one asks.

Tears sting my eyes. I shake my head. If it were the end of the world, being with my baby would make me lose my mind. I would panic, wanting to save her somehow. I don't know if that makes me a bad mother, but it's the truth. I'd be a wreck and my baby would sense she wasn't safe.

I choose him, I say, pointing to the largest buck.

Him? they ask.

I explain: *The girls should be with their mom.*

Three of the fawns nuzzle the doe.

Not him?

I shake my head, fighting back tears.

Ted would be good with the baby. He is calmer, more stable. He would keep her safe at all costs.

The smaller buck huddles the fawn closer to him.

I choose Adam.

I walk over to the larger buck and wrap my arms around his neck, pressing my face into his bristly coat.

If the world were ending, he'd crack open a beer. He'd point out the sunset. He'd sit next to me, his presence enough to lull me into carefree comfort.

Even watching this strange vision play out in my mind, it never occurs to me to wonder if I'm dead. All I know is if the world were ending, I'd want to spend it with my brother.

RINI

This is quite a chaotic start to the Moon Men event. Adam and Margot had a run-in with a deer that left them unharmed but Margot cranky and irritable. When she walked in the house on Adam's arm, they were still arguing about what had happened. Margot wanted to go to the emergency room for fear she might have a concussion. Adam insisted she did not hit her head, but that she passed out.

According to Adam she had been safely wrapped in her seatbelt, airbag cushion over the dashboard. Farah gave her a once-over and declared that she did not present any of the concerning symptoms of brain swelling.

"If I didn't hit my head, why did I pass out?" Margot asks Farah.

"It could have been any number of reasons, including anxiety, fear, or emotional distress. Your blood pressure is fine, your pupils are responsive, and you have no signs of physical injury."

"Shall we cancel the Moon Men event?" I ask.

A chorus of yeses and nos ring out at once.

Margot looks up at me from the couch with daggers in her eyes, like our conversation about her parents' car accident had caused her own.

"If no one wants to make the call, I'll use Ted's words from the first night and elect to keep things on track."

"I'm going to bed," Margot says without acknowledging me. Ted stands up to help her.

"You should feel free to go ahead with the event, but I have to stay with Margot. Just in case," he says.

I lead Rick, Adam and Joe outside to the circle of mats on the front lawn.

"The sky isn't as clear as I'd like, but the rain is holding off and we can see the moon," I say as I remove Ted's spot and re-space the three mats equidistant from one another.

"Lie down on your backs. Make yourselves as comfortable as possible. Bend your knees deeply so that you might bring the soles of your feet together, legs fluttering like a butterfly. I'll come around with these yoga bolsters to prop up your knees because as men your hips were not designed to open that wide."

"Praise the women who give birth," Joe says.

I wonder how good Joe is at his job. He comes across like he's speaking in sound bites. It's off-putting to me, but is "politician speak" one of those things where you fake it until you make it? It's possible not everyone who leads is born with a confident tone of voice.

I walk around to the three men, making sure they are properly set up.

"To be in your feminine means to be receptive, and that begins with your physical body."

Adam stares up at me as I walk past him. He doesn't seem shaken by the deer encounter, which is good.

"Close your eyes. Place one hand on your belly, the other on your heart. Take a few deep breaths in through your nose. When you're full, hold for a beat and then exhale out your mouth.

"Random thoughts may begin popping into your mind. That's a sign that you're quieting yourself, opening up, being receptive. But at this point I want you to let those thoughts come and go. Don't dwell on them."

I let the seconds stretch out into minutes, leaving them alone with their thoughts. After three minutes I provide them with the mantra for the Moon Men event.

"Now that our bodies are prepared, we can begin to share. Sharing is a vital part of community, receptivity, and the divine feminine. Before we begin, I want you to tell the person to your left that he is safe and that you are here to receive."

"Can we go the other direction?" Adam asks.

"No, the ritual must move the energy in a counterclockwise direction. We'll start with you, Joe."

"Rick, you are safe and I am here to receive you."

"Great, now Rick."

"Adam, you are safe and I am here to receive you."

"This is too hokey," Adam says. He sits up and kicks his legs out straight. He could not look more uncomfortable in his skin, exactly as I'd expected.

"Please lie down and continue the circle. We cannot have a break in the energy."

"Joe, you are safe and I am here to receive you," Adam says.

"Now we will have six minutes of silence. Six minutes will feel like an eternity. You will suddenly find yourself overwhelmed with an itch on your leg or a tickle in your throat. Hear me when I tell you that most of these sensations are not real. It's your brain trying to distract you from receiving the collective energy."

"So we shouldn't scratch ourselves?" Joe asks.

"This exercise isn't about doing or not doing; it's about listening. Attempt to discern what is real and what is not. Your six minutes begins now."

The men all squirm. Adam coughs. Joe swats at an imaginary bug crawling on his arm. Rick is able to maintain the most stillness of the three. A gentle alarm signals the end of the silent time. I surreptitiously press the start button on my voice recorder and slide it into my pocket.

"At this point in the exercise, one or two thoughts are nagging at you. Something you said in high school that left its mark and you're still mortified. A situation where you wronged a friend. A time when you used your power to take advantage of a woman."

I walk around the outside of the circle, standing above each of their heads as I offer examples.

"If it happened recently, that's too fresh to be a real wound. I want you to go deeper, back in time to that one thing you convince yourself you are past, but intrudes on you now in this quiet, safe, receptive place."

"And what do we do with this thought?" Joe asks.

"I want you to share it."

"I've got nothing," Adam says.

"I have a hard time believing that," I say, trying to keep my tone light. "Every human on Earth has a moment they would take back. More than one."

"Sure, I'll think about it," Adam says.

"I speak from years of experience that everyone harbors secrets that lay dormant and threaten our happiness," I add.

I let the energy from our conflict settle. A minute later Joe clears his throat.

"When Farah and I started dating, I was in a relationship. It had run its course for me, but I hadn't had the tough conversation. Politicians shouldn't be alone. It's not good for our image."

"Good, Joe, doesn't it feel good to get that out? The Universe can help you carry that burden now. When someone has shared, we repeat the opening mantra. Joe, you are safe and I am here to receive you."

Rick and Adam repeat.

"Adam? Did you think of anything?" Rick asks.

"Nope, not yet."

"I have something, then."

"Go ahead, Rick," I say.

"Something happened with a woman."

"It's important for you to say the words," I encourage.

"It was ten years ago. We were both drinking. Heavily. It was a pub crawl. Afterward we went back to my place. I thought we had a good time."

"So why mention it, Rick?"

"Her sister sent me a bunch of harsh messages, ripping into me. Saying that I took advantage of her sister. That she was blacked out and I should have known. I lost my shit. I wouldn't have sex with someone who was passed out. Never."

"When did you say this happened?"

"Ten years ago."

"And why are you bringing it up now?" I ask.

"The more time that went by, the more I started to recall details from that night. There was one point where I went to get a towel, and when I came back, she'd kind of fallen asleep, but then she was definitely awake again. To tell you the truth I was pretty drunk too. I was focused on my own performance."

"So what's bothering you, Rick? I feel like there's a detail you are holding back."

"A few months later I saw her out at a bar."

"What bar?" I ask.

"Lillian's. She wouldn't even look at me. She was crying on her friend's shoulder. I felt terrible, but also confused. Why didn't she confront me?"

"Why didn't you say something to her?" I ask.

"What was I supposed to say? It was so awkward."

"Always better to say nothing," Joe says.

"At the time I brushed it off, but I don't think I've ever let it go."

"Do you think you're a bad person, Rick?"

"I didn't hold her down and force myself on her or anything like that. I'm not that kind of man. But I should have talked to her. Apologized for the misunderstanding. Instead, I was more scared of what could happen to me than what actually happened to her. I regret that."

"I think you have your answer," I say. "I've said this in many of the private readings, but it's never too late for an apology."

"She doesn't want to hear from me," Rick argues.

"No, she doesn't," I say. "And she is under no obligation to hear you out, nor does she have any responsibility to absolve you of your actions. But you have a moral obligation to apologize, to be open to doing anything that might make this right."

I walk the men through their grounding ritual and ask the Universe to help them heal, but my mind jitters and jumps. Rick said this incident happened ten years ago. At the bar where Andi worked. Could she have known Rick too? No, that doesn't make sense. Also, he said the girl's sister messaged him, and I'm Andi's only sister.

I'm getting paranoid. It's getting closer to my moment and I'm seeing monsters in every shadow. That's to be expected, but I have to stay the course. I know who is responsible for what happened to my sister.

After saying good night to the guests, I walk back to my cottage. I hear a rustle in the grass and freeze. It's probably a deer or raccoon. I wait and let my eyes adjust to the dark.

In the silence, I spot a person walking around my cottage. They look neither small nor large, but I distinctly see a baseball cap. A flash of light sweeps the window. On closer inspection, I'm not sure if they're inside or outside.

"Hey," I say.

Their light shuts off. If they heard me, they must be outside the cottage. I dial Eric, knowing how unreliable 911 is in this cell-tower dead zone, but I don't hit the green call button yet. I let my thumb hover and watch.

"Who's there?" I call out.

Whether it's because of my second attempt to engage them or the fact that I'm inching closer, unafraid, they take off. I hear the soft rustling of someone pushing tree branches out of their way as they run through the evergreens at the edge of the property. I try to track their rapid footfalls, but I can't tell if they're running toward the main house or away from it and toward the front gate. Whoever they are, they're fast. A runner.

I scramble into the cottage to check the security cameras, but by the time I get there, everything is dark. I would have been alerted if someone had approached the gate, so it must have been an inside job. But if it was a guest looking for me, there'd be no point in scurrying away, even if coming to the cottage is against the rules. The intrusion makes no sense and that sets me on edge.

I kick off my fancy shoes and shove my feet into sneakers to investigate in person, but before I'm out the door, my phone screeches with an alert from CNN.

Tropical Storm Clementine takes an unexpected turn, sets its destructive rampage on coastal Georgia overnight.

All I can do is track the storm's progress, but what about the threat that's already here?

Overstimulated and jittery, I flip off the lights in my cottage and watch the main house in the dark. I observe as laptops and televisions flicker and power down as guests move from room to room, settling into sleep for the night. When the house is completely dark, I take to my bed.

All along I've been under the impression I gathered this group for my personal reasons, but what if they arrived with their own agenda in place? To execute a plan that involves me, on the day a psychic told me I'm supposed to die? It's entirely possible, but I'll have to figure out why.

Coincidences that big aren't coincidences at all.

SUNDAY

THE LAST DAY

AIMEE

I rise early out of sheer force of habit. I can't shake my sleep patterns when I'm away from the girls. I don't imagine what they're eating, or worry whether they're brushing their teeth, but the baby's phantom cries wake me with a start at 5 a.m. I've never been away from them long enough to test whether my internal clock would adjust, or how many days it would take.

I turn onto my side and pull the goose-down comforter to my chin, my knees into my body. My eyes adjust to the dark and I take in the strange room. Adam is fully clothed beside me on top of the powder-blue sheets. I open my phone and gaze at the picture of us that I posted yesterday. It really is too adorable. And it has twenty thousand likes already. *Let the love shine through.*

Farah texted with an invitation to sip coffee and watch the sun rise. As nice as that sounds, it's not where I am this morning. I need to expend the energy roiling in me to make sure today is all about forward momentum. I need to run.

I dress in layers. My phone tells me it's sixty-four degrees and clear. It makes it hard to register the tropical storm alert for the area, so I ignore it. Outside, I stretch with wide steps as I make my way up the pebbled driveway. I jog in place to build warmth while I wait for the gate to open, but nothing happens. I jump up and down, but it doesn't move.

"Screw it."

I decide to climb over the fence rather than go back to the house for the remote. I land on the other side ready to take off, but instead I pause. In the silence I hear water lapping behind me and the sound of birds trilling at first morning light. The sky is the deep purple of early dawn. It feels as bruised as I do. In my reading, I held back because I still don't trust Rini, but the memories of ten years ago haunted me all night long.

✦

I used to follow them around. I wore a dark wig and fake blue contacts. Yes, I had too much time on my hands, but so did they. Out gallivanting during the day. Skipping out on life's responsibilities like they were optional. I tailed them to brunch dates and watched them make out on park benches. I followed them back to her apartment. I only let myself cry once.

Her name was Miranda and he called her Mira. Get it? Spanish for "look," as in *Look at this college coed who wants me even though I'm almost thirty.* I wasn't aware he was the kind of man who would make up a nickname. He'd never once called me Aim or Ames. I was just Aimee to him. That hurt.

I waited days for them to have a fight. A bad one. One afternoon she ran away from him in tears, while he stormed off righteously. I had no idea what the fight was about, but I knew that even Adam the adulterer thought he had the moral high ground. He'd probably say, in his estimation, that this girl was being irrational. I could assume this because I'd been her a few years ago, and that was his favorite line to use on me. I was too emotional. What he meant was I had emotions that made him uncomfortable. Anger. Frustration. Rage. Adam couldn't handle anything that wasn't love and unconditional support.

That afternoon, Adam disappeared into a cab and I buzzed her apartment. This was the confrontation I'd been psyching myself up for. I wasn't there to hurt her. She meant nothing to me. She was a pawn in my game. I needed her so I could betray Adam right back. I knocked on the door timidly, signaling that I came in peace. Or at least I came to start a war against him, not her.

She was surprised to see someone other than Adam. She opened the door a crack, but she didn't recognize me. Clearly, she hadn't even had the decency to stalk me on Facebook. I had to push my way into her apartment. My heart raced from the physicality.

"I'm not going to hurt you," I said. "Hear me out."

She was visibly upset, both from her fight with Adam and my intrusion. Her arms were crossed and she gripped her opposite elbows. Her eyes darted around the room, searching for her phone or a weapon.

"What do you want?" she asked.

I took a seat to appear less threatening, a ferocious dog rolling over and showing their belly. I spoke quickly.

"I want us to band together. I know Adam—Professor Flynn—the same way you do."

The lie came out of nowhere, but I knew it was perfect. If I screamed at her, it might push them closer together. But if I could win her over by pretending to be on her side, then we had a common enemy, and she was more likely to listen to me. Besides, why should she think she's special when I knew I wasn't? I continued.

"I had a fight with him a few months ago and he ghosted me."

"You're a student?" she asked, unkindly.

Bitch. I still get carded.

"Grad school," I admitted through gritted teeth. I might have looked young for my late twenties, but that's still really old to a college sophomore. "I followed him today and saw the two of you together."

"You got dumped," she said with a casual shrug. When her shoulder dropped she was visibly more relaxed. She could deal with a crazy ex over a serial killer or a robber.

"There's no pain like a broken heart. It can feel like it will last a lifetime and never heal," I said.

I took my time. I acted like this was hard for me to admit, when in reality I was overwhelmed at the absurdity of what I was doing. There's no guidebook on how to react when you find out your husband is cheating on you, but I'm used to forging new paths. I sat on her couch.

"You should leave," she said.

I was relieved and willingly complied, for the moment. I slapped my palms on my knees and stood up. I moved toward the door, but I wanted to leave her with something to think about. Something that would impress her.

"He's so smart," I said with my back to her. "It's one of the things I love most about him."

I held my hand on the doorknob, waiting for her to speak.

"It's a different kind of smart," she said.

I turned to look at her with a knowing smile.

"Not that he could tell you everything about ancient Egypt," I said. "But that he could create a whole world only for you. Like you were Cleopatra in another life, in his life."

She swept her gaze to the floor, but she nodded.

I picked up a piece of junk mail by the door and found a pen.

"I'm not mad," I said as I scribbled my phone number on the back of an envelope. "I was for a second, but it fizzled away. I wasn't enough to keep him entertained. You probably are and I can help you."

That night I checked Adam's phone. There had been no contact between them after their fight. She was probably waiting for him to apologize. He was probably over the whole thing.

She texted me before midnight, asking if I'd seen him. I was in.

I had to convince her I wasn't interested in a threesome or anything kinky. I imagined being her Cyrano de Bergerac. Then I had to explain Cyrano de Bergerac because she was only nineteen. I told her it was too late for me, but I could help her get him back. Two were better than one. After that, she shared every sweet thing he said and every perceived slight she wasn't sure how to interpret. There had to have been part of me that dissociated from the fact that she was talking about my husband. Or maybe I liked the game of playing with both of them.

It went on longer than I ever expected. Both the affair and my involvement. Adam was not in love with her, I could tell. He lost interest every other day. It should have comforted me, but it made me angrier instead. It was so easy for me to know exactly what to say to get him to reengage with her. Compose a fun, sexy message. Compliment his sexual prowess. Every time he texted back, every time he met her on the corner of Lexington Avenue with a smile, I had the same rageful thought: *I married someone better than this cliché of a man.*

I told her not to sleep with him again. Not so soon. Make him wait, I said. That was for my benefit, protecting whatever was left of my dignity. She didn't listen.

That's when I lost it.

I went to the bar where I knew she waited tables. Adam and Ted were already there. I watched from a table a few feet away. You might think I was working up the courage to confront them, but I was actually trying to calm myself down. It didn't work; I saw red the whole time. Finally I approached her while she waited for drinks at the bar. The worst part, in hindsight, was the smile on her face when she saw me. She probably thought I was going to congratulate her for winning Adam back.

Instead, I double-fisted two pints of beer from her tray and poured them over her head. Her mouth gaped open like her jaw was unhinged. I told her I'd drop much worse on her head if I ever, ever saw her near my husband again. Her face turned white, like she'd seen a ghost.

At the time, I felt a cool satisfaction as I walked out of the bar, even more so when Adam begged for my forgiveness and swore he'd never speak to her again. I thought I'd won. But now, as a mother of three girls, I feel ashamed for manipulating and blaming a vulnerable young woman for what should have stayed between me and Adam.

A mile away from Stars Harbor, the rain pours down from the gray sky without a warning. My running shoes refuse to grip the pavement and I'm forced to slow my pace. I decide that's enough for today and loop back to the house.

I wish my shame was the reason I held back the details from Rini in my reading, but it was suspicion instead. I haven't been able to shake the feeling of déjà vu when I look at her, but I also know I never forget a face, or a name as distinct as Rini. She said point-blank that we didn't know each other, and yet I was compelled to creep around her cottage last night.

Before she returned from the Moon Men event, I had plenty of time to peer through the windows to her neatly made bed, her tiny kitchen, and the wall-mounted Murphy table with stacks of books. The art on the wall was all generic, no photos of siblings or lover's kisses on cheeks. The whole cottage couldn't be more than four hundred square feet.

Nothing inside sparked a connection to Rini, nor did it set my mind at ease. But it's the last day, and if clarity hasn't come by now, it must not be important. It's nothing more than one of those gut feelings that never pans out, the fear that never materializes. As a mother, I know dread well.

With the slick wood and whipping wind, hopping the fence to return to Stars Harbor is trickier. As I jump, my sneaker slips and I land in a puddle. Pain shoots through my foot. I sit to inspect my throbbing ankle. It's not swelling or bruising so I try to stand. It's tender but stable. There's nothing to do but walk it off.

I limp down the long driveway but as I turn the last kink in the path and the highest turret appears, I see someone holding on to the railing. Rini told us there was no access to the turrets, but the movements are unmistakable. There's someone up there. I squint through the rain and the white fog; I see a woman with long dark hair looking out into the distance. Rini.

I consider calling out, but instead I want proof of her lie. I pull out my phone, zoom in, and snap a few shots. My ankle feels stronger already and I hurry inside the house. But when I open my camera to look at the pictures, there's no one there. The turret is empty.

RINI

I n the light of day, last night's fears about this group turning things around on me seem unfounded. They wouldn't *pay* to confront me about the past. They wouldn't listen, rapt, to my astrological advice; they wouldn't drink my smoothies; they wouldn't confess their secrets the way they have over the last two days. But that doesn't mean today is going to be easy. Mother Nature is on the scene with plans of her own.

On CNN, I watch the animated gray cyclone circle over Bermuda before it makes a sharp left turn toward the edge of Long Island and up the Connecticut coast. Fox News, the Weather Channel, ABC—they show the same thing. After all indications we'd escape with nothing more than a little rain, Tropical Storm Clementine is predicted to hit Greenport in less than two hours.

I walk from my cottage to the main house, hugging my cardigan tight around me in the wind. Ted, Rick and Joe pull their baseball caps down low while moving around one of their SUVs.

"Follow me, please," I shout over the gale.

"We'll all gather in the living room," I say as the three men scrape their feet on the welcome mat. The door slams shut on its own behind them.

"Just the wind," I say.

I ring my sound bowl and wait. I move around the room, closing windows. Aimee, Farah, Margot, Eden and Adam have shuffled down the stairs and take their places, the same ones from the first night. On the outside it would appear nothing has changed, and yet the shifts in alliances are palpable. Today, loyalties will be tested under pressure.

"I've got a bit of bad news. Tropical Storm Clementine took a sharp turn last night. She's headed for us now. We're smack in the center of her path."

Adam and Farah slide their phones out of their pockets and the others stretch to see one of the two screens. I watch as they scroll and read.

"I could feel it brewing on my run," Aimee says.

"Some of the guys were planning to leave early, but now I wonder if we should all leave now," Margot says.

Rick stands and jingles his keys in his pocket. "I'm taking off. I can still shoot an eighty-one in this weather and I've got a tee time at Winged Foot," he says.

"That's dumb, dude," Ted says. "Why wouldn't you ride it out?"

"There's no need. I'm not from LA, I can drive in the rain."

"If you're going, I'm still in. I want to get home to my boys," Joe says.

"No one is going anywhere." I hear the edge of panic in my voice and reel it in. "I won't allow it. Even if I did, you'd be pulled over by Suffolk County police before you got to Riverhead," I say with confidence.

Despite my warning, Rick and Joe open the door. A dead crow lands with a wet thwap on the welcome mat. Surprised, Rick takes a big step back, and a gust slams the door shut again.

"Did you plant that?" Eden asks.

"Of course not. It must have smacked into the window, off course from the wind," I say. A chill runs through me. Dead crows represent death and transformation.

A silence settles over the room as each person calculates their next move.

"Is it safe here?" Margot asks.

"Of course. We have a couple of these every year in this area. It will be fine if we take the warnings seriously and stay inside. It's when people start acting like it's not a big deal and try to keep their plans that tragedy strikes."

"Do we need food?" Farah asks.

"All the food for today was delivered early this morning, ahead of schedule, so the locals can stay safe too. And we always have emergency supplies on hand like flashlights and bottled water. However, there is something you can all do." They lean in ever so slightly, listening intently, desperate for some direction. "Because we have a well rather than town water, if the electricity goes out, we lose water too. I will supply water to drink and cook with, but I recommend you fill your bathtub an inch for personal use."

"Got it," Margot and Farah say in unison.

"The wineries that you were planning to visit today are all closed, but I'm going to bring the wine tastings to you. I have a wonderful cellar of the best local bottles that I'll crack open just for this occasion. I won't be able to answer all your technical vintage and flavor-palette questions, but I have a decent working knowledge of my favorites. Does that sound good?"

They nod.

"It's going to be fine. Trust me."

Downstairs in the wine cellar I select several bottles. *Might as well pull out the good stuff,* I think.

Over the last six months, I've wrestled with my fate, whether it was predetermined or not. Today, I can feel it in my bones that this will be my last day, whether it's the psychic's prediction or my own plan back-firing on me. The dead crow is a sign that the messenger of death has arrived on my doorstep. It's time.

FARAH

Rini slips out the back door to gather the bottles of wine. She didn't instruct us to stay in the living room after announcing the lockdown, but none of us have moved. Yet.

I may not feel bold enough to reveal my nascent dreams of partnership with Aimee, but Rini was right. My life is about to change, and it begins with Joe. I beckon him away from the crowd. We wander past the library and the game parlor into a dark den.

"We need to talk," I say when we're alone.

Joe looks puzzled.

"About Beckett," I say at the same time as he asks, "About my former aide?"

"What about your former aide?"

Joe clears his throat. "I thought we'd talk about this when we got home. Is Beckett okay?"

"Now is a good time. Beckett's fine. You go first," I say.

I take a seat on the edge of the chair by the door to signal I'm ready to get into it. My heart starts to race a bit, and not from the storm or the sudden change in plans. Joe is right—I specifically said I didn't want to hear about his work drama while on this vacation, but I'm compelled to have this conversation by something other than my desire to stick my head in the sand. To follow the shame, like Rini said.

Joe closes the half-moon doors behind us. He grimaces. "My former aide is speaking out against me."

"Speaking out? I assume this has nothing to do with your policies."

Joe rubs his hands together and walks to the window.

"She says I touched her inappropriately," he says.

"And did you?"

"No, no, of course not."

"So she's lying?"

"Not really, but it's not the way she's painting it. Farah, come on. I'm old-school. I shake hands. I touch backs. I connect with people."

"You can't say that kind of thing anymore."

"This isn't a press conference. You're my wife."

Am I? I wonder. I've never been a fan of the possessive, generic "my wife," but right now it curdles in my stomach like milk neglected on the kitchen counter. How did we get so far apart? It's as if I woke up one day and the little things I never said had grown into full-fledged secrets we've hidden from each other, from ourselves.

"Are you going to lose reelection?" I ask.

"The emergency polling was inconclusive but not good. Fortunately, I have time. One big news story and this would blow over."

Since I started to have feelings for Aimee, I've repeatedly told myself I couldn't leave Joe for another woman because he's an important politician. The suburb where I grew up is incredibly progressive in its thinking, yet inside our homes, it's like a 1955 sitcom. A man and a woman. Three kids. Sometimes two. Sometimes four. A dog. Never a cat. Cats are for city dwellers. The man makes the money. The woman earns some money (a little or a lot), but her real job is to make the world go round. They have strong values of acceptance, but they have firm boundaries around their beautifully crafted lives. Anything out of the ordinary is dangerous. The message has seeped into my core, and it's this same rigid thinking that won't allow me to be honest about my concerns around Beckett's behavior.

"What about Beckett?" Joe asks. Ready to move on, he takes a seat across from me on the maroon tufted couch.

"I've been biting my tongue a long time, but after his most recent incident at the car—"

"He's doing great, Farah. Stop beating yourself up over that."

"That's the thing—I'm not. It's your passive-aggressive comments that are eating at me. It could have happened to you. It could have happened to the nanny. It could have happened to anyone watching Beckett."

I take a deep breath and let it out in a sigh. This is exactly how our previous discussions have gone before. I dance around the subject, hoping Joe will come to the same conclusion I have, while he railroads the conversation into a different direction. I can't control Joe's reaction, but I can change my approach.

"I want Beckett to get evaluated. He may have ADHD, or behavioral issues, or need developmental intervention. I don't really know."

"You sure sound aggressive for someone who claims they don't know," Joe says.

"The point is, I'm tired of pretending one way or the other. I act like he's fine, or I convince myself of the worst, but in reality I don't know and you don't either. We need a professional assessment."

Joe leans forward, ready to argue the other side of this yet again. *He's a boy, he's high energy* . . . the list of excuses to ignore the issue goes on. But Joe pauses before launching into our usual script. He might actually be hearing me and giving weight to my declaration.

"Yes, yes, I think you're right," Joe says.

"You do?"

Joe stands and begins to pace the room like he's brainstorming. "I'll bring him over to Lottie first thing on Monday. She's the best child psychologist there is."

Although I wanted Joe on board, something about this doesn't feel right. Lottie is a child psychologist, but she's a friend of Joe's. She'll be biased. Possibly easily influenced to support his conclusion.

"I thought we'd start with his pediatrician," I say.

"Lottie knows us. She'll believe us and help us get the ball rolling quickly." Joe approaches me and puts his dry, papery hand on my upper arm. I shake it off. "It's important to make sure we're a unified front right now. With this press, people are going to be looking at us."

"Press?"

"They're going to ask me what it feels like. I have to speak out in support of parents raising neurodivergent children."

"What?" My head is spinning. In one conversation we went from *He's just a boy* to *We're raising a neurodivergent child*? How did we get here?

"You're skipping a few steps, Joe. Let's take it slow."

"You're the one who declared that Beckett needs help with such certainty, but now I'm the one skipping steps?"

"I was being blunt. We need to explore this."

"Are you ashamed, Farah? Ashamed of our son who doesn't fit into your definition of perfect?"

Outside the window behind Joe, lightning flashes. The backyard lights up, but I see far more than that. I admit I almost fell for it when Joe brought up shame. Rini told me to follow the shame. To use it as a moment to reflect rather than react. But after talking to Aimee, I know that I don't feel any shame around Beckett's potential challenges. Joe is using this against me, distracting me from an accusation of his sexual misconduct. It's Political Rhetoric 101.

"What you're saying about getting Beckett an eval, that's about the election, isn't it?" I ask, though it's not really a question.

Joe shakes his head. "Not the election, my constituents. Everything I do is to connect with them and support them."

"You just said one big news story and the aide thing blows over. Or you think this might garner enough sympathy to correct the downslide of the polling."

"You might still be in denial, but I'm sure Beckett is neurodivergent."

"You're not even listening. The whole point of this conversation was to admit we don't know anything. We need professional help. No matter what Beckett's evaluation outcome, I won't let you use our child to further your campaign."

"Well, I won't let you shame me into silence. I'm proud of our son and his learning disabilities."

Although it might look that way on the surface, this development isn't really new and that's the harsh truth. Even when Joe and I switch sides, we are always opposed. But I won't be provoked because the whole world lit up for me in that split second of lightning, and I see this moment, my child, and my marriage with unflinching clarity.

"There's a difference between shame and privacy," I say. "I'm not ashamed of our son, but for his sake, his process for a diagnosis and plan should be kept private from your constituents. To speak loudly about it doesn't mean you're proud of our son. It means you see an opportunity for personal gain. And that happens over my dead body."

I thought being a good mom meant I was never without an answer, and never uttered the words "I don't know"—the traits that make me an excellent doctor. But saying "I don't know" and getting Beckett to the right professional is what makes me a good mom. No. Standing up for him and advocating for his needs, whatever they might be, makes me a great mom. Vulnerability can be a strength in the right circumstances.

With a turn of my heel, I head back to the living room, Joe on my tail. He looks angry, but all I feel is free.

In the foyer, Rini appears through the front door carrying a box of wine bottles. Joe rushes to her aid, ignoring me and acting like everything is fine. Ever the politician. She thanks him for relieving her of the weight. Ted jumps up to help as well. Rini crosses the living room behind the couch and wheels the bar cart from the pantry into the dining room, the way it was arranged on the first night. But that night she had staff to help her; today there's no one here but us.

"Come on," I say to Aimee. I walk into the kitchen where Rini's taking down wineglasses from the cabinet. I pass two to Aimee and grab two more.

"On the dining room table," Rini says.

"Some good years here," Ted says as he unpacks the bottles and lines them up on the bar cart with Joe.

"I like your necklace," Aimee says to Rini. I turn casually to see the two of them face-to-face, inches apart as they squeeze through the doorway at the same time. Aimee is empty-handed and Rini has four glasses between her fingers, Aimee coming, Rini going from the cabinet. Aimee reaches up and touches a locket and key hanging low on Rini's chest. Their intimacy makes me blush.

"Anything in it?" Aimee asks.

"Yes," Rini says, and steps out of the doorway quickly. I busy myself polishing a single glass, hoping to wipe away the streak of jealousy across my heart.

On the last trip to the table, Rini carries a fancy wine opener and a crystal vase. "Makeshift dump bucket," she says when I question the addition.

Each person takes a seat at the dining room table. Rini stands in front of the wall of windows and opens the first bottle. As she recites the description from memory, a flash of lightning whitens the sky behind her. A minute later the thunder rumbles and we all startle a bit.

I can't help but contrast this scene with the bonfire last night. There we gathered in a circle, cross-talking excitedly, jumping from one conversation to another among smaller cliques. The night was warm and full of wonder. There was no hint of icy demeanors and tense silence twelve hours ago. Now, the chill in the air is the product of more than the awkward tension between me and Joe. It's more than the weather.

Eden and Rick have cooled considerably, though I haven't heard them arguing. I keep an arm's length from Aimee because of my nerves. Joe won't even look at me. Margot only half-heartedly trails Adam around the room.

I don't know what it is, but something dark hangs over us all, not just me and Joe. There's no denying it.

"Shall we continue with whites?" Rini asks, clapping her hands. "This one is from one of my favorite places on the North Fork, an aged-oak chardonnay."

Rini's decidedly good cheer stands in stark contrast to the rest of us. She's almost giddy, like she lives for these shut-in storm days. If I'm right, it's something we have in common, and I realize I have a choice. I can let Rini be my mood guide and not get swallowed up by the bad vibes of my companions.

"Aren't thunderstorms beautiful?" I ask. A flash of lightning zips through the sky, lighting up the backyard like a fireworks display.

One of my favorite undergrad psych classes was called Nature & Nurture, a study of human reactions to the natural world. Thunderstorms, my professor said, provide a rare mixture of stimulation and peace, fear and security, power and helplessness, beauty and terror.

I have a feeling we're in for all of it today.

ADAM

After a couple of bottles of wine, Rini concludes our lesson and promises to return with lunch. I head upstairs for a breather, and less than thirty seconds later Margot's knocking on the door. Of all the people who could be intruding, I'm glad it's her and not my wife or my girlfriend . . . or my girlfriend's husband. Being stuck in this house is a disaster waiting to happen, but for now it's contained. As long as Rick doesn't notice Eden's urgent glances, and Aimee and Farah stay in the dark, and Margot feels like she's got some control over the situation. That's a lot of variables. Who knows how long the status quo can last in this pressure cooker.

I grab my keys and a towel from the bathroom. "Help me tape up the side window that cracked last night."

Margot hops into action. "I'll grab a plastic bag from my dry cleaning in the closet."

"And I saw some electrical tape in the pantry. Meet me at the car."

I pull up the hood on my sweatshirt and wait for Margot in the entryway. The rain pours down like daggers. Together, we make a run for it. I grab the passenger-side door, while Margot runs around to the driver's side.

"I think you should break it off with Eden," Margot says, handing me the plastic bag.

Because she's coming at me with a threat, I refuse to admit to the confusion I've felt since last night when Eden said she loved me for the first time. Instead of filling me with promise for the future, her words turned sour in my mouth.

And my doubt has only gotten worse. During our little car spinout, my first thoughts were of Aimee. Not my sister next to me, or our girls at home, but my wife. The only person in the world I committed my life to in front of a hundred guests. After the Moon Men event I went to bed instead of finding Eden. Nothing happened between me and Aimee, but she was in my head.

With my back turned to her in the bed, I kept scrolling to the picture Aimee posted of us yesterday. As the comments rolled in, I found myself convinced. We are the perfect couple. Or we were, but could we be again? Or was it too late and that's why I'd given up? It was a chicken-or-the-egg argument and I kept going round and round. I love Eden; I miss Aimee. I can't anchor myself in reality.

I tell none of this to Margot. In fact, I push this all out of my head.

"Margot, the end is inevitable," I say.

"I don't believe that. You and Aimee could be good again."

I gesture for Margot to lean over and hold the bag in place while I rip off a long piece of tape. It's a tiny crack, no bigger than a pebble, but a hurricane could blow the whole window out, so I don't half-ass it. I pull a second piece of tape and rip it with my teeth.

"I saw that picture she posted on Instagram yesterday. You two are in love," Margot says.

"What do you know about love?" I ask.

Margot drops her hands and backs away, hurt.

"You don't love me?" she asks, her voice small as a child's.

"That's not the same."

"Well, I know what I have with Ted, I know what I saw of you and Aimee in the beginning, and I know what was modeled for me as a child," she says.

I finish covering the window and fall into the passenger's seat.

"Wait. What?" I ask.

This is typical Margot. Last night I planted the seed of evil into our parents' dynamic, and she's doubling down on how perfect they were.

"They were committed to each other and us, and no one else," Margot says.

"You think Mom and Dad were in love? Are you kidding me?"

When it comes to Margot, I avoid the topic of Mom and Dad no matter how hard she pushes. Inevitably, we sound like we lived in different houses with entirely different parents.

"You're pissed off because I'm not buying your car-accident fantasy. Just like you're mad because I don't believe you're in love with Eden," Margot says.

"Don't change the subject. Tell me what gave you the impression of love between our parents. Name one example."

"I don't know. I was young, Adam. But I could feel it. I felt it stronger than anything else."

Margot has a warped vision of love. She thinks the fact that Dad hugged Mom was evidence of his love, but I know he took her into his arms so she would leave him alone to watch TV. He was placating her and her bottomless pit of need, not actually trying to fill it.

"Why do you think I'm obsessed with love, Margot?"

"Because it's a natural human need?"

"Because there was no love between Mom and Dad."

"No love? That's an absurd thing to say. Why did they get married? Why did they bring two children into this world? Why did they stay together for twelve years until they died? Because they were in love. What you're saying makes no sense."

"I don't know how it started, Margot, but what we saw wasn't love. It was demoralizing, the way Dad treated her."

"Stop it."

She turns away from me, but she won't go anywhere. I continue.

"Mom was the textbook definition of a micromanager. She ruled with white knuckles because she was ineffective. Mom didn't have the power to make what she wanted happen."

Margot shakes her head in disbelief. My words are hitting a little too close to home. I push harder.

"The truth is, Mom would have had to love herself more to leave. And she didn't. She wasn't capable. If she had more time, maybe she could have gotten there, but even that is a reach."

But it's not a reach for me. It's not easy to teach yourself what healthy love looks and feels like when no one truly loved you growing up. Nana cared in her way, but she wasn't enough. She was old and grief-stricken and too worn out to be a parent to us. It's taken me years of trial and error—in life and in my writing—to figure out love. Still, the alchemy is not an exact science. It's possible to get it wrong, to confuse love with familiarity, or lust, or insecurity. It happens in my books all the time.

I'm on the precipice of not only understanding what I need and what I can't live without, but also achieving it. That knowledge has to be found inside me, without comparing Aimee and Eden.

Margot crosses her arms and I can tell she's hurt. It wasn't my intention, but it's about time she accepts the truth. She doesn't know how to see things clearly.

"Break up with Eden, or I'll tell Aimee," Margot says, surprising me.

My heart races at the very thought. Would she really betray me like that? I wasn't expecting her to lash out at me, even in words, but she's desperate. She can't control, or validate, or deny the conversation about our parents, so she's latching on to my relationship. In response, I laugh.

"Go ahead, I dare you."

"And Rick too," Margot adds. "I'll tell Rick."

The smirk falls off my face. Rick would lose his shit, and thanks to Tropical Storm Clementine, there's nowhere for me to run and hide. We'd be like caged monkeys.

"He probably already knows. And he wouldn't care," I say, using reverse psychology to throw Margot off.

"Why not?"

"Eden and Rick are in an open marriage."

"What? That's not possible."

"I would've thought you knew, given that he's Ted's best friend."

Two truths and a lie. Rick would, in fact, care. Because it's me and that breaks the rules. The rest is accurate. And if I know my sister, she's going to preoccupy herself with feeling stupid that she didn't know.

I pull my hood up again and make a run for the house. Margot seethes behind me, and I know I've successfully trained her ire on Ted for the moment. But she'll handle him and come back for me.

At least I've bought myself some time to figure out why my feelings for Eden shifted last night and how I actually feel about Aimee. The goal for today is to keep it in my pants, play zone defense, and stay out of the line of fire. Tomorrow, everything will be clearer.

MARGOT

Back in the house, I flop down on the bed, forcing myself to breathe. I feel trapped—by the house, by the fear of a pregnancy test, by my brother's mercurial love—but I don't want to suffocate and panic. I had to remove myself from the forced chill downstairs as people scrolled through their phones and watched TV while drinking wine and eating snacks.

There was a moment last night after Rini told me I'm going to have a baby in a matter of months when I thought I could back off Aimee and Adam and focus on my own growing family, but that was turned on its head by Adam. He really doesn't see a future with Aimee; it's not just this affair that's distracting him. Divorce seems inevitable and I feel more desperate than ever. I want my baby to be around the girls all the time. In case I can't have any more, I want them to feel like older sisters.

If Rini is right, Adam's youngest will be less than two years older than my baby. More than extended family, we will operate like a blended family, one singular unit in multiple locations. How is that going to happen if he's in some sad apartment and can barely keep straight the weekends he has the girls, let alone plan parties and family gatherings? This is where my future becomes bleaker than the girls'. I can't manage all their logistics on top of mine.

Sadly, I threw away my only shot at forcing Adam's hand. I can't make him break up with Eden, and if they're in an open marriage, then Rick won't either. The last option—telling Aimee—isn't really an option at all. That's why Adam laughed—he called my bluff. I'm trying to save them, not destroy everyone in her path.

A strong gust of wind blows and something white floats by my window, catching my eye. But when I look, there's nothing. I need a sign to set me off in a direction that isn't this spiral. The rain pelts the glass with a thud that punctuates every negative thought I have.

Standing next to the window, I remember the dumbwaiter. I pop it open, and once again there is a single tarot card. I can read *THE FOOL* on the bottom. Before I pick it up, I remember what Rini asked me last night. Was it upside down?

I google, *What does it mean when a tarot card is upside down?*

The answer is the card is "reversed," and a reversed card has a different meaning than an upright card. I search *The Fool.*

> **Meaning:** The Fool represents beginning stages. She is inexperienced but lucky. She does not know what to expect but relies on faith.

Right below the definition, there's a distinction I didn't notice yesterday.

> **Upright card (keywords):** Beginnings, Creativity, Leap of faith, Spontaneity

> **Reversed card (keywords):** Chaos, Naivety, Poor judgment

I search *The Empress* again.

> **Upright card (keywords):** Abundance, Nurturing, Pregnancy, Stability

Reversed card (keywords): Domestic problems, Financial issues, Stagnation, Unwanted pregnancy

Those are two very different fates. How can one card mean two opposite things?

I have to find Rini to ask about this. It's important to know.

Ted walks in as I'm on my way out and I'm reminded of what Adam said. I pull him into the room and close the door behind us. My question for Rini will have to wait.

"Why didn't you tell me that your best friend is in an open marriage?"

Ted guides me gently to the edge of the bed. "Margot, you've known Rick for years. He's never exactly been a pro at monogamy, even way before Eden. Making it official didn't feel like a new development."

"Do you two go out picking up chicks?"

Ted stops fidgeting. He looks directly at me and I know I've crossed a line.

"I'm sorry," I say.

Ted sits down on the bed next to me and takes my hand in his.

"You know I would never," he says. "Everything I do is to make you happy."

"Of course I know that." I was acting out of hurt. It feels like a betrayal, like Ted was more loyal to Rick than to me. "So why, then?"

"Why didn't I tell you about Rick's marriage?"

"Yeah."

"Honestly, I don't want to hear about it, let alone discuss it with my beautiful, fun, fascinating wife."

He kisses me on the cheek and I lean into it.

"I came up to tell you that Rini made sandwiches. Gourmet ones. Fancy stuff, " Ted says.

"I'm not hungry right now, but thanks."

Ted starts to close the door behind him, and I call out to tell him I love him.

"Love you too," he says before the lock clicks shut.

I notice the flowers and daily horoscope cards on the dresser across the room. When could Rini have had time to place those? She was making sandwiches while Adam and I were taping up the window. I pick up my card.

···

Good morning, Pisces! Open your eyes today to what you've been blind to, but do so with a kind and gentle heart. You were deliberately ignoring what you could not handle before. You are ready now.

···

I lie down again and close my eyes. I feel woozy and disoriented. Moments from the weekend bombard me.

With Rini: *There's something big coming to you around their death. Some new information, or a new perspective. It's going to be a life-altering realization. Maybe a story you realize is different from the one you've been telling yourself.*

I reach in my memory to the long-ago past, trying to call up the proof Adam wanted. Examples of our parents in love. But all that appears in my mind, over and over, is my father's desk.

When I graduated law school, I decided I wanted my father's old oak desk. Seventeen years later it was in the same condition as it had been in the house, sitting in storage. We were too young to make decisions about their belongings, and my Nana was too burdened.

Cleaning out the desk, I found a variety of key documents: their birth certificates, passports, Social Security cards. I also discovered my father was going to divorce my mother. He had filled out dissolution-of-marriage documents for the State of New York.

At the time, New York required proof of fault to grant a divorce, and the options were cruel and inhumane treatment, abandonment for one year, imprisonment for three years, or adultery. New York held on to this archaic system of fault, rather than allowing couples to claim irreconcilable differences, until 2010. My father selected cruelty.

I don't know if my mother knew about the divorce papers, or the alleged fault, but I can imagine how mad that would have made her. In her mind, if anyone was cruel, it was him. And if anyone was going to leave, it should have been her. But she didn't believe in divorce.

The divorce papers in my father's desk were undated. They could have been from ten years prior, before Adam was born. They also could have been drawn up the day before their car accident.

Divorce doesn't cause car accidents. I know this. But if I'm being honest, I've had questions.

1. The fact that the tire skid marks show them swerving right before the sharp left into the guardrail.
2. The fact that my mother's body was turned sideways so her back was pressed up against the car door.
3. The fact that my father had bruising on both shoulders and both sides of his face, even though he only hit the doorframe on the left side.

The police didn't reveal any of this to an eight-year-old. They probably didn't even tell my grandmother. They declared the deaths an accident. These were details I found in my own personal quest for answers as to why I had to grow up without parents. I didn't ask God; I didn't turn to drugs. My answers were always found in rational assessment; that's how I became a lawyer.

But what if, as Adam asserts, all the arguments I saw between them weren't the passionate flip side of an intense love, but deep hatred and rage?

It's possible that day my father had planned to tell my mother about the divorce, and that's why we were at Nana's. If that was the case, and she had seen that he marked *cruel and inhumane treatment* as his grounds, I can see my mother breaking. Finally. Explosively.

I relax into the bed and let my imagination take over, knowing the answer to my problems is within my reach. A few minutes later, a tingling kicks in and the hairs on my arms stand up straight, like I'm channeling ghosts.

I can't sit still any longer. I open my laptop and begin to write a new story. One I'd been too scared to see before.

THE FLYNNS' LAST DAY, July 1997

Kathy Flynn hadn't slept a wink last night even though she had the entire bed to herself. She replayed the night before over and over in her mind. Adam and Margot were happy to visit their nana so they could have a night alone, Bill's idea. The drive back from his mom's house had been fine. Mostly quiet, a little stilted, but fine.

Bill had eaten his lobster special with gusto. Kathy found it both disgusting and endearing. There was enviable joy in the way he devoured that cockroach of the sea. But as soon as he was finished, Kathy could tell something was wrong. Bill looked like half of his dinner was lodged in his throat. He couldn't swallow and his breathing was labored. Kathy said nothing. Without any clue as to what was coming, she already knew she didn't want to hear it. Kathy opened her purse and reapplied her lipstick, fiddling with her compact to avoid his gaze.

"Kathy," he said.

Kathy waved the waitress over.

"A little more ice water. And then the check."

"No dessert for you two?"

Bill and Kathy said no at the same time. It was the last thing they would agree upon.

"Kathy," Bill started again. "I want a divorce."

The relief Kathy felt bubbled up through her chest and out her mouth in the form of a laugh. In the past few minutes, Kathy had imagined a dozen terrible things Bill might say when he finally worked up the courage: he was leaving her for another woman, he was leaving her for another man, his mother called and something had happened to one of the kids, he lost his job and the bank was foreclosing. This didn't even register as a threat. It was a joke.

"Oh yeah?" Kathy said. "And I want a husband who lifts a finger to help his wife and two kids."

"What does that mean?" Bill said.

"It means we can't always get what we want."

Bill crumpled up his napkin and set it on the table. They stood and walked to the car in silence. Kathy led the way.

"I don't think you understand," Bill said once they were safely out on the parkway. "I've filled out the paperwork. My lawyer has a copy. He's filing on Monday."

Kathy said nothing. She hated fighting in the car. The way their words echoed in the small space, assaulting her. It made her crazy.

At home, Bill took his pillow and locked himself in the guest room before Kathy could resume the conversation.

And now Kathy lay awake, her body exhausted but her mind raging. At 8 a.m. she heard Bill stirring in the kitchen. She wondered how long he'd been waiting for her to come down and make him breakfast. Even though he wanted a divorce, she'd bet he still wanted her apple Dutch babies and bacon.

But he never called to her. Kathy knew he'd left when she heard the car in the driveway. He must have really believed this was over. He had been working himself up to what he thought was the end. Gathering the conviction to meet with a lawyer, making sure the kids were at his mom's, breaking the news in a public place. It took a lot of advance planning and emotional energy—courage, really—simply to get to the point where he could deliver the line: *I want a divorce.*

Thirty minutes later, Kathy heard the garage door slowly open below. She rushed downstairs to the office and settled herself in the chair. She could smell the strong coffee and cheap eggs of the local chain where Bill must have had breakfast. With one meal, he surmised that he could make it without her.

"Bill, you know that I don't believe in divorce," Kathy started as soon as he walked through the door.

"Luckily divorce is fully recognized by the law. It's not something that requires your belief in it."

"I don't think you've thought this through, Bill."

"I've been thinking about it for years. I've been working it out with a lawyer for almost a month. Kathy, you are miserable. I am miserable."

"We aren't miserable; we're middle-aged."

"It doesn't have to be like this," Bill said.

Kathy was so serious about never getting divorced that when Bill had proposed, she'd reminded him that this really was forever. He'd said he would do right by God and their family. But everyone is optimistic when they're young and in love. Still, she'd believed him. As he'd slipped the ring over her finger, he'd promised: *Till death do us part.*

Kathy hadn't been ready for either his declaration or his resolve to see it through. How can you prepare for the things you didn't see coming?

"It's time to get the kids," she said. Kathy needed to buy herself some time, and the drive to the city would help gather her thoughts. Her persuasive arguments.

Bill grabbed the keys from the hook and stormed out the door. Kathy picked up the pace to eliminate his lead. She slammed the passenger door before he even made it around the car to his side.

Kathy had expected a sense of victory as they drove to the city. At least a measure of peace from the frantic vibe of the house. Bill wouldn't get to have control of this narrative, with his mother or the kids. He might even have to listen to her as they drove for forty-five minutes.

But inside the car, the air felt suffocating. She opened her window, but the shrieking wind pierced her ears. That made her more agitated. Why couldn't she breathe?

Kathy looked out the window at the winding road of their town, the lush green trees. She forced an exhale.

"I'm fighting for us, for our family. I'm fighting for you, Bill," she said.

Bill merged onto the Saw Mill River Parkway without a word.

"I want to be happy, Kathy."

A white car with tinted windows honked from behind. Bill tapped the blinker and swerved to the right lane.

"I want that too. For both of us," she said.

Bill turned away from the road to look at her. He shook his head and slowed down as a minivan passed too close on the left. When the minivan pulled ahead, Bill shifted into the left lane. He didn't use his signal.

Kathy angled her body toward him in her seat. She was no longer using just her hands—she was speaking with her whole body now.

"This life could be the better life you're imagining. I admit I haven't been at my best lately. Neither have you. But the kids are getting older. Maybe we could go away for a few nights."

Kathy was spitballing now, making it up as she went along, but she knew she was close to hitting on something that would work. Something that would snap Bill out of this foolish divorce idea. She would fix this.

"A vacation isn't going to cure us," Bill said.

"No, but it's a start. A chance for us to reconnect."

Bill shook his head. Kathy was merely getting started.

"And after a vacation, we could try therapy. Schedule sex once a week. You can't give up on us like this. You can't do this. We'll go to Antigua. Remember that trip?"

Bill's eyes glassed over with tears. He opened his mouth to speak, but nothing came out. He tried again.

"I don't love you anymore. I don't hate you either. There's nothing left between us. Nothing at all."

Kathy turned to the passenger-side window to stop herself from rolling her eyes. Love. Hate. Bill wouldn't know the extremes of love and hate if they smashed him in the face. He was just saying words. Words other people had said. Words used to justify wars.

But Kathy, she could *feel*. She felt the love when Bill tried to make her laugh with a silly dance. She felt the hate when he drank every night, knowing they both grew up with alcoholic fathers. Kathy felt all of it, while Bill never stopped wanting something else.

All Kathy ever heard is what Bill wanted. What was missing. Who was screwing him over. What he didn't have that he deserved. It didn't matter to Bill what Kathy wanted. It didn't matter what was best for the kids. It didn't matter what was right. It was what Bill wanted, period, end of story.

Bill glanced sideways at Kathy. The car picked up speed as they settled into a stretch of straight road.

"What am I supposed to do? Live in misery because you don't want me to leave?" Bill asked.

He was way off on the mind reading, but Kathy appreciated that he was trying. All she'd ever wanted was a little effort. She tried to explain better.

"No, I'm not saying stay and be miserable. I'm saying don't leave because things aren't great. We can make it better. We've been together for too long to throw it all away."

"Too long is the problem. Trash doesn't start to smell better the longer you let it rot."

Kathy nodded slowly, slightly. She turned in her seat to face forward. He was right that garbage doesn't smell better the longer it rots. But her heart raced as she processed this metaphor.

Did he call me trash? In that analogy, our marriage is the trash.

Though there's no way he thinks he's part of the garbage, so it really means I am trash.

Kathy felt dizzy. She tried to focus on the horizon ahead. The trees had helped her breathe earlier, but nature zoomed by too fast. She saw nothing but a blur of green. She couldn't get ahold of anything.

He called me rotting trash.

And now he's not saying anything else. He's not backtracking. He's not adding new words for me to focus on.

All she could think about was the fact that she was trash. The thought consumed her with such force that she could smell it on her. Rotting trash.

Kathy's scalp started to itch, but her arms were paralyzed, glued to her sides. She couldn't scratch her hair, and it became more intense. She tried to casually rub her head on the window, but all it did was slide back and forth. She lengthened her neck to try getting the top of the seat belt mechanism to scratch the itch. That worked a bit. Why wouldn't her arms move? Kathy looked down to see her hands curled into small, hard fists.

I am trash.

Kathy turned her whole body to face Bill, staring at this stranger of a man until he became something else. An animal that would ravage trash. A raccoon or an opossum with beady eyes. She pressed her back up against the window and wanted to scream at him to get away. But she knew nothing she said would matter. So she pulled her knees up to her chest and kicked out.

Before she knew what she was doing, Kathy heard Bill's head slam against the window. Then she did it again.

AIMEE

After the initial burst of adrenaline during our wine-tasting fun, the vibe petered out. Adam, Eden and I played in the arcade while we drank whatever we could get our hands on, but eventually that got boring and annoying. I took a breather to scroll through social media while Adam napped. Dishes and glasses piled up. The Weather Channel was constantly on in the background, giving me a dull headache. I took two ibuprofen and summoned my second wind.

If the past was going to haunt me on this trip, I decided to make it the good past. Before I became a mother and learned to tolerate mess, I loved to have a good time. I wasn't a literal mess yet, but a different kind. A drunk mess. Always in the center of a crowd, shouting too loud, laughing too hard, willing to do anything for a dropped-jaw gasp.

Now, stuck inside this massive Victorian home with a storm raging outside, I invite out the old wild child in me. And she knows how to transform a group of idle people into a party.

I bring down my Bluetooth shower speaker and put on my wedding-dance-floor mix: the Killers, Neil Diamond, Walk the Moon, and Beyoncé. I shout for Rini while I play "September," thinking she'd appreciate the astrological nod in Earth, Wind & Fire. But she's nowhere to be found.

Margot reappears from her room to set up beer pong on the fancy dining room table, and the only time Adam, Eden, Farah, Joe, or I stop dancing is to take a turn competing against each other. Rick and Ted sit on the sidelines with a wad of cash in each of their hands, tossing off hundos to anyone who would eat the cheese that had been sitting out for hours, or chug the wine spittoon, or kiss with tongue in front of them for sixty seconds. I almost convince Margot to do it, but she's allegedly not drunk enough. Instead, we crash onto the couch next to each other.

"I haven't posted one picture today," I say.

"What are you talking about? You've been snapping shots constantly."

She's right—I'm never without my phone raised in the air, capturing the moment a thousand different ways for that one perfect shot.

"But nothing on social media."

"Because this isn't on-brand?" Margot asks.

I shrug, realizing I'm kinda feeling off-brand myself.

"Do you think this place is weird?" I ask. "Weird stuff has been happening to me here."

"That's so crazy that you ask because when I passed out as we spun in the car, I had a vision."

"A vision?"

"It was the end of the world, raining blood, and I was a deer. My brother was a deer. You were a deer. We all were deer."

I'm surprisingly touched that I featured in Margot's end-of-world vision. For a moment, sitting arm to arm, it feels like the old days.

"That's what I'm talking about. Did you ever have something like that happen before coming here?"

Margot shakes her head.

"Do you think it's this place?" I ask.

"Why? Is something happening to you?" She answers my question with a question.

I take a sip of my wine and get to the point. "This morning when I went for a run, I thought I saw someone in the top turret. I tried to take a picture but when I looked at my camera no one was there. Was it a ghost?"

I show her the picture.

"It was probably the fog, I can barely see the house," Margot says.

"You think there's a rational explanation, I'm not surprised."

"Listen, the first night, I heard strange sounds in the walls like the house was haunted, but I discovered they have a whole dumbwaiter system. It was probably just housekeeping. Or the chefs. If you want to get weird, maybe it was a stray animal who got lost in the passageways."

I try to imagine a whole maze of passageways in the walls, not like our Southampton laundry chutes, but something complex enough to deliver food, flowers, sheets, and towels to rooms without disturbing us.

"Okay, I'll give you something woo-woo. I found a tarot card in my dumbwaiter. Two, actually. When I told Rini she said she doesn't use tarot cards," Margot adds.

"Really? Eden said she found a tarot card on her bedroom floor."

"She did?" Margot sounds disappointed, as if she wanted to be the only one receiving magical messages. "Did you?"

"No, no cards for me."

"Do you want to see the dumbwaiters?" Margot asks.

"Now?"

"Let's go hunt for ghosts." Margot pulls me by the hand and we sneak into the pantry off the kitchen. We wait, listening to "Kiss Me" by Sixpence None The Richer and pretending to look for snacks in case anyone followed us. When the coast is clear, Margot places her palm flat on the wall and presses down firmly. A rectangle pops open.

"So cool."

"Get in," Margot says.

"Really? You think it could hold me?"

"Absolutely. You'd have to crouch, but you could fit."

Even though there's no audience, this is exactly the kind of wild thing pre-motherhood Aimee would have done without a moment's hesitation.

"Hold my wine," I say. I slide my butt onto the counter and swing my feet around and into the dumbwaiter. I scoot in and turn around, sitting cross-legged in the box. Margot and I giggle like third graders playing hide-and-seek at recess.

"Take a picture of me," I exclaim. I reach into my pocket, but there's no phone. I must have left it in the living room, where the dance party is still happening.

"Pull your knees up a bit and I'll close the door, send you for a ride," Margot says.

"A ride?" I ask, wide-eyed. "Do you think you can operate this thing?"

"Sure. I'm not even drunk. I've had a couple, but you know we're trying to get pregnant. I don't want to overdo it."

I thought Margot was using "not drunk enough" as an excuse earlier. I hadn't imagined how anyone who had been stuck in this house with endless bottles of wine could be anything but wasted, and yet now that we are alone and in a quiet room, I know she's telling the truth. I can see clarity in her eyes and hear strength in her voice. I trust her.

I nod my head and pull my knees up. Margot slowly closes the door and presses it hard so it locks. She speaks to me through the wood panel.

"There's obviously a whole bunch of passageways, but only a single joystick to maneuver. I'm going to keep it simple and send you up to my room, which is directly above us."

"And then I'll come down from upstairs and no one will know how I did it," I squeal.

Margot gives the door a tap and I wait for the box to move.

"Hold on, I'm moving the joystick but nothing's happening. There must be a button to start the motor," Margot says.

As I wait, I look up and down. Below me is darkness, but there's light peering through the cracks above. I see two ropes dangling in the middle of the shaft. Suddenly there's a loud roaring noise and the box shakes. I press my hands into the walls for balance.

"Found the motor button," Margot says. "I have to hold it down. I let go too quick; that's why you didn't go anywhere."

"Okay," I say, noticing that it's getting warmer in here. "Ready when you are."

Margot presses the button and the box jerks violently. I begin to creep up slowly.

"I'm probably pushing the weight capacity on this thing," I say. Margot either ignores me or can't hear me over the motor.

I look down, and I can see the bottom of her shirt and the top of her pants through the crack between the box and the shaft below. *This is so fun,* I think.

The dumbwaiter stops abruptly.

"Margot?"

Silence.

"Margot?"

"Sorry, my finger got tired pressing the button so hard. Switching to my thumb," she says.

Margot wouldn't be so casual about the starts and stops if she knew it felt like a popcorn kernel in a microwave every time she presses the button. The entire box rattles and shakes. I can feel that I'm both trapped in a small space and hanging precariously, ready for a free fall. As the seconds tick on, the fun is being eaten up, along with my oxygen.

The motor roars to life again, and above me I watch the light from Margot's room inch closer. I begin to count the seconds under my breath. Eight, nine, ten . . . The dumbwaiter stops in place. I'm lined up with the rectangular door, but I can't open it. I press my hands against the wood panel but it doesn't budge. I feel my hands in the dark for some kind of latch or handle, but there's nothing.

"Uh, Margot. We have a problem. I don't think these doors are meant to be opened from the inside."

Once again, there's silence.

"Margot?" I call, this time a little louder. I don't think she's messing with me, but maybe I took our drunk bonding dance party more to heart than she did.

"Margot, this better not have been a sick joke. Margot, this is scary now."

The parlor-trick moment is gone for me. I want out and I don't care who helps me.

"Margot!" I shout.

I hear a click echo in the shaft. A glimpse of movement catches my eye from above. There's another rectangular door space above me. It must go to an attic where they keep supplies.

"Hello?" I call. I keep my eyes peeled in every direction but I see no one. I hear nothing. Was that Rini, or a ghost? The magic I felt in the pantry is gone and the haunting feeling is back.

I begin to pound on the door and shout at the top of my lungs. A moment later the door to Margot's room pops open. I push it wide as a woman with dark hair slips out into the hallway. Rini?

"Wait," I call. I unfurl my legs to chase after her, but I collapse to the ground next to Margot's bed. My right thigh has fallen dead asleep. The pins and needles burn. I hobble to stand, using the desk chair as a crutch, but before I can chase after the woman, I spot the note. It's handwritten in hasty chicken scratch.

You shouldn't be here.

"Aimee?" Margot opens the door to her bedroom as I massage my leg.

"What took you so long?" I ask.

"Ted caught me downstairs. He wanted to dance to the end of 'Watermelon Sugar' before he'd let me go. Are you okay?"

"Look." I show Margot the note.

"Is it a warning to stay out of the dumbwaiters?" she asks.

I'd love to believe that, but even I'm not that delusional. Although it was on the desk in Margot and Ted's room, something tells me this note was written for me. It's the same message I've been getting from my intuition all weekend. Unfortunately, there's nothing that can be done now that the storm has locked us inside. I'm stuck in this house with something or someone who doesn't want me here. And she's getting bolder.

RINI

I didn't get what I needed out of the Moon Men event last night, but I have a new plan. This time I'm not going to hint at the subject, and I'm not going to convince myself there's always tomorrow. I'm going to get what I brought him here for, and I won't stop until I do.

As I turn the corner from my private office hidden upstairs in the second wing, I slam into Rick and Eden. They're standing very close to each other, face-to-face and holding hands. The vibe is intimate but intense.

"Just the woman I didn't realize I needed," Rick says.

"I'm gathering everyone downstairs for a game," I say.

"A game?" Eden asks.

"This is a game I play with the guests who elect to do the group readings since we have more unstructured time."

"Can I ask you something first?" Rick asks.

"We don't need to drag her into this. This is between us," Eden says.

"I was describing the revelation that came over me at the Moon Men event last night. It explains why I personally am attracted to a non-traditional relationship."

"She knows about our situation," Eden says sheepishly. She looks down at her feet, knowing how much more information I have from our reading. That Eden is having a secret affair, that she is craving monogamy with this new man. She doesn't know I saw her and Adam on the lawn later that night. Either way, I would never betray her confidence. That's her fate, not mine.

"She also knows why I'm about to ask you to change it," Rick says to Eden. We both look at him, but I'm not connecting the dots.

"What's the number-one tenet of polyamory?" Rick asks.

"Communication," Eden says.

"And specifically, consent," Rick says.

The dots are merging for me now.

"I once had an experience where the woman suggested I didn't have consent. In the arrangement you and I have, there's nothing unsaid. We are up-front and honest with each other, and with any potential third partner. There's nothing implied. It's all express."

"I don't see what that has to do with the past and this woman," Eden says.

"I was horrified when I'd learned what she thought of our encounter. Horrified. I am not that guy, Eden."

"I know. Of course, I know that."

"I have spent my whole adult life leaning into express consent as if the *quantity* of encounters where I received it could erase that one terrible interaction where I didn't have it."

"That actually makes sense, from a psychological perspective," I add, reminding them that I'm witnessing this very tender and private moment.

"What if we try monogamy?" Rick asks.

Eden's face lights up. "Are you sure?"

In my reading Eden thought she was choosing between two men, one who represented a past decision, another who represented a future promise. She had never considered that the same man could be both.

"I haven't thought about it for long, but it came to me as strong as—"

A bolt of lightning illuminates the sky outside the window. The three of us turn to watch its beauty fade. A crash of thunder follows two seconds later.

"As strong as that," Rick says.

"That seems like a perfect note to go downstairs and gather the rest of the group for our friendly little game. You two can go first," I say.

I walk down the main stairs into the living room, where a full dance party is happening. No one notices me cross the room and pick up my sound bowl. I give it a quick tap with my fingertips.

"I thought we'd play a game," I announce.

Rick and Eden take the center seats on the couch, cuddled together. Aimee turns off the music and the group files into the living room.

"What the hell is this?" Adam asks. His voice is nearly a shout, as if he didn't realize the music had stopped. Eden looks up at him, a quick glance no one else would notice if they weren't already paying attention to their dynamic. Adam recovers but takes a seat in one of the chairs with a huff.

"This is a game I play with the guests who elect to do the group readings."

"Truth or dare?" Ted guesses, his voice slurring on the *th* in *truth*.

"It's called fate or free will. I'll ask about something that happened in your lives, and you say whether you thought it was fate or free will. I will look in your chart to see if I can get an indication of what forces were at play."

"Oh, this sounds fun," Margot says. "Can I go first?"

"Actually, Eden and Rick were here first, so they're up. Okay, your meet-cute—fate or free will?"

"Fate, for sure," Rick says.

"When was it?" I ask.

"Fourth of July, 2020."

"During the pandemic and a Venus retrograde in Gemini. For both of you that's two strong checkmarks on the side of free will."

"It wasn't fate?" Rick asks.

"Does that mean we're not supposed to be together?" Eden asks.

"It means your meeting was a random encounter, but your souls can still be fated," I say. "Soulmates can't miss each other. The Universe will keep trying until you get it right."

I look over at Adam, who wears a grimace. He doesn't like me supporting his current girlfriend leaving him. It's my time to pounce.

"Adam, you've opted out of a lot of my activities, which is obviously your free will, but I have a special question you're fated to answer this weekend."

"When do I get to go?" Margot asks.

I slip my hand into my pocket again and tap the voice recorder. "Fate or free will, your biggest fan falling for you?"

"Did you just say his biggest fan falling for him?" Aimee repeats. "I knew it." She jumps up from the edge of the couch and runs out of the room. Even with the storm raging outside, her stomping and cursing echo through the house. Aimee returns with her arms full of novels. As she makes her way to the couch, they tumble from her grasp with a thud, leaving a tail behind her. I don't understand, but my moment is already getting away from me.

"It's you. You're trying to steal my husband," Aimee says. "You left me a note that says I shouldn't be here. I'm in your way."

"What? No. Aimee, you've got this all wrong," I say. She's confused and thwarting my plan with her projection.

"I saw the books in the library. I thought Adam would be so happy. 'Rini's a fan of your work.' But so are thousands of women. I didn't put it together."

"What are you talking about?" I ask. "Those are Audra Rose novels."

"And you're his biggest fan. I got it. Don't treat me like I'm dumb," she says.

Aimee's voice grows louder as she drops the pile of Audra Rose novels on the wood floor. She picks up a single book and rips a handful of pages out, then tosses them into the air like confetti. Adam remains silent. Across the room, Margot stares at her brother. I wonder what she thinks. What she knows.

"I should have known," Aimee says. "From the moment I saw your picture, I thought you looked familiar. I must have seen you around our apartment in the city. Sneaking off from a rendezvous before the wife got home."

"No, Aimee, none of that is true," I say.

"Of course you'd gaslight me. Just like you tried to do in my reading. Suggesting that if I lose Adam maybe I'll gain something better, when you really just wanted me out of the picture."

Aimee grunts and tears out more pages. She crushes them in her hand with a fist of fury.

"Adam," Margot says.

"Aimee, wait," I say. "You're right about my vague familiarity. But it's not me. Adam's biggest fan was a student of his. My sister."

"Your sister?" Aimee repeats.

"Andi," I say.

Everyone in the room looks at Adam, other than Eden, who looks down at the bottom of her wineglass. Adam appears genuinely confused, and I remember. She wanted to start fresh in college. She was planning to go by her given name. "He had an affair with my sister, Miranda."

ADAM

I could not have written a more perfect way out of the mess that's been unfolding in the last day than what Rini has set up for me. Ten minutes ago I went up to my room and from around the corner, overheard Eden reuniting with her husband. The scene was sweet—a little bit of sad backstory unfolded into a full-fledged declaration of love—but it sent me into a panic. If Eden was with Rick and I'd successfully abandoned Aimee, I would be alone. That was impossible. Unthinkable. Unbearable. But now I have a chance to reunite with Aimee in a grand way. I had been leaning in her direction, but fate made the decision for me.

I had an eerie feeling of déjà vu around Rini too. But she looks nothing like her sister, not really, the way our daughters Dylan and Clara bear little resemblance to each other. Now it makes sense why Rini was trying to force some confession out of me at the Moon Men event, after laying the groundwork in my reading, saying I had unpaid debts from ten years ago. Her whole shtick has been a farce.

"Don't let this woman get into your head. Mira is old news. We've been through that," I say to Aimee.

I hug Aimee and kiss her hair, her forehead, her neck. I tell her I love her. I love her so much. The more I hold her and touch her, the more my initial fear of being alone and anger at Eden fade. Maybe my affair with Eden was supposed to be brief, an instrument to bring us back to our rightful partners.

"Aimee, you're the only one I love. No one else has ever made me better the way you do. You've always been the one."

Aimee looks up at me, her eyes searching my face for reassurance.

"I know, we've been through a rough patch. But I never stopped loving you, not one tiny bit."

It's not a lie. Perhaps an exaggeration. But I do believe I love Aimee the best. It must be why I subconsciously picked Eden, who was in a poly relationship. I was looking for relief from feeling like a bad husband and father when Aimee was so focused on the needs of the girls while ignoring mine. I wasn't looking for a way out. I was wrong.

"And now I can see how much you still care"—I gesture to the ripped pages on the ground, the sign of her fury—"and that our relationship isn't all a social media facade for you. That's all I ever wanted. I was afraid you'd never give it to me again."

I trace my thumb along the dried tears streaking her face.

"Really? You think we can be good again?" Aimee asks, her voice small and delicate.

I nod, staring into her beautiful blue eyes.

"Really?" Margot repeats. Her voice is harder, but full of hope. This is what she wants too, even if I told her hours ago that it wasn't possible.

"Really," Eden confirms. I look behind me and Eden is safely wrapped in Rick's arms, beaming at me. She doesn't want to reveal how she broke the rules and betrayed Rick as much as I don't want to admit that the affair Rini's conjuring up from ten years ago wasn't my only one.

"Not all of us have a happy ending," Joe says, glaring across the room at Farah.

"Hey, Rick, kick Ted," I say. Rick nudges Ted, who has passed out on the chair next to him. He's not even hungover yet because he's still clearly drunk. But it doesn't matter. I want an audience.

I drop down to my knee. "Aimee, will you marry me?"

"What?" she asks.

"Marry me all over again. Let me reclaim my love and commitment to you from this moment until death do us part."

Lightning and thunder strike again.

"Excuse me, I'm the one who has something to say," Rini says. "And I wasn't finished."

"Why are you talking?" I ask, annoyed that she's ruining my moment.

"Because it's my house."

"Right, your astrology house. Are you even a real astrologist? According to me and my wife, all you did was further your own agenda in your so-called readings."

"Stop it," Margot shouts, putting an end to my Rini takedown. She squeezes her eyes shut and presses the heels of her hands into her head as if the pressure could make her explode. "I cannot take it anymore."

I stare at her, but she won't look at me. She is not about to ruin this elegant exit. She better not. I'll kill her if she did.

MARGOT

The living room is as scattered and confused as I am. Aimee stands there dopily looking up at her cheating husband, unsure what to say or do with his second marriage proposal. Pages of Adam's novels trail like tears from the library. Joe and Farah look sad, like they're at a wedding thinking they'll be alone forever, while previously poly Eden and Rick look like blissful witnesses to the potential joy of monogamy. *What is happening?*

"Stop it," I shout. The sneaky omissions, the sudden revelations, the doubt, the lies. "I cannot take it anymore."

I need fresh air.

Through the sliding glass door, I step outside into the rain. I fight the wind to make my way across the lawn, water collecting in beads on my hair and sweater. I reach the dock and sit cross-legged on the wooden planks. The drama of the storm feels like student theater compared to the telenovela inside.

Is Rini a fake? Could she have falsified all of those glowing reviews? Does that mean I'm not pregnant? I desperately want to take that test now, to know what I can believe in and what I can't.

And what about Adam and Aimee? A few hours ago Adam said they were broken beyond repair; now he wants to recommit. Was it all for show, or was Eden a huge mistake, as I'd suspected all along?

Do I need to have faith in Rini's reading of my star chart for the things I want to be true? What if we had never come here this weekend—would it be real anyway?

Does what I want even matter?

A clap of thunder booms out of nowhere, as if in response to my question. It feels as if all of the oxygen has been sucked out of the air and I can no longer breathe.

Farah and Aimee approach, their heads down against the wind.

"Are you okay?" Farah asks.

I shake my head no.

"Where does it hurt?"

I point to my throat and my chest.

"Are you having a panic attack?"

I shrug.

Adam appears, slipping his arms around Aimee like he can't stand to be away from her for a minute.

"What's going on?" he asks.

"Adam, go inside and get her a paper bag to breathe into," Farah says.

"Paper, in this weather? Not plastic?"

"If you want to suffocate her, sure."

"Shouldn't we just get her inside?" Aimee asks.

I shake my head violently. I already feel like the whole world is closing in on me. I couldn't possibly go inside four walls again.

"Adam, get a whole bunch of paper bags and bring them to her. One will have to hold up," Farah says.

Farah kneels down next to me. She pulls my knees up to ninety degrees and pushes my head between them. "If it feels okay, close your eyes," she says.

As soon as my neck releases and I tune out the world around me, I feel better.

"Aimee," I say, the word coming out as a whisper.

"Aimee, Margot is calling you," Farah says.

Aimee sits down cross-legged next to me and leans her face close.

"Are you sure you want this?" I ask.

"This?" she repeats.

I nod toward the house, the ridiculous scene that unfolded before us.

"Your brother? Of course. Why wouldn't I?" she asks.

"What if he's a cheater?"

"I forgave him for what he did ten years ago."

"But what if it's not about what he did ten years ago? What if that's who he is? Someone who needs a woman. Our mother is his God-shaped hole. I've tried to fill it, but my unconditional love is not enough. Just like my father is mine. It's why I chose Ted, who would literally do anything to protect me."

"We all have our shadow sides," Aimee says.

"But, Aimee, what if Adam is a man who wilts if for a split second he doesn't feel adored? And when he doesn't feel adored, he doesn't sit down and say, 'Can we make a plan to connect?' He instead acts out like a child having a tantrum to get the attention he wants."

"Oh, I'm very good at ignoring tantrums," Aimee responds.

We're talking past each other.

"I know, I've seen it with the girls. But that might be why he will always fall into the arms of someone else."

"Always? Are you saying this has happened before?"

I am already betraying my brother more than I can stomach. I cannot answer her question.

"It's happening now," Rini says. I didn't hear her arrive, but I should have known she wasn't going to give up on whatever she had to say. "I saw him and Eden having sex on this very lawn after the first night."

Aimee cannot process any more conflicting information. It's too much to handle, and her protective rage takes over. She shields her eyes from the rain and looks up at Rini.

"Who invited you out here? You're a liar and a manipulator," Aimee says. Her timid voice stands in opposition to her harsh words.

"A first-class fake," Adam adds, his fist full of brown paper bags. They turned to black mush between the house and the dock.

"Get away from us," he says, throwing the paper slop at Rini. The bags hit Rini and cling to her chest in wet clumps.

Rini wipes away the mess while she runs back to the house. I can hear her muttering under her breath, crying or cursing him.

"Farah, can you see if Ted has passed out again? I need him," I say.

When it's only the three of us left on the back lawn, Aimee and I stand.

"Adam," I beseech. He stays silent, refusing to accept he's been caught. I can understand trying to avoid it, but the moment to come clean is here. Instead, he's leaning in the other direction. How can he be so cruel to Rini? And why won't he admit what he's done to Aimee? I briefly wonder. But I already know the answers: because he can and because he doesn't have to. He does what he wants and never has to take responsibility. It's always been that way.

I remember watching the very first episode of *Friends*, "The One Where It All Began."

Monica gets raked over the coals by her parents, about her middling job, her lack of a husband, her general failure to live up to their standards. Monica, in turn, encourages her older brother, Ross, to share his news, knowing it will take some of their parents' judgmental heat off her.

Finally Ross spills his guts. He is getting divorced. His wife left him for a woman, but she's also pregnant with his child, whom he wants to raise with the new lesbian couple. And what happens? Their parents look at Monica with disappointment and say, "And you knew about this?"

My mother had warned me, *If you clean up their messes, they start to think you're the one who made them.*

She said it when I was five years old and putting away the crayons Adam had left out. She said it when I was eight years old and picking up the Cheerios dust that Adam and I had stomped into the floor tiles. It wasn't just that I'd help, but that I let him pretend he needed my help, encouraged his helplessness. I did it because it made me feel powerful.

If you clean up their messes, they start to think you're the one who made them.

Like when Adam told me Eden was on this trip because of me.

Technically you brought her. She's your husband's best friend's wife.

Or when he shattered my memory of Dad.

Margot, that wasn't love. That was demoralizing, the way Dad treated her.

His problems, made my problems. His version of events, made mine.

My brother and sister-in-law stand over me with their arms wrapped around each other in such a deep and loving gesture, and there's not a selfie stick in sight. It's wonderful, but is it real? Would I even know?

The rain makes everything a little blurry, even in my mind.

Is this the true Adam and the true Aimee, or are they characters in "The One Where They Push Margot over the Edge"?

FARAH

Inside the house, Ted is in the kitchen and has inexplicably shifted from nearly passed-out drunk to wired. Joe's talking his ear off while they wait for another pot of coffee to brew. I think he's had more than enough.

"Margot needs you," I say.

Ted sprints ahead as I jog back toward the center of the action. Aimee and Adam embrace in the rain. It would be romantic if it weren't for the allegation that he's currently having an affair, in addition to the one Aimee apparently knew about ten years ago. I cannot hold my tongue any longer.

"Aimee, what are you doing? Rini just said Adam is having an affair with Eden. Eden, a woman under this roof with us, someone who is part of our friend group."

"Well, Rini's a fraud," Aimee says.

"And what about Margot? Is she lying too? Because I heard her subtext loud and clear."

"What?" Adam snaps.

"Oh boy," I say. "And then there's that reaction. Doesn't exactly scream *innocent* to be angry at your sister for revealing your dirty secret."

"Margot was asking me tough questions, trying to unearth what I want. She wasn't tattling on her brother," Aimee says.

I can feel my patience wearing thin. Aimee will counter every infer-
ence I make. She needs new information. Straight from the source.

"Why don't you go inside and ask Eden? Her reaction might be all
you need to confirm or deny. You had a feeling on that first night. You
made me go through his stuff with you."

"You went through my stuff?" Adam asks. His victim meter is off
the charts.

"I didn't make you," Aimee says to me.

"That's right, you didn't. Because I would do anything for you. That's
my bad."

I can't take any more of this. This entire group has the primal responses of a trapped animal. Their instinct has no rational thought; it's
all lashing out.

"Don't listen to her," Adam says to Aimee. "She wants you to break
up with me so she can control you. All she does is order you around like
you're her nurse."

The underlying connection between me and Aimee's-mother-the-
cold-nurse is meant to be hurtful, to both me and Aimee. It's true I'm
confused about my feelings for Aimee, but I'm pushing her to do the
right thing. To confront the truth and then decide how to move forward.
I'm not secretly hoping she divorces Adam and falls in love with me, at
least not consciously. And not yet. It's too soon to know. Adam's warped
words send me back toward the house.

"Wait," Margot calls. I turn to see her cross the lawn to Ted. He
opens his arms and pulls her into a warm hug away from the cold rain.
It's a genuine display of love that comforts me, as opposed to the farce
of Adam and Aimee.

"Part of the concern here—for me too—is whether Rini is a fraud, a
fake astrologer," Margot says. "Well, in my reading she told me I'm going
to have a baby in nine months' time, which would mean I'm pregnant
right now. I have a pregnancy test upstairs."

"You do? We agreed there'd be no tests this weekend," Ted says.

"I know. I found it in the bottom of my suitcase this afternoon. I didn't buy it or pack it, but it's there. It must be old," Margot says.

"Lucky," Ted says with a weak smile.

I jump in with the obvious conclusion. "So if the test is positive, Rini was right and Aimee confronts Eden for her side of the story."

"And if the test is negative, we run Rini back to her cottage and head home the minute it's safe. Let's allow fate to have a say in what happens next," Margot says.

"Deal," Aimee says. Adam and Ted agree reluctantly. I nod my consent in time with a bolt of lightning flashing through the sky. On the mark of the rumble of thunder, the five of us begin the slog through the wet grass to the main house.

"Not so fast," Rini yells. She's put a hoodie on over the mess Adam splattered on her. "You're not coming back inside my house until I get what I need from you."

RINI

This moment is not what I expected. What started as a defense of my sister has become personal. Adam and Aimee have attacked my character, my business, my studies and skill.

"I did have ulterior motives in bringing you all here, but that doesn't mean I'm a fraud. I've been studying astrology since I was fourteen years old, and every reading I shared came directly from your charts. For one of you, and only one of you, I chose my narrative with an agenda."

"Which one?" Aimee asks.

"Adam. Adam is the only one who I'd known had hurt my sister before you showed up. I had no idea that you had a role in the way it played out, Aimee. I figured that out hours after your reading. You added to her trauma."

"I'm sorry," Aimee says.

"What do you want, Rini?" Margot asks.

Margot is leading me exactly where I wanted to go. But one piece of this picture is still missing. "I want Adam to pay for what he's done," I say.

"What did I do to your sister anyway? Or what do you think I did?" Adam asks.

I stutter here, because I don't know the full extent. But I know enough. That she was a teenager. That he was her professor. That he was married, stringing along a much younger girl with hero worship.

"You had an inappropriate relationship with her, just like you did with Eden, which you're still avoiding taking responsibility for. These aren't isolated incidents; this is your character. Your actions have consequences. You can't chase your every whimsical desire and expect everyone to fall in line. You have to pay for what you've done."

My declaration is punctuated not only by a clap of thunder but by the unexpected slam of a metal door. The bulkhead doors of the basement. When a figure appears around the corner, I cannot hide my elation. I was beginning to doubt this confrontation would happen. It's nothing short of a miracle, my dying wish coming true.

Andi steps into the storm. My sister is outside, in the presence of other people, for the first time in years.

◆

Hiding my sister away in the walls of the house was her idea, not mine. I thought moving away from the city would begin to cure her, like slowly sipping a magic potion. In Greenport, I gladly went out and got jobs to pay for the work, while Andi binged YouTube tutorials. But as the house started to show signs of life, nosy neighbors and enterprising press came knocking at the door. They wanted to know what two young girls were doing with decrepit property. They were aggressive, or worse, underhandedly kind, trying to ingratiate themselves for information. Andi couldn't take it. She refused to go outside, ever, for any reason.

That ushered in her third nosedive, and for me, the most devastating.

Andi got the idea for a secret room from YouTube, a BBC interview with Anthony Horowitz showing the hidden office where he wrote all his masterpiece novels. I came home from my shift and she showed me the video. It was cool for a workspace, but what Andi was proposing was different. If word got out, she would be a freak. I would be a monster.

The story would be front-page news. Andi pleaded. *We could build a place for me. To be safe. To be happy.*

Still, I wanted to say no. I wanted Andi to feel safe, but I also wanted her to rejoin the world of the living, which meant engaging with society, its roses and its thorns. I was afraid that would never happen if she went so far as to live in a secret apartment in the walls of the house.

I tried to get Eric to say no so I could blame it on him. At that point Eric was the only person in Greenport who had ever seen Andi. There were rumors of two girls living here, but no one could confirm or deny it. Andi made phone calls—never Zooms—and refused to come to the door for vendors, but she trusted Eric, and he never let her down. If Eric noticed that Andi didn't leave the house—not to join us for dinner, not to go out to bars, not even for a grocery run—he didn't say anything.

When I shared Andi's idea with Eric, he was the opposite of judgmental; he was so accepting that he went straight to the practical. He said if he added the modifications to the planning designs, they'd become public record. He wanted to confirm that would negate what he assumed was the whole point—to make sure no one would know Andi was there.

When we understood the risk he was taking by building an unpermitted apartment, I knew he deserved to know the whole story—as much as I knew, at least—starting from our father leaving to the night she dropped out of college, our mother's intolerance, and Andi's increasing agoraphobia. In the end, knowing what Andi had been through actually brought her closer to Eric.

"I'll get them to grant you a certificate of occupancy for the house and the cottage. If you ever sell this place, you're going to have a lot of problems with that illegal addition," he'd said.

"I don't ever want to sell this place," I said, dreaming of the business on the horizon.

"Not in our lifetimes," Andi agreed, comforted by her secret spaces.

I thought Andi and I had a shared vision, but we were never truly on the same page. Stars Harbor was a dream come true for both of us, but in two very different ways. This fundamental divide would remain hidden for years. Until I had my death date.

With my fate sealed, I had broken up with Eric, pushed him away to protect him, but I couldn't do that with Andi. Besides, to say I would be abandoning her in six months when she couldn't face the world alone felt beyond cruel. So I had to help her without telling her. I directed all my energy into figuring out how to provide for her when I was gone. The first thing I did was create a will. I left everything to her, which was mainly my bank accounts and Stars Harbor.

After meeting with the lawyer, I felt strong knowing the business would legally pass to her upon my death, but that security faded when I considered the logistics. Andi knew astrology as well as I did; I'd taught her well. She did all the intake forms for new guests; she helped me generate charts and prepare narratives for the readings. Andi could do everything it took to run Stars Harbor behind the scenes. But she could never trust strangers.

Feeling the pressure of time ticking by, I got my answer by watching *The Real Housewives of Beverly Hills* when one of the women said, "It's never too late to say you're sorry." She and her sister apologized and hugged it out, not only ending a years-long feud, but also taking care of issues that hadn't even seemed directly related.

Not willing to place my future in the hands of reality-show editors, I conducted my own research. While no one would call it a cure, there was a lot of support—from Reddit personal anecdotes to articles from psychologists and mental health experts—for the healing power of an apology.

I started myself. Late at night, in the safety of the dark with Andi, I would deliberately reminisce with the intention of making amends for losing my grip. The days I couldn't bear another minute carrying the burden of a dependent when I'd been abandoned by the parents who were supposed to care for us. I'd felt terrible for the times I had snapped at her for her depression, or tried to shame her into eating when she was severely restricting. I cried when I said I was sorry for those moments of weakness.

Stop beating yourself up for being human. I appreciate everything you've done for me, she said. A sincere apology and genuine forgiveness. After every late-night sisterly therapy session, I swore I could see a change in Andi.

To continue the healing tour of my final six months, I tried to reach out to our father, but he said he had nothing to apologize for and that Andi's problems were her own. *You turned out well,* he said. I hung up on him. I tracked down our mother, but reception was spotty where she was traveling in Marrakech. *I raised you both to adulthood. Andi even longer. When you have kids of your own, you'll appreciate how much I did for both of you, especially as a single mom. Maybe then I'll get an apology.* She hung up on me. No intergenerational apologies were coming.

And that's when I knew the person who would make the most dramatic difference, and I hatched the plan that could let me die believing Andi was healed, or at least well on her way. A few targeted email blasts and Instagram ads, and the future was in motion.

Andi didn't know why I thought it was important for us to confront Adam this particular weekend. When I showed her the reservation list, she nodded without hesitation. But as the weekend approached, she refused to come up with a script or a strategy with me. I knew she'd need my help, but she wouldn't talk about any of it.

I didn't want to wait until the last possible minute, so I originally floated the idea of Andi appearing during Adam's reading on Friday night. She balked. When I got scared after the Moon Men event, I wanted to wake everyone up and do it then, before the clock struck midnight. Andi passed on that idea as well. She went radio silent. Given that we've all been trapped in the house, I couldn't coordinate with her for an alternate plan.

But as she reveals herself in the storm—with emotions already heated, confidences betrayed, loyalties tested—I see that Andi had her own agenda, and it could not be more perfect. It's the exact right moment.

Lightning flashes, illuminating Andi, her face drawn tight.

"Oh, holy hell, this house really was haunting me," Aimee says.

"Who is that?" Margot asks.

"Miranda, the woman Adam had an affair with ten years ago," Aimee responds.

"She's my sister," I say.

No one speaks for a moment as I try to ease my way into this final negotiation. I've been preparing for months, but it's all coming to a head so quickly. It feels surreal. Andi is outside at Stars Harbor in the presence of other people.

"Rini, you're making a mistake," Andi says.

I turn away from the group, shocked and confused by my sister's words.

"You have the wrong target," Andi adds.

"It's not Adam?"

Andi shakes her head.

"See," he says, taunting me.

"It's me?" Aimee asks.

Another no from Andi.

"It was Ted," Andi says.

ANDI

Fate is real. That, you cannot deny. If you didn't believe in fate, you'd never believe my story. Even if you did, it's hard to get your head around. That's why I never told my mom or Rini. And yet, it happened. The Universe conspired to bring it all together.

Fate is real, but it's not always kind.

It was fate that I chose Professor Flynn's creative writing class ten years ago. It was fate that our bodies brushed and there was electricity. I didn't even think to ask if he was married. I was nineteen years old and out of my house for the first time. In the beginning, all I knew was he was talented and sophisticated. Over the course of the semester he confided in me, sharing so much about his life —his parents' deaths, his MFA war stories, his meddling but lovable sister—but nothing about a wife.

It was fate that she found out. And it was fate that Ted was there the night Aimee attacked me and Adam abandoned me. It was fate that Ted assured Adam he would get me cleaned up and home safely.

Ted was primed to be my savior and he knew the role well. He comforted me, called Adam a loser and a wimp, winning me over as soon as Adam was out of earshot. He pulled clothes out of his gym bag for me to change into. *They're clean*, he said.

When I came out of the bathroom feeling embarrassed, he told me I looked cute. Ted was kind and gentle where Adam was commanding and self-assured. Ted was deferential where Adam took the lead. He was everything I needed in that moment and he was everything Adam was never going to be.

I was the one who kissed him first, right there in the middle of the bar, wearing his gym clothes. And when he pulled away and led me out to the back alley by the hand, I thought he was being a gentleman. Knowing the trouble I'd just gotten myself into, I asked him point-blank if he was married, or engaged, or in a serious relationship. He told me no with zero hesitation.

Our chemistry was immediate, his mouth on mine in the alley behind the bar. When he suggested we spend the night together in a hotel, and that hotel was the Gansevoort, I was swept away by the luxury. We changed into robes and flopped on the bed. When he said we didn't have to do anything if the moment had passed, I thought he was a saint. It was the perfect one-night-stand scenario, like a scene from my favorite teen drama.

It was fate that I got pregnant during our one night together.

I hadn't wanted a relationship with Ted, because of the timing and because of his connection to Adam, but I never doubted my desire to keep the baby. My family had fallen apart after my parents' divorce, and to be honest, I was desperate for someone to love. Boys had caused me more pain than I'd expected. Even when the romantic love filled me up, the relationships had left me emptier than before. I wanted this baby. I needed this baby.

I didn't know where we would live or whether my mom would approve, so I told no one. I worked as many shifts as possible to squirrel away money and to hide my morning sickness, which happened in the bar bathroom during the afternoon and night too.

About a month after I found out I was pregnant, I had a crisis of confidence. I had decided I could do this on my own, whether my mother helped or not—but now I was asking myself if I should. My father abandoning me shaped my entire life. Would my baby feel that pain too? I didn't know if I could subject another generation to that trauma. I decided I would share the news with Ted. I would tell him he had a choice too. He could decide to be a part of the baby's life or he would have to promise to stay away forever.

Ted saw different choices.

ADAM

Mira looks like a mirage. She stands before us, beginning her story, and she's as stunning as she was ten years ago. Her skin is like porcelain, milky white, as if it hasn't seen the sun in a decade. Her dark thick hair reaches to the belly button I once kissed. She's an optical illusion summoned by the harsh atmospheric conditions. At one point, I actually rub my eyes like a total cliché.

But as she continues to talk, my horror grows. I'm in stunned disbelief that Ted tried to steal my girl. I'd told him I wasn't in love, and he knew I was choosing Aimee when I ran after her and left Mira—Andi—with him, but would he really stoop so low?

As if in response to my question, Ted scoffs at Andi. "Don't believe a word out of her mouth. I've never seen this woman before in my life," he says, his eyes locked on Margot.

My sister shifts nervously, and I watch her gather her resolve.

"Ten years ago Ted and I were already living together. He proposed right around the time you're talking about. None of this would have happened," she says.

"I'm having a hard time believing it myself," Aimee says. "That after her relationship with Adam, and my encounter with her, Ted randomly crossed her path and did something horrible to her? What are the odds? Maybe she's mistaken."

Andi is now as soaked as the rest of us who have been standing out in the rain. She is shaking, but it's not cold enough to produce that reaction. She's that scared.

"I'm not lying," she says, barely audible above the din of the storm. Rini is by her side, and I can't tell if it's rain or tears—or both—streaming down her face.

"Yes, she is. She's hell-bent on ruining our lives," Margot cries. "The two of them, they're liars."

Margot charges Andi, but I grab her arm. "Ted's the one lying," I say. Margot recoils from my assertion. I turn to Ted. "You know her."

Ted looks away from me and pretends to study Andi's face. I don't know who he thinks he's kidding. She looks exactly the same, immaculately preserved.

"Ted was there that night. Aimee, you saw him. We were at a high-top table when you dumped drinks on Andi at the bar," I say.

"That's right," Aimee says. "I followed you to Lillian's where you were meeting her. That's when I saw red. Ted was there."

"I actually asked him to take care of her while I went after you," I explain. I've known Ted for over fifteen years now, and to think he could have kept a secret like this for a decade seems unlikely. But I can't fathom why Andi would lie about any of this.

"Why didn't you tell me it was Ted?" Rini asks her sister. "This whole time I've been targeting Adam."

"I couldn't talk about what he'd done, Rini," Andi says. "It didn't matter what you knew and what information you were missing. I knew when Margot booked the retreat he would be here. I had seen their wedding announcement in the *New York Times* a year after our weekend at the Gansevoort."

"Weekend at the Gansevoort?" I ask. "This wasn't a one-time thing?"

Andi shakes her head, but she hasn't looked at me. Not once, even after all we shared. She won't look at Ted either. She's been speaking directly to her sister the whole time.

"I tried to warn you all weekend, Margot," Andi says.

"Okay, that's it. We're done here," Ted says.

"Exactly. Let's go," Margot adds.

Ted and Margot start up the lawn toward the house, but no one else follows.

"None of you are leaving, not until we get to the bottom of this," Rini says.

Ted and Margot look frustrated, but they don't move. Aimee, Farah and I turn back to Rini and her sister.

"I need to hear more. Go on," Farah says.

ANDI

Ted was surprisingly easy to find. He'd given me his real name, first and last. He'd shared what he did for a job, and the gym bag he was carrying that night had the name of the bank where he worked. I called him at the office and left a message saying I needed to talk. His voice-mail box sounded like the man I'd met: confident, not aggressive. Ted called me back an hour later.

"I thought you'd never call," he said.

"Were you waiting for me to?" I asked.

"Of course. I had a great time that night. I thought you did too, but it's been almost two months, so I assumed I was wrong."

"How do you know I wasn't waiting for you to call?"

"Because I put my name in your phone and said if you wanted to do it again, I was up for it."

He was telling the truth, but I had forgotten. The morning after our first time together, I'd been disoriented. Aimee had attacked me, Adam had abandoned me, and I'd had a one-night stand with Adam's friend. A lot had happened and it was just starting to sink in.

I wasn't sure if I'd hooked up with Ted to make Adam mad. I wasn't sure if Adam would be mad. Would he take it out on me? Would he blame Ted? It turned out worse than either of those. Adam didn't care about me at all. But those motivations didn't matter anymore; Ted and I had something bigger than us to discuss.

"I'm working tonight, but I can probably get out around ten p.m. Do you want to meet after my shift?" I asked.

"Perfect timing. I've got a work thing, but I should be able to sneak away by then."

"Please let me know if you can't." I worried that I sounded whiny and needy, but Ted responded with kindness.

"I wouldn't miss the chance to see you again," he said.

Ted was true to his word. He picked me up in the alley outside my bar at 10 p.m. We made out there for a while, but I didn't want to chicken out and not share my news. I recommended another bar where we could talk and where I knew I wouldn't get carded. In the vein of our first encounter, he opted for luxury over practicality. *No one checks IDs when you're spending a couple of hundred dollars*, he said. At the fanciest restaurant I'd ever seen, he ordered a bottle of wine and a half-dozen appetizers. I was starving and he thought I was cute for eating without inhibition.

"Well, you might not think it's cute in a few minutes."

"Impossible. I will always think you're cute."

"I'm pregnant," I said. He looked at me, eyes wide, and I forged ahead, the rest spilling out of me. "I'm going to keep it. I've made up my mind. I just want to get our story straight if you reject having a part in the baby's life. You can't change your mind when she's ten-years-old."

Ted shook his head and a grin slid across his face from ear to ear. He pulled me in for a hug and wouldn't stop kissing my face. I was stunned, and after the waiter came around to ask if we needed anything else, Ted ordered more food while I sat in silence.

"You didn't even ask if it was yours," I said.

It was his, but I'd expected him to try to deny it. I'd been with Adam, but we'd always used condoms. That night at the hotel, Ted didn't have any and I told him it was okay.

"We had unprotected sex. This is what happens when you do that," Ted said.

"I wasn't lying when I said it was okay. I'd just had my period. I thought ovulation was weeks away."

"I don't care about how this happened. I only care that it did. We should celebrate."

"Celebrate?"

"Let's go away this weekend. New England is gorgeous this time of year."

"I can't. I have to take extra shifts at the bar."

"No you don't."

"I do," I said. Ted looked like he wanted to argue, and I secretly wished he would declare that he'd take care of me and the baby for the rest of our lives, but I think we both sensed it was too soon.

"What about a few nights in the city? At the hotel where we conceived this little nugget. Surely you can get off in the middle of the week."

"Tuesday's my day off, and I could probably swap shifts to get Wednesday too."

"See, it's perfect," Ted said.

We met in the lobby of the Gansevoort at 5 p.m. on Tuesday. I was debating whether I should hug him or kiss him, but he picked me up and twirled me around until we were both laughing and dizzy.

We went upstairs and didn't come out again for two days. The first night had its fair share of awkward moments, but they were dodged by me letting him take the lead. He talked me into a drink to loosen us up. A few sips couldn't possibly hurt the baby, I reasoned. When he brought out a baggie full of vials and pills, I had to hold myself back from freaking out. Instead of asking if he was insane, I explained that I wasn't a typical big-city teen. My mother had sent us to Catholic school, and she'd made us get jobs to build character and help contribute to the family from a young age. Thankfully, Ted didn't seem to care that I wasn't into drugs. He didn't push me to try anything. He said he didn't know my partying style yet and wanted to come prepared. That he brought drugs to celebrate my pregnancy was a red flag, but I assumed he needed time to change his ways.

By the end of the second night, I couldn't get out of bed, I was in so much pain. I did everything to hide it. We watched TV while cuddling, and I prayed it would pass. At first, I was sure I'd had a flare-up of IBS from the rich food he was ordering. When I ruled out gas, I thought it was a urinary tract infection from all the sex we'd been having. But my instinct told me it was something worse.

While Ted slept soundly, I experienced the worst physical pain of my life. Sobbing and scared, I writhed around the bathroom floor, the cold tile offering the only relief I could find. I thought something was wrong with me. Really wrong, like I might die. I prayed to God to let my stomach tear or my appendix burst, as long as my baby was safe.

I was so exhausted and embarrassed by the time Ted woke up that I told him he could leave. I called through the door like it was nothing but a stomach bug. *I have the late shift at the bar and it doesn't make sense to go home and come back, so I'll shower and get ready for work here.* He said he was sorry I didn't feel well and blew me a kiss goodbye.

Twenty minutes later I was in the hospital, bleeding into my black uniform pants at an alarming rate. I could no longer deny that I might be having a miscarriage, and for the next five hours I obsessed over the fact that the Universe was telling me I didn't deserve anything good, that God was punishing me for being so unlovable.

"You'll have to contact your OB to complete the termination in the next forty-eight hours," the discharge nurse said. "We don't do D&Cs unless the mother's life is in danger."

"Okay," I said, trying to scan the paperwork to understand what she was saying.

"I'm not sure why you came in here. Yours was a normal response to the pills. If you had read the directions, or contacted the clinic who gave them to you, you wouldn't have wasted our valuable resources. We're all overworked."

"I came in here to save my baby from miscarriage. Isn't that what happened?"

I will never forget the way that nurse studied my face, unsure if I was an idiot or there was something clinically wrong with me.

"You can't change your mind after you've taken both doses of the pills," she said.

The last time I saw Ted's face flashed in my mind then, how happy he was when he left me on the floor of the hotel bathroom. He knew what was happening. He blew me a kiss goodbye.

FARAH

Once Andi said the nurse was upset, I knew how the story ended.
I had the extra beat to take in everyone's reactions. Shock rippled
from one face to another.

"He forced an abortion on you?" Aimee exclaims.

Margot faints then. Her knees buckle and her torso folds. She lands
on the grass with a wet thump. I look at Ted, all of us do, but he doesn't
move. If looks could kill, Andi would be long gone.

Adam is the one who moves toward Margot. He lays her out flat
from the awkward angle she's crumpled in. Watching Ted, I move closer
to Margot.

"I'm checking her vitals," I say, crouching next to her. Ted doesn't
even glance over. He's locked on Andi.

Margot's heart rate is a little slow, but nothing concerning. She's
breathing fine. But this is her second fainting spell in as many days.
She's not well.

"How?" Aimee asks. "How is that possible?"

I stand from Margot's side, and Adam sits down and puts her head
in his lap. I explain.

"The first night he must have slipped mifepristone in her drink.
It blocks progesterone and stalls the pregnancy. The next night when

she could barely move, that was the misoprostol; it empties your uterus."

"Farah, stop it right now," Ted says.

On one hand Ted's veiled threat should frighten me. This is a man who took advantage of a vulnerable young woman and then violated her in ways I cannot fathom even reading on the worst dark-web threads. And yet, all I feel is my doctor's God-complex. I am invincible. I stare him in the eyes and continue my explanation.

"The second drug can be taken one of three ways, but it can't be swallowed like the mifepristone. It has to remain under your tongue or in your cheek for thirty minutes. It can also be inserted vaginally."

Aimee's hand had been slowly creeping toward her mouth as the story went on, but now it flies down to her side and her hands press together into fists. "You lured her to a hotel room, assaulted her by drugging her drink, and then stuck pills inside her under the pretense that you were making love to the future mother of your child?" she asks.

"I did nothing," Ted says.

I check Margot's vital signs again and notice she's awake. I don't know how much she's heard, but she appears to be in shock. She stares at the sky above as the rain pelts her face.

"I need to see what I have upstairs for supplies," I say. "I can't be sure I'm getting her pulse right with the chaos around us."

There have been times in the five or six years I've known Margot that I've thought Ted must be the perfect husband. He's quiet but not boring, supportive but not condescending, loving but not possessive, and most importantly, he's tolerant of Margot's neuroses. I've thought, *Why can't I fall in love with someone like that?* I married Joe, the guy who is always the center of attention, who has a story for everything, whom everyone wants to crowd around. And now I might have feelings for Aimee, another person who shines in the spotlight. *What I wouldn't do for an easy and simple Ted*, I thought as recently as last night when Ted skipped the Moon Men event to stay by his wife's side.

Hindsight is twenty-twenty when it comes to guys like that. Either they die peacefully at an old age surrounded by generations of love, or they are exposed for the psychopaths they are, and spend the rest of their lives in jail. It's too soon to tell which direction this one is going in, but my gut tells me to believe Andi and Rini. They have nothing to gain by lying, unlike Ted, who has everything to lose if the truth comes out.

As I run toward the house, the wind picks up and I can feel that things are about to get much worse.

MARGOT

sit up and my vision goes black. The voices around me come in and out like I'm opening and closing a door between us. I blink my eyes and my head spins.

"Did I pass out again?" I ask.

"This time there was no airbag," Adam says, helping me sit up.

"You hit your head on the wet grass. Farah went to get some of her doctor stuff to check you out," Aimee adds.

"I'm fine," I say. "Ted?"

He doesn't hear me. I push myself up to stand and fight the wave of nausea creeping up my throat. Adam helps me balance myself.

"Ted, I need to talk to you," I say.

"Now? You want to talk now?"

"Yes, now."

I move past Rini and her sister, ignoring them, and reach the dock, away from the group. The wind picks up as Ted and I walk over the water, but we forge our way to the floating dock, as far away from the others as possible. I lose my footing but Ted grabs me before I fall. I consider that this isn't the safest place in a storm, but it will give us the best chance of privacy.

"Margot, you're not listening to any of this, right?"

"Ted" is the only word I can eke out before my throat closes up. He wraps his arms around me and presses me into his body. I smell his sour alcohol breath and remember how much drunker he is than I am. I don't know what to think, what to believe. If Andi is telling the truth, that Ted did those horrendous things, it would make him a monster.

That couldn't be the man I know, the man I married. The man I love. Could it?

I think of the tarot cards, the ones left in the dumbwaiter only for me. The ones Rini knew nothing about.

The Empress, upright: pregnancy; reversed: domestic problems.

The Fool, upright: new beginnings; reversed: poor judgment, naivety.

If they were left by Andi, who said she was trying to warn me, then their intended meaning was clear. And yet I saw what I wanted to see, a promise for the future rather than a glimpse of clarity into the past. I've always willfully ignored the signs that disturbed me. I did it with my parents' marriage. With their tragic death. With Adam. With Ted too?

I remember back to that time before Ted and I got engaged. Our two-year dating anniversary was coming up, and I had a feeling Ted was going to propose. We'd been talking about the future and engagement rings and our favorite time of the year for weddings. Despite my firmly held career ambitions, I suddenly became more desperate for him to propose than a woman approaching her thirties in the 1950s. Aimee and Adam were already married and I knew they'd start having kids. I wanted the same. Adam and I would morph from orphans into a superfamily.

It was easy to ignore the nights Ted stayed out until the morning. Or the unexpected business trips. I was so close to getting what I wanted that I glossed right over those incidents. And in hindsight his odd behavior felt like a blip. Last-minute jitters before a well-planned-out, highly orchestrated proposal. There was nothing to ask about. Nothing to dig up. Until Andi appeared from the hands of fate with a horror story to ruin my life.

AIMEE

I fight the urge to take out my phone and snap a picture of the gray storm clouds cast Martian red from the late-afternoon sun hidden behind them. I want to video the flashes of lightning that divide the sky. To record the thunder that shakes the wooden piles of the dock below us.

This compulsion is not to post on social media, but to capture tangible evidence of the day the past came crashing back into us. Me, Adam, and apparently, Ted. Somehow I knew this was coming, as far back as the drive to Stars Harbor two days ago, but I could've never grasped the extent of it.

When Margot took Ted out to the end of the dock to confront him about Andi's confession, Rini started to follow. Adam stepped up, blocking her.

"They need a minute," he said.

Rini complied and since then, we've been loitering on either side of the dock's entrance: Rini and her sister on one side whispering, Adam and I on the other.

"Do you think he could have done that?" I ask Adam. "That's a pretty wild story."

"Which makes me more inclined to believe it. I don't know Andi to be a liar."

"Do you know Ted to be one?" I ask, feeling defensive that Adam would stick up for his ex-mistress over his brother-in-law. Though somehow Adam's use of "Andi" over "Mira" comforts me. When he adopts the name that Rini used for her sister over the one he gave her when they were lovers, that opens up the space for some objectivity.

"I know Ted is a man who will do anything to protect what's his. We've all heard stories of clients his colleagues have tried to poach," Adam says.

He's right. That's the reason Ted does so well at work. He's quiet but cutthroat. Calm but merciless. We have heard the stories, but Ted tells them like he's the victim and then the savior. Now he's cast as the villain.

Like the rain that seems to be bouncing up at me from the dock below, my whole perception has been turned upside down. Ten years ago, I called Andi the villain. This weekend I understood my part in that same role. And now Ted is stepping into something worse than our petty crimes, into a truly heinous act.

"With Margot too," I add. "How many times has he gone above and beyond to protect Margot's feelings from being hurt by even the slightest comment?"

Ted's personality comes off as a strength in his role as a husband. He's fiercely loyal to Margot. He always follows through. But how far would he go to protect her?

Adam nods. "And remember, this all happened ten years ago. He was more desperate. If he'd knocked up another girl, Margot would have dumped him in two seconds flat. Goodbye Flynn trust fund, goodbye family connections. And they were so close to getting engaged. He had it in the bag."

Could he have really gone to these lengths? I watch Ted animatedly explaining to Margot without being able to hear a word. He can barely hold his footing on the floating dock, bucking up and down in the waves, and yet Margot maintains her composure as always. I've never been more afraid for her. This is not the time to be calm.

RINI

Ted was the one who had done the unthinkable. I had no idea the extent of the violation Andi suffered. Ted showed no remorse while listening to my sister unburden her pain. We're never going to get an apology. And even if we did, it wouldn't be enough. Not for what he did to Andi.

I watch as Ted and Margot ascend the ramp of the floating jetty and stroll toward us. The storm whips their clothes and hair against their bodies.

Andi steps from the lawn to the dock, drawn to them like a moth to a flame. I follow behind her. Ted moves with the confidence of someone who has never lost a match of "he said, she said," and as they approach I assume he's persuaded Margot onto his side.

By the time they get within a few feet of me and Andi halfway down the dock, I'm frozen with rage. Ted drops Margot's hand and ushers her in front of him. Margot moves quickly past Andi and then me, without making eye contact. She doesn't notice that Ted has stopped inches from my sister. I can barely pick up what he says to her over the howling wind.

"I told you that if you ever contacted me or my wife, it would not end well for you," he whispers.

Ted moves so quickly that I don't have a chance to react. He grabs my sister and throws her into the stormy water.

FARAH

As I run through the house, I notice it's a wreck. In the foyer, I trip over Aimee's sneaker, laces outstretched and tangled in knots. From the kitchen I hear the fridge beep, its door ajar. A trail of novels drips like tears from the library to the living room.

In the background, I hear a television, Eden and Rick whispering and laughing.

"We need all hands on deck in the backyard," I yell. No one responds. I take the back stairs two-by-two up to my suite and return before the next flash of lightning.

With supplies in hand, I pause at the floor-to-ceiling windows, and the scene unfolds in slow motion. A bright blue raft drifts across the lawn. It levitates and dances in the crosswinds of the storm. My friends move around the backyard as if in a poorly choreographed ballet. Tiptoeing, running, leaping. The sky flickers with light, brilliant then brooding. It's so strange, but serene.

When I swing the French doors open, the chaos assaults me. The wind howls. The floating dock has accelerated from rocking to crashing up and down against the water. Thunder booms. The storm feels more urgent. More dangerous. The eye has passed and we're in the thick of it. Aimee screams. I break into a run.

"What's going on?" I yell.

Adam and Aimee stand at the edge of the dock, anxiously watching. From the window I couldn't see Rini and Ted thrashing in the water. They're fighting the current so they aren't swept out to sea. Andi rolls on the dock in a puddle of water, coughing.

"What happened?" I ask.

"Ted threw Andi in. Rini charged him, caught him off guard, and they went in together. Andi got away but the two of them won't let go of each other," Aimee says.

"Don't just stand there," I shout to Adam and Aimee.

"I'm not getting in; I've been drinking all day. Shots, beer chasers, and countless bottles of wine," Adam says.

So has Ted, I remind myself. Despite their size difference, if Rini wanted to kill him, she probably could in these circumstances. But not without killing herself too.

"Of course not. Look for noodles or rafts, any kind of floatation devices. There's a shed right there."

Adam sprints in the direction of the house and I turn to Aimee.

"How long until the EMTs arrive?" I ask.

Aimee's face turns white. "It happened so fast," she says.

My stomach clenches. Help isn't on the way yet. I run calculations in my mind. This doesn't look good. With my emergency room voice, I instruct her to call now.

I jog out onto the dock and Aimee follows with the phone to her ear. Even closer, it's impossible to see Rini and Ted below the roiling waves.

"The call won't go through," Aimee cries. "It's not ringing. It's not doing anything."

"Keep trying. 911 shouldn't require cellular service."

"I am trying." She fumbles the phone and it slides across the dock before stopping at the edge. She scrambles to pick it up. We are losing precious time. Ted and Rini have been underwater for several minutes; their lungs must be close to capacity.

"Where is Margot?" I shout. No one answers. I scan the dock and see her slumped against a pole, catatonic. I need to check on her.

Adam returns with an armful of life vests and two rafts. He dumps the rafts in the water, and within a split second, they fly off by air and by sea, caught in the wind or the current. Ted's head breaks the surface and he calls for Margot like a child to his mother. Margot doesn't move, not even a blink. Rini pops up seconds later. She opens her mouth wide, drawing in a huge gulp of air.

"Swim to the raft, Rini," I yell.

Rini doesn't acknowledge me; she has her sights set on Ted. She slams her mouth shut and lunges on top of him. They disappear again under the water.

"Aimee, EMTs?"

"The call went to the wrong cell tower. They're transferring to Greenport police now," Aimee reports.

I scan the water again. With the rain, I've lost sight of the last place I saw Rini and Ted.

"How long?" I ask.

"She said the roads are full of debris. They're coming, but it's going to take longer than usual."

There's no debating what I have to do. I pull off my socks and dangle my legs in the water. A mere thirty seconds to acclimate will help my body avoid shock.

Doctors know to avoid putting themselves in harm's way. We're not trained rescue workers. We're the ones needed after the rescue. If I get hurt, I won't be able to help. But I also know that assistance isn't coming and we are losing time. They've been under too long.

RINI

It feels like Ted and I will be struggling and fighting forever under this water, so I'm surprised when in a single moment he goes limp. He drifts away from me toward the bottom of the water in slow motion.

And then I soften. It's such a relief that I swear I'm smiling.

I choose to float for a few moments before breaking for another breath. This feeling is so ethereal and perfect I don't want it to end.

ADAM

Even though Farah and I have never been fans of each other, I can't let her go into the water. If we get these people out, she's the one who's going to have to save them.

"Farah, don't. I'll go," I say.

I pick up one of the six life vests I found in the shed by the cottage and buckle it on. Without hesitation, I jump in and regret it immediately. The water is shockingly cold for summer and the current is strong. Luckily, the adrenaline takes over. I can't afford to look like a coward. Ted and Rini break the surface and Ted spots me. He waves as Rini surfaces behind him.

"Help," Ted yells.

Rini jumps on Ted's back and pulls them under again.

When I reach the spot where they last went under, I dive down to find them. The water is murky. The shades of green are my best indications of direction, along with the temperature. Army green and cold, I'm going down. Yellow green and warmer, I'm heading toward the surface. This I know. But I have no idea how I'm going to get these two apart and onto land.

By some twist of fate, Rini lets go of Ted. I grab hold of his shirt, but he's not rising to the surface. He must be caught on some of the seagrass at the bottom. I yank once and Ted moves a little. I yank a second time and his body shoots up another few inches. It's progress, but now I've overexerted myself. I let go of Ted and go limp, letting the life jacket buoy me back to the surface.

With a second round of air, I dive under and pull Ted's body from the brush.

"Aimee, throw me a life vest," I call out.

She throws one but we watch it get carried far to the left of me. Aimee processes the trajectory and adjusts. She tosses two more into the water and the current brings them straight to me.

"Nice job, hon."

I wrap Ted in a life jacket and prop one under his chin to keep his mouth and nose out of the water although I'm not sure it will help. He looks unconscious.

Once I reach the dock, Aimee and Farah pull while I push Ted from underneath. We have him out of the water in less than a minute. I head back for Rini.

RINI

I keep floating, drifting in the water outside Stars Harbor. Impossibly, I see Eric swimming toward me and my smile grows bigger. *Wait, Eric's not here.* I'm supposed to call him later, when the guests leave.

"Eric, I was hoping to see you," I say.

How can I talk under water? And why does Eric look frightened when I'm clearly glad to see him?

I wait patiently for him to reach me, but his growing silhouette turns everything black.

When my vision returns, I'm floating on the water. It's not the Long Island Sound in the middle of a storm. This water is salty and warm and so blue. The sky is clear; a gentle breeze carries the smell of honeysuckle.

"Wow," I say.

My voice echoes off the water. There's not a soul in sight.

"Wow," I say, this time louder.

Suddenly I hear a splash behind me. I'm not afraid of what it might be. All I feel is peace.

"Hey."

I recognize Andi's voice. I turn to her with joy. But there's no one there. I tread in circles, waiting to spot her, but there's only the quiet lapping of water in response.

"Andi? Where are you, Andi?"

"Hey," she says.

I push the water around me back and forth. I don't see anyone. In the distance is nothing either. No buildings, no beaches, no boats. It's water as far as the eye can see in 360 degrees.

Andi's head pops above the water.

"I was right behind you the whole time," she says. She wipes the water from her nose. "I was practically touching you."

"Where are we?"

"The most beautiful place I've ever seen," Andi says. She turns her face up to the cloudless sky above us. She's right about that.

It's the most glorious body of water I've ever been in. I've never experienced beauty like this in person. If it were a photo, I would have thought it was all Instagram filters and tricks of light.

"Why didn't you tell me that today was the day you were going to die?" she asks.

In a flash of anger, I want to ask her why *she* didn't tell me about Ted and what he'd done to her. But instead of feeling the anger, it materializes as a lightning bolt through the sky behind me. It hits and then disappears. And I know my answer. Andi was protecting me like I was protecting her.

The sky changes again and the sun peeks out from behind a white fluffy cloud. A vibrant rainbow spreads across the sky. I think about hugging Andi, and as soon as I acknowledge my thought, she's in my arms embracing me. I stop treading water to squeeze her tighter and an unseen force holds me up. The laws of physics don't apply, and that's the confirmation I need. This isn't real.

I'm dead.

This is exactly how they described it in the books. Specific to me, but always the same. My ideal person in my ideal place. Eric led me to Andi by the water.

"I'm sorry for what happened to you," I say. "I love you."

"I love you too. Both of our plans were half-baked, so maybe the lesson is two heads are better than one?" Andi asks with a laugh.

But I can't agree with her. There was no way out of my death date and I don't regret keeping it from her.

"I'm glad it ended this way," I say.

"There could have been a different way," she says.

I shake my head.

"I would die for you all over again if I could," I say.

Andi smiles at me until my vision fades to black.

FARAH

At work, I shut off my personal brain. My own moral, political, and philosophical decisions are cut off with a decision-tree tourniquet. If this, then this. Doctors memorize courses of action so that we don't need to think about basics in emergency situations. I don't have to consider the person in front of me. There is no regard for race, gender, creed. I assess organs and functions. When I explain this to people, they have a hard time believing me. Who am I if not Farah playing my role as doctor? It's not for most people to understand, but it's true. I have two minds. And this is why doctors shouldn't treat people they know.

I roll Ted onto his back and stare at him.

His lungs are filled with water, my doctor brain warns. But my conscious brain counters.

He violated that woman in unimaginable ways.

He's about to go into cardiac arrest.

He took her choice away from her.

Save him.

Let him die.

I pound on his chest as hard as I can. With that out of my system, I get to work. I pinch his nose and lean over his mouth, but on my way down, I catch a glimpse of Andi. She looks stronger than she has since she emerged from the house. As Adam drags Rini's limp body through the water, Andi's watching her sister with such intensity, as if her desire alone could empty Rini's lungs and restart her heart. In turn, I watch Andi and imagine her as one of my clients, the women who call my office in a panic because they're losing their pregnancy, the women who waddle into the hospital in physical pain but are crying for the existential pain of knowing what it means that the bleeding won't stop.

My doctor instinct is strong, and it will serve me well because I know how to make impossible choices. Choices that would paralyze a normal person. Ethical choices, like whose care takes priority over another's. I stand and move away from Ted.

I wait for Rini.

MARGOT

I can count the number of unwanted epiphanies I've had on this lawn. The realization that the timing of Ted's pregnancy confession yesterday couldn't have been a coincidence—whether he recognized Rini or not, a primal instinct told him to get his story out first before I heard the real one. I also vividly recall his aloofness and disappearances before our wedding. And though I didn't see it with my own two eyes, it dawns on me that Andi didn't slip and fall into the water like he said. He didn't even reach down to help her. Instead he seemed to be willing her to die.

I didn't pass out again, but when Rini and Ted hit the water, my brain hit a wall. That was the last thing I remember. The rest comes in nonconsecutive snapshots. Farah shakes me. I slump down against a pole. Adam dives under the water. Andi looks away from me.

And then I'm present. On the dock. Farah hovers over Rini and barks out orders. She takes vitals. She digs in her medical kit. Aimee calls out time. I watch from the corner of the dock. A loose kayak skims the water far out in the horizon.

The rain slaps us sideways and I can't discern which way is up.

"Please," I call out. My voice is raspy. It hurts to breathe. Andi hears me. I can tell because she's watching me now. I speak only to her.

"If he did as you said, he should live and suffer the consequences.

He will go to trial. He could go to jail. But you'll never get justice if he's dead."

Around the front of the house the ambulance siren screams. Joe, Eden and Rick emerge from inside the house, unaware of the devastation that rained down on us while they were safe and dry inside. Two EMTs run around the house to the backyard. Farah shouts information at them.

"Male and female in cardiac arrest when we got them to surface. I administered 0.3 milligrams of epinephrine to both patients."

"Why do you have multiple EpiPens?" one of the EMTs asks.

"I'm a doctor. And I have a son with an allergy," Farah says.

The other EMT steps away from Rini and inspects Ted.

"The male, thirty-nine, was submerged for six minutes after last breath of oxygen, twelve minutes in total. The female, twenty-six, submerged for twelve minutes after last surfacing, seventeen minutes in total," Farah explains.

Another stranger is part of the group now too. He holds Andi's hand and looks like he wants to cry but has to hold it together.

My sobs break free then. I cry like an overtired toddler.

"It's going to be okay," Aimee says, rubbing my back.

"Vitals?" one of the paramedics asks.

"None," Farah says.

"For either?"

"None," Farah repeats.

"For how long?"

"Two minutes."

"Get the paddles," the paramedic yells into his walkie-talkie. "We need to get them out of the rain to the defib."

"I know it looks scary," Aimee says. "But Farah is an exceptional doctor. She has help now. All these people here, they will save them."

The EMTs carry my husband off on a stretcher to the hospital. My chosen family—the one person I never thought I'd lose—is drifting away from me.

I fall to the dock and press my face against the cold, wet wood.

FARAH

I don't call it. I'm in the hospital in an unofficial capacity. But I'm there when the emergency room doctor makes the declaration.

"Time of death, 4:44 p.m."

THREE MONTHS
LATER

AIMEE

After we left Stars Harbor, I insisted that Margot move into our house—and Adam move out. Selflessly risking his life to pull Ted from the stormy water, and then going back to do it again for Rini, was reckless but honorable. Those final acts were his saving grace, and the only reason I didn't file divorce papers as soon as we got home. Still, a break was nonnegotiable.

In my reading, Rini had told me that every loss makes space for gain. Although I was terrified to lose my family and our picture-perfect life, I was finally ready to take that risk. Truth be told, the alternative was no longer feasible. I could no longer ride along with every plot twist and turn Adam dreamed up on the fly. His books might need to continually raise the stakes, building to an over-the-top climax, but real life requires more stability than fiction.

Moving Margot in, at the same time as Adam was leaving, helped ward off too many questions from the girls. They were happy to have their aunt in the house for a while.

Since Adam doesn't feature prominently on my social media accounts, I originally had no intention of exposing our separation. Yet something compelled me to share that I was struggling. A small voice in the depth of my belly—a whisper that didn't understand algorithms and high-engagement content—told me to tell the truth. The messy truth. I wanted to admit that no, I didn't have it all under control, and no, I didn't have it all figured out.

Farah, on the other hand, knew her relationship was over after Joe was willing to use their son to save his political career. Beckett is thriving in occupational therapy twice a week, but Joe and Farah are in mediation to dissolve their marriage. I'm decidedly unsure whether our separation is the first step toward Adam and me divorcing or whether, like my photo shoots, this is one of the dozens of tries it takes to get it right. And it's okay to let the future remain out of focus.

I don't know . . . yet. But I will.

That was the takeaway of my first "honest" post, which was viewed by 350,000 users in its first twenty-four hours. My following has continued to grow by tens of thousands with each post. Most of my grid is still populated with adorable pics of the girls, but my sad Solo cup of wine gets shared twice as much. I was worried Margot would see my admissions as betrayal, but she's proud of me for not going to extremes and instead trying to find peace in the middle. It proves to her that I've changed.

She's also got a lot more on her mind than my loyalty to her brother.

I thought nothing of it when Margot found herself exhausted and vomiting regularly after Ted's funeral. She was in distress. But when the weeks became nearly two months, I begged Farah to run some blood tests to make sure this wasn't anything more than extraordinary grief.

Turned out it was something more: the cruelest twist of fate. Remember all those fainting spells Margot had that weekend at Stars Harbor? They weren't from stress. After five years of unsuccessfully trying to conceive, Margot was pregnant. It was what she'd always wanted, but now this blessing was awash in darkness. Margot is carrying the offspring of a—I won't say it, because my nurse mother warned me against speaking ill of the dead, but you know what he was.

I told Margot she had choices, but she refused to consider the multiple reasons in favor of termination. She is convinced that if there's any ounce of evil passed on from Ted's DNA in this miracle baby, her nurturing will overpower his nature. Again, I'm not so sure yet.

Farah and I make a great team caring for Margot—she's the medical guru for the challenging pregnancy, while I'm the emotional support. The three of us are bonded deeper than I could've imagined before our astrology retreat weekend.

Even after they move out, I expect to keep Margot and her baby close, not only because I love my sister-in-law and my future niece or nephew, but to make sure her judgment isn't as clouded as it was with Ted. I'll be her eyes wide open. The best thing I took away from Stars Harbor was a healthy dose of skepticism.

ANDI

Margot's demand for a homicide investigation around Ted's death was granted, but it proved inconclusive. I was vocal about Rini's act being nothing short of heroic. The other witnesses—Adam, Aimee and Farah—were mostly silent, each for their own reasons, but even hard interrogation could not produce compelling evidence that the events of that evening were anything more than a terrible accident fueled by alcohol and a raging tropical storm. I say it was fate.

Margot, on the other hand, had a whole sordid story of what had transpired that afternoon. The police tried to take her seriously, but she had too many strikes against her as an unreliable witness, including her blackouts that weekend and her distraught widowhood. In the end, her story of unseen connections and twisty acts of vengeance, while fascinating, didn't hold water with the prosecution.

"Write a novel," the detective said. "I hear it's therapeutic."

If she ever considered it, Margot didn't say. But it stuck with me. Maybe I have a disturbing tale in me that's almost ready to come out.

Over the first few weeks I asked myself whether Ted's death was justice. Did he deserve to die because of what he did to me ten years ago? Did he deserve to die because, when confronted all these years later, he refused to admit his wrongdoing and suffer the consequences of his actions? Did he deserve to die because he threw me into the water with the intention to drown me?

Did Ted deserve to die at all?

I don't know how to answer that. But I know I didn't deserve what he did to me. We don't always get what we deserve, good or bad.

Watching my sister die for me changed my life forever. The very next day, I woke up and vowed to run Stars Harbor as she did, with as little interruption as possible. With Eric's support and quiet protection, I'm getting stronger every day. I've accepted that I will never trust strangers, but I've also realized I don't need to in order to face the world. It's more important to trust myself. I never would have tried if Rini hadn't sacrificed her life for me, and now I'm slowly learning.

After a few private-invitation test runs, Stars Harbor officially reopened for the winter holidays and we've been booked solid. I might not be as gracious of a host as my sister, but after doing charts with her for seven years, I'm nearly as confident as she is in a reading. Early feedback has been overwhelmingly positive.

"New Year's Eve booking went live this morning," I tell Eric when I climb into his truck. "We incited a bidding war."

"How many groups were in the running?"

"Six. We ended up at $5,000 a night."

Eric whistles low and long.

"It's all for her," I say.

New Year's Eve is the highly anticipated weekend of Rini's return. Beginning with the next calendar year, we'll run Stars Harbor together.

Eric and I walk into the rehabilitation facility together, but he hangs back in the hallway to let me greet her first.

"Are you ready?" I ask my sister. She nods.

It's time for me to return the favor and take care of her.

RINI

On the Friday before Thanksgiving, I am officially released from the rehab facility where I've been living. Over the past months I've regained my cognitive ability, my motor skills, and my memory. All the things I lost on the day I died. Which, thanks to Farah, is now the day I was reborn.

Sometimes I dream about being pulled under that bright blue fantasy-island water, through the murky green Long Island Sound, and back into the world where I took my first breath after so many minutes of being gone. Somewhere else. Somewhere in between. I wonder if this is what it's like being transferred out of the womb. Shocking, cold, but ultimately a relief.

Since I came back, it's been a whole new life. Eric proposed to me the day I opened my eyes. I asked him to give me some time to think about it. Technically I was still a newborn, I joked. There's no doubt I love him and want to spend my life with him, but I don't have much experience in making plans. Not ones that work out, anyway.

Given that my target among the final guests at Stars Harbor missed the mark, I think I need to work on communication. I want to take things slowly. Andi, on the other hand, has jumped in the deep end. From new five-star reviews to reports from the vendors and stories from Eric, she's facing the challenges of her new life with grace.

"I'm ready," I tell her.

Andi bundles me up and Eric carries me to his truck, though it's a warm November day and I can walk myself. We ride in sweet, thick silence, like a body pillow I can collapse into.

When we pull up to the deer gate—Eric driving and Andi in the back seat—I break into quiet sobs. The doctors warned me that I might experience sudden and strong emotions, and I'm unexpectedly overwhelmed by the sight of the welcome sign for Stars Harbor Astrological Retreat.

Eric and Andi have stepped up in ways I could never have imagined, and as hard as it is to let them help, it's been a constant reminder that I don't have to shoulder every burden on my own, as I did before.

"Are you okay?" Andi asks.

I nod, not even bothering to wipe away the tears.

"You get what you get and you don't get upset," I say.

This new life is even better than the last. I don't know how I got so lucky.

ACKNOWLEDGMENTS

I am endlessly grateful to the people who edit, design, sell, and share books. As a little girl who felt lonely in the great big world, I was never alone with a novel. Later, as a mother, I found comfort in fiction, a reminder that a captivating world still existed outside of my new identity. As a writer, I discovered community with those of us digging up our wounds to tell stories. I hope I've provided that same comfort, perspective, or entertainment to at least one reader.

To my agent, Claire Friedman, for your decisive action and unwavering support. There are no words to express my gratitude for your guidance in making my lifelong dream come true. I have never given up the reins so completely as I did to you when this novel went on submission, and it was the best decision I've ever made because it led me to Natalie Hallak.

Natalie, my appreciation for your edits knows no bounds; specifically your trust that there's more talent inside me than I think, and your willingness to toss out off-the-wall suggestions that set my creativity on fire. I am so grateful for what you saw in my original submission, as much as your refusal to leave it at that. And thanks for letting me be weird.

How lucky am I that I get to collaborate with not one but two amazing editors at Atria? Kaitlin Olson, we've only just begun working together but our shared Capricorn moons and Pisces placements are already adding up to a creative and productive dynamic.

Being published by Atria Books had been a dream of mine before I even knew what an imprint was, and now that I'm "on the inside," it's no longer a fantasy but a beautiful reality. I have to thank Elizabeth Hitti, Ife Anyoku, Maudee Genao, and Gena Lanzi for that.

I could not have finished this book and pushed her out into the world without Alissa Lee. You were there as this book started to come together in Henriette's class at Grub Street, and you answered my plea for a reader a year later. Soon we were regularly exchanging entire manuscripts, meeting on Zoom to brainstorm, attending retreats together, and revealing our personal lives in bars and cars on both coasts. Your guidance, sharp insight, and encouragement shaped not only the revisions on *The Astrology House*, but me as a writer.

Christie Tate, your decade of friendship is written all over me as a mother, friend, and author. We started putting words together to make sense of our ambition bumping up against our legal careers and motherhood. We kept putting more and more words together to tell stories. You led the charge into the publishing world and never let me fall away while your rocket soared. I am so grateful we get to explore all the new places together.

I have written several novels that live in the proverbial drawer, but the only reason I wrote one worth reading is my *Pop Fiction Women* co-host, Kate. Together we fell down many rabbit holes of astrology until I knew enough to write a character who had to grapple with her own fate. Our interviews with authors allowed me to see that a life publishing novels was possible, and that I wasn't doomed because of past failures. Our continuous conversations (on and off camera) push me to new heights. Thank you for saying yes.

I learned to take myself seriously as a writer at the Northern California Writers' Retreat in 2017 and I learned to enjoy the rollercoaster ride to publication at the same retreat in 2023. Deep gratitude to both authors-in-residence, Stephanie Danler and Kirstin Chen, as well as my workshop leader, agent Michelle Brower. Heather Lazare, you create magic when you put people together at NCWR. Part of that magic came from my roommate Caro Claire Burke (she and I were the only two adults who rejected the single room and requested to sleep next to a stranger). JJ Elliott, you made us a trio, and I emulate you in life and publishing. You two have seen me through my lowest lows on this journey and I am thrilled I get to thank you in this way (the acknowledgments of my published novel!! Can you believe it?!?!).

Shaun Bernier, the first time I heard you read your words, I knew we'd be friends . . . and then I found out you lived half a world away in Singapore. Fast forward to 2023, after years of trading pages and emails we celebrated your birthday in person, overlooking the Pacific Ocean, our families in tow, and I guess I wasn't wrong.

Every Wednesday evening in 2021, fifteen small rectangles met on Zoom in the Grub Street Novel Generator led by the inimitable Henriette Lazaridis. These people helped me water the seeds of this novel. Shaun, Sarah, Melissa, and Katherine Ouellette, your early feedback shaped this story in ways I could not have done alone.

Henriette Lazaridis, there is something about your teaching that goes straight from my brain to my writing fingers. I began putting words together in your "Seed of a story" class, reached "The end" in your novel generator, and learned to evaluate scenes and structure in your revision class. I cannot separate this book from your guidance. Thank you.

Emily Giffin and Ashley Audrain, you are personal and professional heroes of mine. Knowing I'd been burned in publishing before, your relentless enthusiasm gave me the courage to get my hopes up.

Writing is less solitary than I imagined, and that has made all the difference. To my writer people, Grace McNamee, Amanda Churchill, Sara Cutaia, and Tanya Friedman, your work keeps me inspired and your support keeps me motivated. To my reader friends, Samantha Marrin, Laurel MacDonald, Karri-Leigh P. Mastrangelo, and Jeanie, for always sharing books and opinions. To Carol Newman Cronin, our 100+ check-ins have held me accountable and lifted my spirits.

It might be strange to thank your yoga teacher in the acknowledgments of a book with an actual corpse, but Jean Koerner has shepherded me through many transitions in my life: from practitioner to teacher, from woman to mother, and now from writer to author.

Michelle Weiner, thank you for our long conversation about birth order, singletons and siblings, about New York and LA, about building a life and making it count. The adaptation will be *I Would Die For You*.

On *Pop Fiction Women*, we've had many incredible conversations with writers who have left their mark on me. Thank you to every single woman who gave your time so generously to create art and discuss it with us. You've become my community and I'm so grateful. Thank you especially to Katy Hayes, Ashley Audrain, Rachel Koller Croft, Sarah Pearse, Mary Kubica, Carola Lovering, and Avery Carpenter Forrey for reading early versions of this book and sharing your enthusiastic support.

Elisabeth Baker prompted me to buy my very first astrology book and upgraded me from casual to committed. I've been researching this novel my entire life, but I used the following books and Instagram accounts as my guides: @costarstrology, @solelunastro, *The Only Astrology Book You'll Ever Need* by Joanna Martine Woolfolk, *You Were Born for This* by Chani Nicholas, and *Signs & Skymates* by Dossé-Via Trenou. Any inaccuracies or inconsistencies in this novel are my own, done to preserve the narrative.

To Reggie, Bernie, Katie, Stan, Nancy, and Denise, for your over-the-top support of me and my novel. You have gone above and beyond in your own ways, and it touches my heart.

To David and Johnny, for not being anything like the brother in this book and for tolerating all the ways that I'm like the sister. And to Danielle for putting up with all of us.

Ian, you have supported every iteration of my career with steadfast love. From learning how to read a land survey to taking each yoga class

I taught, you never hesitate to jump in with me. Of all your roles, podcast producer and story editor are my most treasured. Thank you for spending countless country walks hashing out plot twists, organizing timelines, and sketching pictures of docks. I sincerely don't know who I would be without you, and I don't want to either.

Luke and Chyler Jade, when you were born, I came alive too. You helped me write this novel—and navigate this life—in ways you could never imagine. You've been aware that I was a writer from the time you were small, but when things really started to happen in publishing, you were as excited as I was. You make me proud every day. Just to know you is a gift.

Finally, thank you to my parents for a childhood of unconditional love that allowed me to (eventually) find the audacity to create, and then call it a life. This all begins with you.

ABOUT THE AUTHOR

Carinn Jade is a lawyer, writer, and cohost of the *Pop Fiction Women* podcast. Her essays have been published in *The New York Times, DailyWorth,* and *Motherwell.* She has attended the GrubStreet Novel Generator, Yale Writers' Conference, and the Northern California Writers' Retreat. Carinn grew up on the North Fork of Long Island and lives with her family in New York City. *The Astrology House* is her first novel.